Where Heaven And The Bronx Met

a novel

Cooper Kalin

OPUS PRESS | WASHINGTON, DC | 2016

©2016

ISBN-13: 978-1-62429-095-4

Cover painting by Petie Russo

OPUS PRESS
Originally printed on Opus, an Espresso Book Machine located at:
Politics and Prose Bookstore
5015 Connecticut Ave NW
Washington, DC 20008
www.politics-prose.com // (202) 364-1919

This book is dedicated to

Danny Cooper
who in sickness and in health
always pointed to Christ.

"Choose God."

Students ask, "Why does
God allow a world filled with suffering?"

"Why do we?" I reply.
"He showed us the way."

Corporal Works of Mercy
feed the hungry
give drink to the thirsty
clothe the naked
shelter the homeless
visit the sick
comfort the imprisoned
bury the dead

Spiritual Works of Mercy
admonish sinners
instruct the ignorant
counsel the doubtful
comfort the sorrowful
be patient with those in error
forgive offenses
pray for the living and the dead

Literary scholars tell us that Herman Melville's "Call me Ishmael," in Moby Dick, is a classic opening line. I don't have a classic line like that but I can tell you Herman is buried in Woodlawn Cemetery, in the Woodlawn neighborhood in "da Bronx." Ishmael and Moby are not. Manhattan real estate was too valuable for cemeteries, so writers, entertainers (Duke Ellington, George M. Cohan), the rich (Woolworth, Belmont), and others got shipped up to the Bronx. We already had our own stiffs in the Bronx. We still do. Some are in this story.

The story is well known. It is good vs. evil. Darkness vs. light. Cain vs. Abel. Archangel Michael vs. fallen angel Lucifer. My tale takes place in my beloved Bronx but evil and goodness are everywhere, in all five boroughs, across nations, and the universe. A cosmic battle. Yet, also, an individual battle. A battle of the soul. We all play a part. Yes, even the indifferent and apathetic. The theologians and philosophers say that they may be the most guilty of sin. They choose amorality but we are not allowed to be Pontius Pilate and wash our hands of guilt. We must resist injustice and evil.

What is my part? I'm still figuring it out, day by day, prayer by prayer. I'm not one of the indifferent or apathetic. I'm a God guy, an old altar boy. Like you, I'm a work in progress. I'm evolving. Unlike you, unless I'm seriously mistaken, I was recently asked to step up to the plate in this game of life and eternity. Who asked? No less than God, Himself: the Boss, the Chief, the Big Man, Yahweh, Father, Son, and Spirit, Allah, Brahma, the Buddha and his one thousand other names.

Prologue

He has given his angels charge
over you to guard you in all your ways
Psalm 91:11

I awoke to a balding, middle-aged man bending over me. His hands were touching my head and my chest. What was going on? Praying over me? Robbery? Was this real? A dream? I closed my eyes and when I reopened them, he was still there. Nope. Not a dream. He was making the sign of the cross over me. Last rites? Who was this guy? A priest? How did I get propped up against a rock with my worn and faded rugby blanket wrapped around me? It's usually in the trunk of my car.

"You've had an accident," he stated as if reading my mind.

"Huh?"

"We hit black ice on the road, and then had quite the roller coaster ride."

"We? ... What's with the we?"

"Yep. I was right there with you as the car rolled and then rolled again. Quite the circle dance," he offered.

I gazed around. A silvery light from a half moon filtered through the swaying tree branches and danced on the twisted wreck of my car. Or what once was my car. It rested on rocks, inches shy of the Bronx River. It's a shallow river but there's enough water to drown in, especially if a car is on top of you.

"You were in the car?" Cobwebs, thick like those in grandma's attic, hung in my brain. "I don't remember you being there? ... I think the Rangers hockey game was on the radio."

"I joined you in the last minute of the ride. We rocked and

rolled. The car groaned and moaned and you joined the chorus. A different kind of choir than I'm used to. By the way, Girardi scored the winning goal."

I usually pump my fists after a Ranger victory, but not this time. Instead, I gazed at my companion.

"How badly am I hurt?" I finally managed to ask.

"You're fine. That was taken care of."

"Huh? ... You lost me again."

"Your shoulder was broken and you had cuts on your forehead and near your left ear. That's why you have blood on your shirt. A concussion, also."

"Was broken? Had cuts?"

"Let's just say I have a healing touch. We'll leave it there for the moment."

I studied my Good Samaritan. He looked just like Lou Grant of the old Mary Tyler Moore show. I blinked and then blinked again. Sure looked like Lou. I saw a slightly heavyset man with a balding head and a kindness to his face. Wait! Lou Grant never wore wire-rimmed glasses. And I never remember him in a red flannel shirt, worn brown cords, and work boots unlaced at the top. Nor red socks with hearts on them.

"You started to pray the moment the car went out of control. The Our Father and then an Act of Contrition. You even managed to slip in a Hail Mary before the car came to a rest," he told me matter of fact. "You lost consciousness. An invitation of light came to you but it was just beyond your reach. A line from one of your favorite songs by Martyn Joseph, 'A man leaves the darkness when he follows the Son' penetrated your misty dream. You wanted to say yes to this invitation of light but you hesitated. The light faded with your dream."

"How can you possibly know all this?" The confusion in my

brain banged around like a silver ball in a pinball machine. Make sense out of it. Not possible at the moment. I probed my head tenderly for any damage or soreness but nothing shouted out.

"Hallucinations!" I finally blurted out.

"No. I'm all too real." He grinned mischievously.

"Who are you?" I asked. "And why the chuckle?"

"Because you talk to me every day."

"How can that be? I talk to no one every day. Not even my mom or my dear sister Brigid."

"Prayer," he said softly.

My eyes widened. "Are you God?"

One

We have only this short life in which to prove our love.
St. Bernard

My name is Kevin McCarthy, also known as Mac. I've also been called mook, shmuck and nastier things. You see, I'm a teacher. What haven't teachers been called in playgrounds, in graffiti over urinals, and now in cyberspace?

I teach religion at Dorothy Day High School, a Catholic school in the Bronx. I love working at a school named for Dorothy. I've adopted her as my patron saint. Well, not a saint yet but she's on her way. She's in the first step of the four steps needed for sainthood in the Catholic Church. Servant of God, step number one, recognizes that the person lived a holy life. The next step is Venerable. We are in awe of the person's Christian witness. Two miracles need to be attributed to Dorothy in the last two steps. The first miracle earns her the title Blessed; the second, she would be canonized – sainthood. The miracles are proof of the saint's closeness to God.

Dorothy inspires me. A twentieth century American, she was similar to the saintly Mother Teresa, working with the poor, the forgotten, the overlooked in society. Throw in Dr. Martin Luther King Jr., crying out against injustice; the holy outlaw Berrigan brother priests, advocating fiercely against war; and Mother Jones, fighting against labor abuse of children and adults, and you've got a great patron saint. Mother Jones said "Pray for the dead and fight like hell for the living." That was my Dorothy.

In the opening days of school, I always share Dorothy's story with my students. She "stands for those who think of themselves too damaged or too sinful to do anything meaningful for God," noted

Father James Martin, a Jesuit priest. Her example allows me to introduce the concept that life is a journey up a spiritual ladder.

I put on my white board a crude drawing of a ladder daily; its rungs extend into the clouds. It's a reminder to the students of their lifetime spiritual journey, one rung at a time. The idea comes from St. John Climacus, a 7th century Byzantine monk. His treatise, *The Ladder to Paradise*, a spiritual classic, outlines thirty steps, beginning with renunciation of earthly pleasures, and includes ascending a ladder to the perfection of faith, hope, and charity. A famous icon shows Christ greeting pilgrims at the top of the ladder. The pilgrims on the ladder are urged on by angels but there are also demons attempting to pull them off. Not an easy ride on an escalator, but a hard grasp of the posts and a lifting of the feet, heavy at times, to the next rung.

Dorothy surely climbed a spiritual ladder. As a young woman, she searched for life's meaning in the isms: anarchism, socialism, and communism. She partied with the best of them, smoking and drinking like there was no tomorrow. She had an abortion. At one point, despair had her look at suicide as an option.

Dorothy stepped firmly onto her spiritual ladder with the birth of Tamar, her daughter out of wedlock. "No human creature could receive or contain so vast a flood of love and joy as I often felt after the birth of my child," she said. "With this came the need to worship, to adore." She surrendered to God and became a Catholic. She began attending daily mass. Not easy to do. I'm still working on the daily mass thing; most weeks I achieve it. If I miss morning mass, it's usually the day after rugby practice. My body clearly lets me know that an early morning wake-up is not in the cards.

Dorothy, a journalist, wrote for *America* and *Commonweal*, two Catholic publications. An assignment to cover the Hunger March for the Unemployed brought her to Washington, D.C., in

1932. On December 8th, the feast of the Immaculate Conception, Dorothy went to mass at the Basilica of the National Shrine. The largest Catholic church in the United States, the Basilica contains over 70 chapels honoring Mary. A mixture of Byzantine and Romanesque architecture, the Church combines round arches, thick walls, domes, and mosaics on its walls.

That December day found Dorothy on her knees in the Basilica's crypt, a throwback to the catacombs of ancient Rome. Feeling aimless and lost, she prayed that "some way would open for me to use my talents I possessed for my fellow workers, for the poor." There's an old saying: be careful what you pray for. It floors me to think that soon after, her prayer was answered. Like she had a direct line to the Big Guy. Maybe she did. Later in life, Dorothy wrote "we usually get what we pray for..." Not sure that applies to me; I've been praying a long time to shed my Bronx brawler self. As I said before, I'm still a work in progress.

Dorothy returned to the New York apartment that she shared with her brother and his wife. A few days later, a knock came at the door in the early afternoon. Her hospitable sister-in-law welcomed a gray-haired man into the apartment. Peter Maurin, with a thick French accent, said that he had read articles Dorothy had written in Catholic magazines. He greeted Dorothy with "George Schuster, editor of *Commonweal*, told me to look you up. Also a red-haired Irish communist in Union Square told me to see you. He says we think alike."

Peter proceeded to give her "an entirely new education." Catholic radicalism. He urged her to not give lip service to the Gospels but to live them out. As Jesus said, "... *as you did it to one of the least of ... my brethren, you did it to me*" (Matthew 25:41).

I'm one of nine children; Peter had me beat by a baker's dozen.

He was the eldest of twenty two kids from a French peasant farming family. He spent nine years as a La Salle Brother, an order started by St. John Baptist De LaSalle, a priest, to teach the poor. Believing his calling was elsewhere, Peter left the Brothers. He crossed the Atlantic and came to North America, working any job to support himself. He made a decent living teaching French but he had a deeper calling. He became a wandering ascetic, possession free, and taught the radical side of the *Papal Encyclicals*, writings issued by Popes, to anyone who would listen. Feed the hungry. Clothe the naked. Honor the laborer. He was a walking Gospel message. Meanwhile, he prayed for a collaborator in living out the Gospels. Someone to build the Kingdom with him. You can guess where this is going.

Dorothy's prayer brought her Peter, and his prayer, Dorothy. They became a formidable team, and founders of the Catholic Worker movement. Thus began a lifetime of peace and justice work. Their solidarity with the marginalized led to the Catholic Worker paper. It railed against social injustice, especially the plight of suffering laborers, who struggled to pay bills and feed families, while business owners focused on profits and the fatness of their bank accounts. Then the duo started shelters, called Houses of Hospitality, and organized farming communes. I've always admired that they embraced a lifetime of voluntary poverty and works of mercy. Dorothy became pro-life on every issue and was arrested many times protesting non-violently for women's rights, civil rights, workers' rights, and against nukes and war.

Her legacy of the Catholic Worker continues today. The two CW houses started by Dorothy in the lower east side of Manhattan still operate, joined by other CW houses in the nation and the world. Saintly people who work 24/7, assisting the poor, the forgotten, the overlooked. Not sure I could "be on" the whole day. I welcome the quiet and solitude in my apartment after the school day, a much needed time to regroup and re-energize.

I've often asked Dorothy, a pacifist, for help from above in my own struggle with violence, in my thinking that violence is an option in dealing with problems at times. Bronx boys learn to fight, kick, claw, and head-butt our way through life. We're scrappers. We know it's wrong and some of us make it out of the cycle. I turned to Gaelic football, martial art, and rugby for healthier outlets.

I definitely have one thing in common with Dorothy. Like her, Jesus is my lifeline. I want to absorb the violence and anger in His name. I want to make violence impotent. Have I been successful? I've stumbled along. The last bar fight never a distant memory. Two steps forward and one step back. With Dorothy's help and God's grace, I keep trying. As the men and women in Alcoholic Anonymous meeting rooms say, "one day at a time."

Two

Learn to see God in the details of your life,
for he is everywhere.
St. Theresa of Avila

The Dorothy Day school is just south of Fordham Road in the Bronx. Fordham Road runs east-west from the Harlem River to the Bronx Park, home of the Bronx Zoo and the Botanical Gardens. Thank the zoo for saving the buffalo! Yeah, it's a true story. Look it up.

My school is diverse and co-ed with about 800 kids. Latinos, Blacks, Caribbeans, Africans, the EYErish from North Bronx, and EYEtalians from Throggs Neck and Pelham make up our student body. Throw in some Albanians, Filipinos, and Indians from India (not the island of Manhattan and twenty-four beads). We also have some Jewish students, who missed getting into the selective prestigious public school, Bronx High School of Science. No shame there. Me, neither. It was for the really smart kids. So like the Jews in my school, as they say in Yiddish, I'm a putz, too.

I'm a bachelor-for-life Catholic school teacher. Every school has them. We say yes to everything. Coaching, cafe duty, service projects, retreats, whatever. Did I mention plumber for overflowing toilets? I bought the whole program. I believe in kingdom building. We're baptized to do it and it's my core. "To do and to teach," as Brother Willie, the athletic director, as well as teacher, coach, and all around good guy, tells us. We try to change lives for the better. It's exciting and exhausting. All in His name.

*   *   *

My strong faith began early in life. I'm talking about when I was a kid. Fourth grade found me as an altar boy and I still vividly recall the first time I served at mass. I thought I messed up but Father Delamater told my mom afterwards that I had done a fine job. I still serve at mass, now as a Eucharistic minister. Prayer has been my companion for as long as I can remember. *"Lord, I believe; help Thou my unbelief"* (Mark 9:23) has not been one of my supplications. I'm simply in love with God.

Teaching religion is my vocation. Trying to move students up their spiritual ladders energizes and fulfills me. I'm a fool for Christ and the students know it. Boy, do they know it. My booming voice fills with passion when I talk about Jesus and the Gospels. In the words of St. Paul: *"Woe to me if I do not preach the Gospel!"* (1 Cor 9:16). Teenagers quickly pick up on phoniness or insincerity. That's never been a label hung on me. I live my faith and belief in Jesus inside and outside of the classroom. I try to live each day looking through the eyes of Christ. "...to see Jesus in every human being," said Eileen Egan, a peacemaker. Successful all of the time, nah, of course not. Sinner, yeah, but at least I keep trying.

Students often want to find God on their own. "I'm spiritual" is the comment I often hear from them. It boils down to vague new-age imagery. A quick calculation of the time being spiritual – or not – usually shows the spiritual emperor has no clothes. Jesus prayed alone in the garden and the desert, and on the mountain. But he also prayed with the community in the temple. We need a community to nourish us. Dorothy Day caught the paradox well. "Christians must live in a state of permanent dissatisfaction with the Church yet keep in mind that we don't save the Church, the Church saves us."

No church, synagogue, mosque, or temple will ever live up to expectations. All are made up of people who stumble and sin. We must get up and keep trying for God. *"My soul is restless until it rests in thee,"* according to St. Augustine.

*   *   *

School mornings often find me at 7 A.M. mass in the school chapel. The intimate and beautiful chapel has a wooden crucifix on the fieldstone wall behind the altar. Mary flanks one side of the cross, Joseph the other. The stained glass windows on the right side of the chapel depict three scenes from Dorothy Day's story. The first has her feeding the poor at a Catholic Worker house. Jesus stands in the food line. In the second, she's in jail, one of numerous incarcerations for non-violent protest against war and nukes, or for civil and worker rights. Jesus shares her cell. The third and last one has her praying in front of the Tabernacle with Jesus behind her with His hand on her shoulder. To the left of the windows, a bronze tablet lists the seven corporal works of mercy; the one on the right proclaims the seven spiritual works of mercy.

The chapel is an integral part of our school. Its location puts it front and center opposite the main doors. It also plays a daily role in my school life. At morning mass, and periodic visits during the day, I center and focus on seeing Christ in all people, especially the students. I encourage students to go to the chapel, kneel, pray, and talk with Jesus daily. I urge them to keep working on moving up their own spiritual ladders.

Father Tim Coy, our campus priest, always has a lop-sided smile and a twinkle in his Irish American eyes. He's a holy man, maybe even mystical. Mystics are the highest form of pray-ers. Like a prophet of old, he has a beard. His happens to have untrimmed tufts of hair that have sprouted with little order. Sometimes, a morsel of food from his breakfast or lunch plays hide and seek in it. He has a bit of the absent-minded professor about him, possibly due to his mind being elsewhere in a contemplative state.

He is often elsewhere physically. Like many priests, he is stretched thin due to the shortage of priests in the Church. We share Father Tim with a local community college where he's the chaplain. Sundays find him helping out with Mass at two nearby parishes. His hectic schedule is always full but he, like other good priests, marches on and leads the flocks in His name. May the Spirit carry all of them.

In Catholic schools, class starts with a prayer. Easy? No, not by a long shot. Creating the sacred regularly in the school day and throughout the year takes effort. I use different methods, including traditional prayers, music, the Church calendar of saints and seasons, current events, and the Holy Spirit to move them. "Let us call to mind the presence of God" begins the prayer and "Dorothy Day, pray for us. Live Jesus in our hearts forever" concludes it.

All academic disciplines begin class with a prayer because all education, including math, science, and English, is through the eyes of God. The wholeness of this approach brings the search for truth in all subjects. In Christianity, Jesus is the Truth. A living God. Pilate asks the most famous question in the Bible, "*Truth, what is that?*" (John 18:38). In our Catholic schools, we ask "Who" not "What." Jesus is the Who: "*I am the Way, the Truth and the Life*" (John 14:6). We spend our lives journeying to discover Jesus, the springboard for all study.

Our teaching shows our students how to live in the Christian example. Religion classes provide the cornerstone on which the other disciplines build. Our search for faith brings us to the infinity of math, the writings of Dante and Milton, the art of Michelangelo, the music of Bach, and the historical journey of saints and prophets.

At Dorothy Day HS, our Christian teaching carries into the sports program. The principal, Sister Sam, wants coaches to focus on nurturing the athletes, teaching values, and discipline. Our culture pushes that winning is everything but not Sister Sam. No recruiting, she has told us. She's not an avid sports fan but she's seen enough to know that the recruiting of athletes at the high school level has reached a fever pitch. "Here at Dorothy Day, in our building, we will recruit the minds, bodies and souls of the athletes for Christ," she has said.

*   *   *

Teaching is an art. When the bell rings, it's game time. A teacher better have his or her A game ready for forty-five minutes. A cast of characters walks in the door five times a day, each class averaging twenty five students – one hundred and twenty five students – every school day. Names to learn, personalities as well. That's critical. You find out quickly enough who can be teased, who is sensitive, the shy ones, the extroverts. Trust me, each class has a distinct personality.

You're a maestro directing conversation, imparting information, and trying to keep everyone focused and involved. You try for an Oscar winning performance every day. Students and teacher know when a class hums.

Exhausting, you bet. Fulfilling, for sure. It's a vocation. Hard to survive otherwise. Roughly thirty percent of new teachers leave the profession within five years. It's a tough job. Vocation or not.

*   *   *

The twenty-minute morning walk to school always gets my juices flowing. I love the pulse and rhythm of the Bronx. At the early hour, the city is a medley of noise, sights, and smells. An impatient driver honks at a garbage truck backing into an alley or at a pedestrian to clear out of his way. The elevated train, commonly referred to as the El, rumbles by with wheels squealing on the track as it curls to the right. "Tax-ee," I hear numerous times. Workers walk by, cradling steaming cups of coffee, while munching on bagels with "a schmear." The cream cheese oozes out, leaving a thick white stash above their mouths. Drivers, like jockeys, move from one lane to the next, maneuvering to pick up a few more yards on their daily commute. And then there's Mrs. Tilak. Always in the morning.

Mrs. Tilak comes into view halfway into my walk. She runs an Indian restaurant on White Plains Road under the El. I call her "my holy Hindu." She sees God in all living things. She always dresses in a colorful sari. We share a love of the color green. This led me to grant her honorary Irish status. Her colorful saris are accompanied by the traditional Hindu red dot on her forehead, the seat of concealed wisdom. Bindi, the fancy word for it, comes from Sanskrit. It literally means a drop or a dot. It symbolizes spiritual vision. When I see someone with the dot, I am reminded to be centered in God. It's one of my many sacramental reminders pointing to God. Too cool.

Mrs. Tilak's restaurant has become an oasis for the working poor. A night out. A treat. Everybody says she loses money because of the low price of her large-size portions. She always dismisses the portion concerns with "TLC, tender loving care, costs nothing." The working poor, those with full-time jobs but little left over after rent and necessities, have a night of dignity. Yes, in a small Indian restaurant with worn tabletops and faded curtains. But always clean, and a cloth napkin by one's table setting.

To me, Mrs. Tilak is Kama, the Hindu goddess of love. I tease her for dating Krishna, an incarnation of Vishnu, one of the three principal Hindu deities. He's often depicted as a handsome man playing the flute. His fine image fills an entire wall in her restaurant.

"Top of the day to you, Mrs. Tilak" is my daily greeting. "I do believe you've swept that sidewalk as clean as it's going to get."

"And the rest of the day to you," she responds. We both always chuckle at her using the Irish response I've taught her.

A wave good-bye and I continue on my way. Within five minutes, I usually hear "Hey, Mr. Mac." Smiling, Mr. Abdul waves a hand out the window as he drives by in his gypsy cab, one of the non-yellow cabs operating in the boroughs outside of Manhattan. Most are legal, some not.

An immigrant from Indonesia, Mr. Abdul is a Muslim pacifist. He non-violently knocks our kids' socks off when he guest speaks at the school about Islam. Jihad, or holy war, is an internal battle between good and evil, he explains to them. He declares that evil can be beaten if one is centered in prayer. And pray he does, all over the Bronx, a minimum of five times a day. Kneeling on his prayer rug and facing Mecca, he can be seen in parks and on the streets, oblivious to the urban noises crashing and swirling around him. His rug is an island of calm in a honky-tonk city. What a great witness to the love of God.

Driving his cab on the city streets, he scours the streets for junkies and drunks. Saving them from the slavery of addiction is his mission. His compassion allows him inside the pain of those addicted. He helps them see the light again.

Ah, the beauty around me. The goodness of these people never fails to pump me up early in the morning. The Bronx, you gotta love it. Its living, breathing, Christ-like self.

Three

All sins tend to be addictive, and
the terminal point of addiction is damnation.
W.H. Auden

Thursday

A hundred pairs of eyes and a hundred pairs of ears. Necessary elements for a good teacher to be effective in the classroom. A teacher's radar operates continuously. A constant search for distractions and for students that are upset, happy, tuned in, disengaged, on cell phones...the list could fill up a page.

Today, my first class of the day "kicked butt." In the high school world, a rockin' first period is hard to achieve. The teenage beast is programmed to sleep at that time of day. If schools had no afternoon sports, the perfect learning time would be 10 to 5. Conversation closed! As we know, sports win. The younger children should start earlier as they are bright-eyed a lot sooner in the morning than teenagers. Something about buses and waiting for them on dark mornings prevents that from happening.

Yesterday's revelation of drug dealing in our school bothered me, but was no surprise. I've been at this game for many years and I've definitely seen drug problems in schools. My kids are street-wise. They would get today's message. I used poor beautiful Mexico as my starting point.

"Young people of Dorothy Day, Mexico, our neighbor, has two dozen victims of drug wars already this week. Some were bad boys in the drug business while others were innocent victims. Two were young children of a rival dealer, slaughtered to send a message. The beheading of a journalist – another message. No need to go to Mexico to talk of drug violence. Does anybody in this room of Bronx students not know of a friend, neighbor, or family member who got hurt in the drug world on our streets?"

Everybody has known someone. Some of my students were victims. Robbed to feed a habit. They felt my passion which came easy as drugs have touched most everyone in the Bronx in one way or another. Even my own family.

"Someone gets hurt to bring you or others drugs. It may be the dealers. It may be the good guys – cops, Mexican soldiers, innocent kids, journalists, the drive-by shooting victim in the wrong place and time, the ruined life of a junkie and his family."

A pin dropping could have been heard in the classroom.

"You are good people, the temple of God. We have read St. Paul; we are God's finest earthly creation. Good people should never be part of this deadly 'recreation.' To paraphrase St. Peter: keep sober and alert, drug free, for your enemy the devil is on the prowl like a roaring lion, looking for someone to devour."

No one stirred. All eyes and ears focused on me.

"When peers pressure you to do drugs, which they will if it hasn't already happened, tell them you want no part of the cycle of violence. You'll blow them away. Be a non-violent witness."

"Hypothetically, Mr. McCarthy, if I grow my own pot, avoid-ing the middleman, and smoke it, would that be morally okay?" asked Chris Petrizzi, who always thinks outside of the box.

My students love situation ethics. I avoid them. For them it's black and white, clear-cut. I prefer a larger moral blueprint.

"Are you a dope or doped up?"

"Neither, Mr. Mac."

The class laughed, no one heartier than knucklehead Chris. Most teenagers like kidding around and the lightness it brings to a class. Some students you can tease and my radar is pretty good at discerning which ones. The knuckleheads, I fondly call them, roll with any punch and add to the levity of the classroom. I've made mistakes, and I know immediately by the look on a face. The first order of business after class is to talk with the student and apologize for my jocularity. Afterwards, I make a mental note, never again with that one.

"Don't bug me with situation ethics, Chris. If my car is out of control, do I stop by hitting the old man or the group of children?"

Of course the whole class wants to debate it. "Hit the old man; he already lived a life…"

I interject. "If you want to get high continuously, join me for mass. To quote Jesus '…*anyone who drinks the water that I shall give will never be thirsty again…*'" (John 4:14).

The class yells out in unison, "Amen, Mr. Mac."

I often end my class a few minutes early to have time to talk with students. First, I put on music: Christian rock, gospel, rap, traditional rock, or classical. Then I walk up and down aisles to touch base with students. Today, I whispered to Manuel Navarros to see me after class. My teacher radar had zoned in on the tall, lean yet muscular young man looking uncomfortable and squirming in his seat, when I gave my drug speech.

"My brother, you danced in your seat when I talked about drugs. Am I right?"

"Ummm… not sure. Maybe."

Maybe gave me the opening.

"How can I help? I'm here for you. Just like your parents are here for you. They work hard so you can go to Dorothy Day."

"I know… I know. They're giving me a chance that I wouldn't get in El Salvador. They woke up to a dead body in their village every day. Fled a brutal civil war. Came here with nothing and started again. Worked jobs... any job they could get. I don't forget."

Many Americans get hot under the collar about immigrants coming here, especially if they are illegal. According to Elie Wiesel, a Nobel Peace Prize winner and a Holocaust survivor, no human being is illegal. Undocumented, yes; illegal, no! What are these people guilty of? They want an opportunity to live in peace and provide a better life for themselves and their children. Sounds familiar, huh? It's what we all want.

Have I brought this up in my class? You betcha. I teach the Gospels.

"So, how can I help?"

"No one can. It's complicated. I'm on my own."

"I've known the great Navarros family for three years now. We have prayed together. You never walk alone."

"You and Jesus are tight but sometimes He seems far away... and the streets are rough."

"Does this involve the new kid, Rico Ponce?"

He averted his eyes, unable to make contact.

"Gotta go. The bell," he said.

"If you need me, you know where I am."

"Sure thing." Nervous Manuel flew out the door, never looking back.

The day resumed its normalcy. Cafeteria duty followed my two Church History classes. Cafeteria duty – no teacher likes to see it on his schedule. But I'm attuned to the teachings of Christ. I understand the opportunity He has put before me. The saints remind us that there is God's work in even the most trying of jobs.

Cafe duty becomes an extension of our classroom and vocation to serve Christ. Certain cafeteria jobs need to be done and each one provides the chance to be Christ-like. Today I'm the faculty member who must establish order on the food line. I have learned each student's name. As always, I focus on the individual and, depending on the circumstance, comment: "How's your day going?" "What's the matter? You look upset," or "Your smile lights up the room."

A brief notice of students by a faculty member goes a long way to brighten their day. Am I envious of teachers assigned class coverage instead of cafeteria duty? Of course. They have time to correct papers, while covering a class. They miss an opportunity, however, to bond with three hundred students they might otherwise not have gotten to know. Cafeteria duty. God has a sense of humor.

I relished my free afternoon after school today. My freshmen basketball team exited the season with a loss in the semis. Coaching the junior varsity baseball team would start up shortly in early March. I had planned to take a break from coaching after the basketball season but Brother Willie had another idea. He asked me this way, "If you don't coach 'em no one else will and we cancel the program. Twenty more kids on Bronx streets." Ouch. Not exactly asking. My solid Christian guilt said yes. Could you have said no?

After school, I worked on my lesson plans, corrected papers, responded to emails, and made phone calls to parents. A full-time job. Yeah, right. Not even close. Make it two or three jobs rolled into one. Oh, I know. I get all those vacations – summers off. Teachers hear that frequently. Well, the way I figure it, after I add up all the time I put into a school day plus the work before and after school, and on weekends, my weeks are much longer than forty hours. Sixty hours is more like it. Counting up all the hours, summer vacation really comes down to about two weeks.

I made my way to the administrative offices to speak with Sister Sam. A necessary follow-up on the drug situation at the school and my suspicions as to the particular student involved. The kid was no good. Harsh words from a teacher but I call it like it is. Redeemable, I doubted it. It could be his upbringing, the crowd he hangs out with, or the lure of money and perceived prestige. Not sure what caused him to go astray. But surely he had managed to bring the blues to our little kingdom of God here at Dorothy Day. My heart weighed heavy for Manuel. The veiled threat of violence hung in the air.

Four

Turn the other cheek...
Luke 6:29

Thursday afternoon

Before the first rugby practice of the season, I headed home to my end of day snack. I washed down cheese and crackers with swigs of chocolate milk from a pint bottle. I put on my practice clothes – old familiar friends, consisting of a well-worn, heavy, gray-hooded sweatshirt and sweatpants. I stuffed my cleats and dry clothes for post practice into my faded blue duffel bag.

Give blood. Play rugby. You also give sweat, tons of it. Tears, absolutely not. One's skin is given over to cuts, scrapes, and abrasions; the body to soreness. By the end of the game, you're sweaty, smelly, muddy or grass-stained, depending on the conditions of the pitch, and in some cases, covered with goose droppings. Yeah, you heard right, goose droppings. Bruises, colored deep blue and black, come sooner rather than later. You definitely wake up with them the next morning. That's the price a rugger pays for running, tackling, hitting the ground, getting piled on, passing the ball, and heading to the goal line.

Rugby requires all you have physically throughout a game. Substitutions are rare, usually only for injuries. No pads or helmets in rugby. Not like the popular sport of football where players wear heavily padded protection, get frequent breaks on the sidelines for oxygen, are substituted for regularly, and only play offense or defense but not both. In rugby, you're on the field for every play.

Rugby makes me feel alive. The intensity of the action on the field leads to an adrenaline rush. I love the game, especially, the camaraderie with the other guys, or at least most of the other guys. In anything, there's always the exception.

I'm an okay rugger for the White Plains club in Westchester County, north of the Bronx. I usually play the B side, the second team; infrequently, the A side, made up of the best ruggers on the team. At six foot three and one hundred and ninety five pounds, I'm fit enough to play a second game with the C side, a game that nobody in the first two games usually wants to play. I could be a better rugger but it's not a priority in my life as it is for some. God is my priority; service to Him includes teaching, coaching, family, and friends. Rugby provides my need for a healthy physical outlet.

Rugby practice is usually routine. Yet surprises happen. I warmed up with short sprints along the sideline in the cold and yesterday's left-over snow, which had already turned gray and gritty. My buddy Jerry, aka the Professor, ran at my side. He teaches rhetoric at a wonderful local college, Manhattanville. He's a secular New York Jew. We have great conversations about life and Yahweh, usually over a pint or two. I pray that he will know the love of God. He's taken baby steps. As the chosen people say, "Next year, Jerusalem."

Practice started with the Professor and me avoiding the hard physical contact. A philosophical difference with the coach. We hate beating ourselves up in practice, especially before the first game. The season does that soon enough. No one is 100% ready to go at the first practice.

Tonight we practiced a ruck and maul drill – a ball possession technique for the forwards. It was meant to be a walk through with mild contact. Halfway through the drill, someone picked me up and slammed me hard onto the pitch. The frozen ground felt like concrete. Bone jarring. The wind knocked out of me, I lay flat on my back with Johnson, aka Pretty Boy, on top of me, grinning for all to see. He always struts like a peacock and avoids the hard work on the pitch. He takes advantage of legal rugby hits but most everyone views them as cheap shots. He's a pompous A side ass. Every team has one. Full of himself, he considers himself the face of White Plains Rugby and gives little or no credit to the other fourteen players who get him the ball. He crows like a rooster amongst chicks. Sorry, Johnson, time to end the delusion.

Pinned under the weight of Johnson, my juices were flowing; my adrenaline peaked. I slapped Johnson's head back with a forearm to his face. I grabbed his GQ hairstyle and pulled it toward the ground. Head and torso followed. He lay on the ground and I sprang up and jumped on top of him. I landed several left and right crosses. Drawing my fist back and down, I powered it up – a haymaker – to his face. Serious contact with his left cheek. Ruggers pulled me off before I could release another bomb. He staggered to his feet and challenged my manhood for a clean hit. I called him a coward as he talked tough with the team between us.

We huffed and puffed for a few minutes and paced back and forth. The coach mercifully ended practice. My black mood turned even fouler as I regretted my actions. My street fighting man side is always just a reactive moment away. My good friend, the Professor, could sense I needed some space and walked me around the field a few times. Nothing said, just solidarity of presence and understanding. Breathing exercises helped me to regroup. I asked God and the heavens for help in controlling my anger and my violent side. I need to get better at this. Some day.

I refused the usual after practice beer offerings, and headed home. I turned on the radio to listen to the New York Rangers, my favorite hockey team. A treat, for sure, but hockey is almost impossible to follow on radio. The speed of the game, and European names lead to chaos and confusion. "Ovechkin, one timer, Lundquist saves, long rebound, Zuccarello has it, ensuing rush, he dekes, score!" Yeah. Fist pump for the Rangers.

I merged onto the Bronx River Parkway and headed south. The parkway runs approximately twenty miles, and parallels the Bronx River, thus its name. When I crossed the border between Yonkers and the Bronx, my car hit black ice at a turn in the road. A blur of trees passed by the window as the car spun. Controlling it was out of the question. Not an option. A Hail Mary was. "Pray for us sinners now and at the hour of our death."

Blackness.

Five

For now I have seen the angel of the Lord face to face
Judges 6:22

Thursday night

Roars of laughter greeted my inquiry of "Are you God?" Wave after wave of mirth from my Good Samaritan swept around and over me. Eventually, amidst the laughing fits, he sputtered out "not even close."

"Are you a saint? ... A prophet? ... An angel?" I asked.

"Bingo. Number 3," he answered.

"Michael, Raphael, Gabriel...?"

"Nope, not one of them. You named me."

Could he be... Was this... Daniel? The name I gave to my guardian angel when I was a kid. The one I talk to in prayer every day. Never seen in person... Well, maybe, not until now.

Jesus told us of guardian angels in scripture (Matthew 18:10). The belief that angels guard the righteous was ancient and Jewish. An angel rescued an imprisoned St. Peter. *"Then suddenly the angel of the Lord stood there, and the cell was filled with light. He tapped Peter on the side and woke him... the angel next said, 'Wrap your cloak around you and follow me'"* (Acts of the Apostles 12:7-8).

"Daniel?" I asked. He bowed with the exaggeration of a thespian. I added, "Like St. Peter's angel, are you here to save me?"

"Well, that's the rub. Right now your life is on pause, kinda like the button on your remote control. Frozen in time. You're hovering between life and death." Our eyes locked, tighter than security bolts on a Bronx door.

"To use the Irish culture you love, you are invited by God

Himself to choose life or death."

Say what? Did I hear that correctly? A long silence. I looked intently at him.

"Himself," I finally managed to say. "Jesus H. Christ, you have a sense of humor."

"I'm all too serious." Daniel continued, "Kevin, you have a degree in Theology. What did you learn about angels? Something, I'm sure."

"They do God's will," I answered. "They are depicted with wings and non-wings, weapons and staffs, musical instruments and beautiful voices. My knowledge of angels comes mostly from St. Thomas Aquinas and his classic, *Summa Theologica*. According to Tom... I saw your look, Daniel, yeah, I said Tom... there are various levels of angels. Archangels are the elite; the marines, rangers or seals, you might say. Angel Thrones are adoring monks praying, Seraphim Angels are scholars of knowledge. Angel Powers, like an army, keep evil in check. And, of course, you and the guardians. My answer is inadequate and incomplete, but I'm really not ready for academic comps at the moment." I gazed around and then added, "Considering the circumstances... Daniel, we're outside on a cold blustery winter's night, inches from the river and you're quizzing me about angels."

He paused, scanned the area, took the whole scene in, and then looked at me.

"The million dollar question for you," he said gently. "Do you wanna...? Let me reword that. Would you like to be an angel? A formal invitation. You're invited to become an angel."

Moments passed before I found my voice.

"An angel? Me? Did I hear you right?" I asked. "In no freakin' way did I ever think I would be asked that question."

"Himself sends the invitation," he said.

"Himself? ... Did you say Himself? ... Blow me away. I must be delusional from the accident." Closing my eyes, I inhaled deeply, trying to get a grip on my swirling emotions.

"Has anyone ever refused the offer? I assume there have been others."

"Absolutely," Daniel responded. "You too might prefer to move on to eternal life, with the hope, of course, of walking through the Pearly Gates." He continued, "Your body will be found soon enough. Your brother, Patrick, the police officer, will be notified and he'll be the one who informs your mother. Brigid will comfort her the most. Many people will think that drink was the cause of the accident but no worries there. The autopsy will prove otherwise. You often pray that you are ready to meet your Maker. The choice is yours."

My wheels churned as thoughts rushed through my head. I tried to get a firm grip on all that was happening. Refuse an offer from the Big Man. Not an option in my way of thinking. I ended up relying more on my guts than my brain.

"Daniel, you know me well from prayer. I want to do His will. Tell Himself, I'm in... I think."

A sad smile crossed Daniel's face. "I understand your hesitation. I'm glad and nervous for you. You will know joy and great danger."

"Trust me, I already know danger. My car danced its way down the embankment and turned into an accordion. I'm propped up against a rock next to the river and blood stains my clothes."

I paused to catch my breath. "An angel... here... in the Bronx?"

"Kevin, you won't be the first Bronx angel – you might be pleasantly surprised. As it is stated in the New Testament, '... *you have entertained angels without knowing it*' (Hebrews 13:1) and have seen them face to face."

30

"Wild! ... When was that?"

"Show time," responded Daniel.

*   *   *

Yankee bat day. A give-away promotion. We were kids, 6ᵗʰ graders. We took the 4 train down to the stadium. We got our free bats. A grand day, indeed. At the station on the way home, some older Manhattan kids pushed us around and stole our bats. Our buddy, Sean Michael Burns, put up a fight. They busted him up pretty bad with the bats. While they crowed, he tried to crawl away and ended up falling onto the tracks. Sprawled there and unable to move. The sound of an oncoming train froze everyone except a thin black man with glasses. He calmly jumped down on the tracks, and easily lifted Sean. Cradling him in his arms, he hopped up onto the platform. He lay Sean down, and gently ran his hands over Sean's injuries.

The train roared into the station. The Good Samaritan stood up and walked onto the train. Never a word. Never a backward glance. The Manhattan kids, the thugs, ran as we crowded around Sean. He was fine, no injuries, no nothing. What the...? The Daily News ran with the story for a while but the rescuer was never identified or seen again.

"An angel? Is that what you're telling me?" Sean had always said he felt something special that day.

"Of course, Kevin."

*   *   *

Brother Anthony, a Trappist monk, has made the cloistered monastic grounds of Spencer Abbey, in Massachusetts, his battlefield. Evil

31

will not enter. The monks bridge the heavens and earth in choir and work, which fuel and renew their love of God daily. On weekly retreats, lay people get swept into the holiness of the place as they strive to grow closer to God. They center themselves by listening to the monks chant several times a day in the church, by attending mass, and by making time to reflect and pray on their own.

Gentle Brother Anthony could never have been a warrior angel for God. It's not his nature. He chose his service of adoration in choir, prayer, and monastic rule. And can he chant; his voice soars to the heavens.

His hero growing up was not a sports figure but King Kamehamaha, who united the Hawaiian Islands. Legend states that Haley's comet, streaking across the heavens, announced the King's birth. He taught his warriors to deflect and catch spears. Anthony loved that story as a young boy and as a result, he committed himself to a lifetime of deflecting violence. His weapons are chastity, poverty, and obedience. Anthony always conveys to others that even in holy cloistered ground the monks are engaged in combat versus dark forces. The power of the Holy Spirit sustains the monks.

"By true prayer a monk becomes another angel, for he ardently longs to see the face of the Father in heaven," *said St. Evagrius Porticus.*

*   *   *

I pensively worked my way through the passing images. I know Brother Anthony well. He has become my spiritual director on my annual week-long retreat in the monastery each summer.

"An angel must choose the path that is faithful to his own story," said Daniel. "You, Kevin, are a Christian in the Catholic tradition. You can serve the light in that wonderful story."

"I think you're forgetting something. I have a side to me that's not angel-like. I'm still a bit of a bar brawler, at times. And I do like my drink."

"All angels are warriors in one way, shape or form. The man who saved the boy on the tracks. Did he not have the courage of a warrior?" He went on. "Mrs. Tilak waging a war against hunger with her dignity. Surely, she's a warrior."

"Huh... Mrs. T? ... An angel?"

Daniel simply nodded.

"That's a wow!"

He continued. "Mr. Kenji Yokonama. A true warrior in your way of thinking."

Mr. Kenji, an ageless Japanese man, had taught me martial art. My mother had offered all of her children lessons in Irish dance or music. Neither interested me. Mom gave the okay to substitute martial art instead. In later years, the Lord of the Dance, a celebration of Irish dance and music, exploded in culture. As the old Shaker song goes, "I'll live in you if you'll live in me – I am the Lord of the Dance," said He. I regret not dancing with the pretty Colleens then and now. However, as a boy, a Bronx boy at that, dancing was considered wimpy. In my family, only my sister, Mary Claire, became a dancer. She's the life of every party.

Mr. Kenji also taught budo, a way of life with physical, spiritual, and moral dimensions. It focuses on self-improvement, fulfillment, and personal growth. Mr. Kenji, like all noble martial art instructors, emphasized self-defense and being an officer and a gentleman. He let us know, however, that as children of the spirit we must stand up to evil in any form, be it gangs, bullies or whatever else that lurked in society's shadows. He drilled into us that evil must be fought.

*   *   *

After martial art class, most of the students, accompanied by their parents, headed for ice cream. Meanwhile, Mrs. DiGerolomo was determined to walk back by herself to her Italian neighborhood. Mr. Kenji offered to walk her home. Ten minutes into their walk, three punks accosted them. An old man and a woman posed no threat to these three hoodlums. Or so they thought. Little did they know.

Mr. Kenji offered them everything; money, credit cards, you name it. The leader, wielding a knife, strutted, weaved around them, snatched their stuff and then grabbed Mrs. DiGerolomo's hair. Mr. Kenji sprang into action. He seized the wrist holding the knife, and quickly and easily disarmed the young man. The punk's knees buckled and he howled from the pain in his hand. Stooping down, Mr. Kenji picked up the knife, pivoted, and threw it into the chest of the assailant with a gun in hand. His short life ended with a stunned look. Before he hit the ground, Mr. Kenji stepped forward and pulled out the knife. With a low whirling complete circle move, and with the knife flashing in his hand, he lunged and slashed the third punk reaching for his gun. The knife slashed his arm to the bone just below his biceps. The gun clattered to the ground at the same time as the punk screamed and then fainted. Another whirl, and Mr. Kenji faced the leader, now back on his feet and stepping forward to threaten again. This time with a gun. The speed of Mr. Kenji surprised him. The knife slashed his throat and he went down. Never to get up. The sound of his gun firing as it hit the ground lasted longer than he did.

The assault ended in a minute, maybe a little longer. Two cop cars with sirens blaring and lights flashing arrived within minutes of the 911 call. Telling their story to the cops lasted longer than the attack. The cops were amazed that small Mr. Kenji had tamed three beasts. Two dead and the third permanently injured; his arm would never be the same again. A reminder to last him his whole life.

Excited to learn Mr. Kenji's story, the media pursued him. Eventually, the story moved on. The media wanted more from Mr. Kenji but he always had the same answer to every question. "We tried to give our money but they wanted more. Evil must be fought." Soon after, Mr. Kenji told his classes that he, too, must move on. His work was done here.

He had the perfect neighborhood send-off. The Italians cooked the food and the table groaned under the weight of lasagna, eggplant parmigiana, meatballs and spaghetti, thick crusty Italian bread, and platters of cheese and prosciutto. Meanwhile, the Irish supplied the drink. Beer and Irish whiskey. And yes, a bottle of o'sake! A grand night for our hero.

*   *   *

"An honorable warrior, Mr. Kenji," commented Daniel.

Silence. "In the Still of the Night," a doo wop song, came to my mind.

Daniel broke the silence. "And now the rules."

I managed to nod.

He smiled at me. "In essence, it comes down to this. There are no rules per se. It's part free will and part evolution. Very human-like. You are being offered a great opportunity and power. But only you can decide how to use God's gifts. You get to set the bar. You will have to learn to harness the power."

"Not good enough. I need more. This teacher is confused."

"Take for example, your five senses. You will be able to max them out if you choose. Your hearing will increase, your vision, whatever you want. It's up to you. Your vision can increase in more ways than one. Physical as well as spiritual insights. You'll be able to heal quicker, you old rugger." He smiled and then added, "You can increase your language skills to more than your Bronxese if you desire. Whatever you need in your fight against darkness will be available. You choose and develop the capabilities."

"No way. I mean, really?" I stammered. Daniel responded by speaking Irish with a brogue, followed by Italian, French, and Spanish.

I thought of the future possibilities. Presently, I'm content with my American facsimile of a brogue. Also, I know when the Italian guys are cursing me out. French? I could show off with my hockey buddies by singing the Canadian national anthem in French. It would earn me free beer from my friends. We road trip once a year to Montreal to watch the Rangers play the Canadians. The French-speaking lassies would be swept off their feet. Learning Creole would enable me to speak with Haitian parishioners.

Fluency in Spanish excited me the most, as I kinda lost out on the opportunity growing up. My high school Spanish teacher became deeply depressed and suffered a breakdown after the death of her husband. Teaching and learning disappeared. The students, sympathetic to her grief, said nothing and the administration never picked up on what was happening, or I should say, not happening in the class. She retired at the end of the school year. Not soon enough. My Spanish learning took a direct hit.

"Kevin," Daniel chuckled. "Montreal mademoiselles? Think bigger, deeper, and higher! Remember, all your new skills will evolve only if you are centered in the Lord. You're a good pray-er but you must get better. Grace will be your sustenance. Your patron saint Dorothy Day said about the little boy and his loaves and fishes and the feeding of the 5,000..."

"Let God use us like that little boy and He will multiply our gifts like the loaves and fishes," I interjected.

"A big advantage for us is only God gives grace. Only He can make you stronger, faster, holier... on the other hand, evil is unable to give gifts to its forces; it can only seduce the weak side of man and fuel man's violence, greed, sexuality..."

What was happening here? What is going to happen? Difficult to imagine. More thoughts flashed by. Why me? Was this guy for real?

"Yes, Kevin, it's daunting and overwhelming. Rest assured you will never walk completely alone. The Lord and the communion of saints, prophets, and angels will aid you. So will I. I'll check on you, guard you, as well as guide you. I'm spread thin, however, and don't have the luxury of focusing on just you. I'll inform my band of angels about you but they fight on-going battles and will be unable to give you their undivided attention."

"You must think in terms of being on your own," he continued. "You need to get battle-ready: mentally, physically, and spiritually. Be cautious as evil has its minions. Devils on earth evolve at varying degrees and skill levels. You'll sense them and they you. Some cloak, however, making them difficult to see, to know. Some are new, like you, and some ancient like our leader, Michael, the archangel. You'll battle them in a manner of your own choosing. Be ready. Most likely, as early as tomorrow, you will be detected and put on their radar. Soon you will be tested in the battle of good and evil. You may live a day longer or a lifetime. No promises."

"Fight the devil and his troops? I'm not sure this body's ready to do that. This Bronx guy may be tough but we're talking the devil here."

"You'll evolve. Physically you'll stay six feet three with strawberry blond hair. And no worries, your thick, droopy blond mustache is going nowhere. But with grace you may become this."

The dark night brightened with a shimmering white light. In front of me stood a warrior angel, a burning sword held high in one hand, a shield, four feet across, in the other. Sparks cascaded from gold points on the outer edge of the shield. The ends of his wings, also tipped in gold, extended out one foot on either side of his massive silver armor.

Momentarily, I closed my eyes, dazzled by the bright light. When I reopened them, the balding middle-aged man stood before me once again.

"*...the shield of faith,*" I whispered.

"*and the sword of the Spirit*" (Ephesians 6:16-17), added Daniel.

Silence.

I gazed at him intently and then looked over at the wreck of my car.

"Why me?" I finally whispered. "A kid from da Bronx."

"Mother Mary called herself '*his lowly handmaid*' (Luke 1:48). Yes, even she who was sinless felt unworthy of the Lord's calling. Bronx boy, we know sinless doesn't fit you," he said with a twinkle in his eye and a raised eyebrow. "Nor did it fit your Patron Saint Dorothy. You teach Church History and know saints come in all shapes and sizes, rich, poor, black, white, Asian, Latino, native American, and to quote you, purple and green."

He went on. "You try, that's your strength. You sin and then get up and try to be holy again. You go to confession. And most of all, you pray. That's a definition of saintliness."

"I pray to become the person God wants me to be. To try and imitate Christ. To go through the day looking through the eyes of Christ. To sin no more." And then with silliness, I added, "Until my next confession."

Daniel's eyebrows rose once again.

"Remember Daniel, humor." He smiled.

"As an angel, just like as a human, God wants you to keep trying and evolving up that spiritual ladder. Like Dorothy did," said Daniel. "You're not guaranteed success as an angel. Failure and sin will be part of the journey. Temptations will not cease. Always be ready to fight your sinful weakness or else you will be useless in the cosmic battle. Stay centered and become that awakened walking contemplative you always want to be. The devil will try to disturb your oneness with God and keep you from knowing peace."

Daniel's eyes bored into mine. "Remember," he cautioned, "no quitting. If you turn from God and give up the fight, you will lose your new powers. Then you won't last long. The enemy particularly delights in fallen angels. Choose carefully your path. I need to leave. A cop will soon find you. Any last questions?"

"In all seriousness," I replied. "I want the wisdom of Solomon to do His will."

"You got that right. Keep asking in prayer. You will need it. You have barely checked your Bronx macho side as a human. Now, with more power, you will need to double your efforts. We need God-centered angels not cowboy ones. Our enemy will use any weakness against you... us. I pray that your faith may not fail."

A police car stopped on the shoulder of the parkway above us. I looked up at the flashing red swirl of the cruiser's light and then returned my gaze to Daniel.

In the book of Genesis (28:12) it is written: *"...there was a ladder set up on earth, and the top of it reached to heaven; and behold, the angels of God were ascending and descending on it!"*

No ladder for Daniel. He had simply vanished.

Six

Miracles do not, in fact,
break the laws of nature.
C.S. Lewis

Thursday night

A lone police officer with flashlight in hand slowly made his way down the hill. The light panned over the area and came to rest on the car. He whistled a sharp warning note. I startled him with an "Officer!" from the darkness of the rocks. His flashlight found me and lit up my face.

"You survived this?" he asked incredulously. His flashlight again surveyed the wreckage. He started to call for an ambulance.

"No, officer. I'm okay." I stood up.

"Impossible. I'm no state trooper but I've seen a fair amount of wrecks and the damage they can do."

"Really. I'm okay."

"It looks like you used up one, maybe more, of your nine lives. A bleeping miracle."

I looked the young officer in the eye. "A miracle, indeed. I hope to use my remaining lives in service of the miracle worker."

His eyes squinted as he looked at me. "I'd be getting religious too after what you went through." Once again, his flashlight lit up the twisted and crushed car, lying on its side, inches from the water.

"Amen."

"What's your name?" asked New York's Finest.

I told him. He wrote it down. I waited. I knew what would come next.

"Well, I have to ask. You look like my boss, Captain McCarthy, minus the mop of hair. The color is the same, and you have similar builds. And this accident is close to Woodlawn. You related?"

"Yeah, brothers." My clan of nine siblings all have variations of strawberry blond hair. It's the McCarthy look.

"I'll see him, tomorrow. Should I tell him?"

I looked at his badge and took in his name. "Sure, Officer McIvor."

"I saw the snowy tire tracks leading off the road and the shoulder." He hesitated a moment and glanced down at his writing pad. "Snow and ice? Drink? Or both?" he finally asked.

"Fair enough, officer. I think black ice. No drink, not even a drop."

Visibly relieved by my answer, he commented, "I'm Irish but you Woodlawn Irish have a rep and a half. The captain is a good guy but he is my boss. I had to ask. Let me test you for alcohol so you get a clean slate. Then, I'll drive you home."

"Officer, you handled that well. The Woodlawn Irish have a drinking rep, well deserved, at times. Let me get my stuff. I have a friend who does towing. I want to give him the job tomorrow."

"No problem, McCarthy."

I gazed at the river. It shone in the moonlight, and its surface barely rippled. A calmness came over me. As I walked slowly up the hill beside McIvor and took one last glance backward at the wreck, I thought: You're one blessed Irish guy: don't mess this up.

Seven

The spirit of the Lord shall rest on him
Isaiah 11:2

Thursday night

McIvor, a cop in the five two precinct, headquartered at Webster Ave. and Bainbridge Rd., would have to leave his precinct to take me home. Not unprecedented but not encouraged either. McIvor's no dummy; my brother, a New York Police Department (NYPD) captain and his boss, would be happy with the break in protocol.

The captain, the oldest son in my clan of nine siblings, is named Patrick but he has always been called Paddy, a common Irish name. The name led to the infamous label the police paddy wagon. In the 1800's, some Irish, a number of them named Paddy, a bit taken with drink or with criminal activity, got arrested and placed in the police wagons for the ride to the police station. Over time, the police vehicles acquired the Irish name. It's not exactly bragging Irish history but a fact is a fact.

Paddy is a neighborhood success story. A Notre Dame graduate – it's a big deal in my neck of the woods to go to what is considered the top Catholic university in the country. He lives over in Riverdale, a three square mile neighborhood in the Bronx. The northernmost point in New York City, its western border along the Hudson River, offers a magnificent view across the water of the Palisades, steep rock cliffs in New Jersey, free for the taking.

We Catholics tend to do our geography by parishes. We often greet new acquaintances with the query what parish are you from. Riverdale is St. Margaret's Parish. We tease Paddy for living with the upper class Irish in Riverdale. "The Irish-lace crowd" we call 'em. In the old days of Tammany Hall, when the Irish ran NYC, Paddy would have gone far. The days when the Irish were kings of the city are over. Let it be noted though that we still have a lot of fight left in us.

McIvor talked away, leaving no opportunity for reflection on my encounter with Daniel. He grew up in northern New Jersey. I told him in a lighthearted way that I wouldn't hold it against him. It was the usual banter between a New Yorker and a neighbor from the Garden State. Weehawken, a town across the Hudson River from Manhattan, he calls home. It has a main claim to fame. Aaron Burr fatally shot Alexander Hamilton in a duel on the Weehawken cliffs overlooking the Hudson. Dueling was illegal in New York so they rowed over to Jersey.

McIvor always wanted to be a New York City cop. He loves his job; it's the commuting over the George Washington Bridge that he hates. Known by locals as the GW, it spans the majestic Hudson and connects Jersey and The City. Traffic simply is a fact of life in the metropolitan New York area. Traffic reports on 1010 WINS or 880 CBS AM radio, given every ten minutes, always blare out info about delays on the upper or lower decks of the bridge or both. Forget the Cross Bronx Expressway, heading east and west to and from the bridge on the New York side. You could laugh at the word expressway if it wasn't so painful idling away hours sitting on that road. For the city that never sleeps, one could take a good nap waiting for the traffic to move. A honking horn – or, most likely, horns – announce loud and clear that it's time to inch forward.

Officer McIvor dropped me off at my house. Indeed, there are houses in the Bronx, sometimes, whole blocks and neighborhoods, like my beloved Woodlawn. More often than not, neighborhoods have a few houses nestled between apartment buildings. I live now in one of three duplexes sandwiched between apartments on Valentine Avenue below Fordham Road. I rent the ground floor from Louisa Todisco, an elderly Italian lady, who stayed put in the Belmont neighborhood, when most of her neighbors headed for the suburbs. Dion, the lead singer for the Belmonts, left the area, also. Arthur Avenue, named after U.S. president Chester A. Arthur, and the primary thoroughfare in the Belmont neighborhood, however, is still full of Italian restaurants, and smells of garlic bread, pizza, tomato sauce, and pasta dishes served on tables with red-checkered cloths and burning candles stuck in empty wine bottles.

My landlord Louisa had reached out to my local Catholic high school to see if a teacher needed housing. Fearful of living alone, she wanted the security of someone "safe" in her house. The neighborhood rests on the police radar as a high crime neighborhood. McIvor's surprised that the Captain's brother lives here.

"Jersey boy, whatta you know?" I pounded him in my New Yorker style, by way of a thank you and a good-bye.

I let myself into my apartment. My large foyer is where I hang up my sweaty, muddy, wet, and sometimes, bloody, rugby clothes on metal hooks. My mountain bike leans against the left-side wall. It's not for mountains but for the New York City equivalent, potholes. Aka pits of despair. From the foyer, it's a straight shot to my bedroom, living room, and then a small kitchen. Immediately, I walked to the bathroom, off the kitchen to the right, to wash away rugby grime.

I showered, letting the hot water stream in rivulets down my body. Minutes ticked by but I had no desire to move. Questions, doubts, and disbelief swarmed in my mind, though none of them took firm hold. Finally, after unsuccessful efforts to cut through my jumbled emotions, I got out and toweled off. I performed my post-rugby check for injuries. Black and blue bruises on my arms and legs, the usual ones, had already made their colorful appearance. From the accident, none at all that I could figure.

I followed my nightly routine. In the larger picture, nothing would ever be routine again. I lit my prayer candle and put on reflective harp music. Usually, night prayer involves an examination of conscience of my daily behavior. Tonight's prayer activity took me in different directions... to Daniel and future possibilities. I felt a strong urge to talk with God and listen to his answers. *"To you I call; for you will surely hear me, O God"* (Psalm 17:6).

The Lenten season usually finds me cutting back on beer as part of my fasting. Not tonight. A cold one in hand, I settled back on my hand-me-down couch. Thoughts of Dorothy made me hesitate before taking the first sip.

In 1965, she and nineteen other Catholic women urged the final session of the Vatican Council to "Put away the sword." They fasted ten days, drinking only water, to highlight their call for the Council to condemn weapons of mass destruction, and to support nonviolence in the fight for social justice and conscientious objection to military service.

I gazed at the cold beer, the bottle sweating beads of water that moistened my hand, and pursed my lips. Obviously, not a solid beginning to my Lenten fast. That's why you're on the road to being declared a saint, Dorothy, not me, I thought.

Hey, wait. Dorothy were you an angel here on earth? Was that how you were able to do it all? Your unceasing witness for nonviolence... enduring arrest and jail time for protesting non-violently... writing and publishing a newspaper that cried out for the poor... feeding the hungry with bread and soup... providing service to others morning, noon, and night at Houses of Hospitality. Maybe, just maybe, all done on "angel juice."

How would I serve? Like Dorothy? Or...? The "how to serve"

swirled through my mind.

Teaching angel? I love my teaching vocation. Yet awesome academic, I'm not. Let the record show, however, that I'm smarter than my teenagers. In my clan, Paddy of Notre Dame, and sister Molly of Boston College, are the family's bright academic lights. But I'm no dummy. I went to a fine college, Manhattan College, in the Bronx run by the La Sallian Brothers. The name of the college, long removed from its days in the borough of Manhattan, confuses some. Adding to the confusion is that this fine order of Brothers was started by a priest, St. John Baptist De LaSalle. Go figure. Graduate school for a Master's degree in Theology found me still in the Bronx at Fordham University. Even with that Jesuit education, I'm no college professor type.

A religious angel? Monk? Brother? Priest? Deacon? I have prayed often over a religious life but like the great St. Augustine of Hippo, I keep saying to God, "Not yet."

The coach angel? I've never been an "x and o" guy, plotting out strategies. I keep good kids off the streets so trouble doesn't find them. Outside of hitting a great fungo, a practice fly ball, my coaching ability is lacking.

Warrior angel appeals to me the most. I'm from the Bronx and fighting was part of growing up. Bar brawls and street fights often settled arguments in my neighborhood. Violence is the first and easiest of solutions for humans. It has the "sexy" look of good guys crushing bad guys and of immediate results versus planting seeds as a teacher and a coach.

Unlike the beautiful pacifist Quakers, the Catholic Church believes we have a duty to defend life from the womb to the tomb. The Church's Just War theory gives the government the right to defend. One cannot initiate violence but one has an obligation to defend the innocent. While not officially a pacifist church, the Catholic Church, however, has a rich history of pacifists in its flock over the years. The list includes Dorothy Day and her Catholic Workers, the Berrigans, St. Jaggerstatter, an Austrian pacifist who refused to serve in Hitler's army, and oh yeah, Jesus. Maybe, in the future, the Church should study the lives of its pacifists and develop a Just Peace theory. Food for thought.

I'm an altar boy type but my patience has limits. Prayer keeps me calm with kids. I understand the growing pains of youth but adults are a different story. I figure they know better. Even though I'm usually centered with an inner peace, I sometimes fly off the handle, especially at injustice, poverty, suffering, and the struggle to survive in the world. Always something to work on. The list grows longer.

The prayer candle flickered and burned. Tonight's prayer relieved my angst and pent-up emotion. Breathing and mental exercises quieted my mind. The Chinese martial art of tai chi, took me deeper with deliberate slow body movements. This brought about an increased state of mental calm and clarity. Kata, a choreographed pattern of martial art techniques taught to me by Mr. Kenji, led me to a higher state. Squat kicks followed slow-motion ones. I finished with speed punches, pretending my punches met with resistance.

I danced with shadows flickering on the living room walls. I danced with the Lord of the Dance!

Eight

If you are a theologian, you truly pray;
if you truly pray, you are a theologian.
St. Evagrius Ponticus

Friday

When I woke the next morning stretched out on my couch, my candle still burned. Pink and red streaks in the sky announced a new day. A fitful sleep left me physically tired but my mind jolted into overdrive. Disbelief, shock, confusion. Wistfulness for what was. Trust, hope in the future. All these emotions churned in the cauldron of my thoughts.

I uttered "Holy Hannah," my exclamatory expression for anything that surprises me. The encounter with Daniel surely qualified.

My juices started flowing with a cold shower followed by two cups of tea. I ran late out the door, put my head down, and hoofed it quickly to school. Driving my car, obviously, not an option.

I approached the day in my usual way with morning mass in the school chapel. A dozen of us regularly attend but today our numbers doubled in size. The Lenten season of the church adds to our core group and renews the flock.

The first rays of the day streamed through the stained glass windows, unleashing the red, blue, and yellow colors to dance on the floor and the chairs. The colors appeared heightened in intensity, most likely due to my charged up imagination.

"...the Body of Christ...," Father Tim intoned. A grace-filled moment. A fabulous way to start the day.

Today's test on Black History: Saints, Prophets, Movers and Shakers led juniors to linger at my doorway before entering the classroom. They touched the wooden mezuzah, a Jewish sign of faith, with their fingertips and whispered a prayer. Some recited the traditional Jewish prayer, called the Shema: *"Hear, o Israel, the Lord is our God, the Lord alone! You shall love your God with all your heart and all your soul, and with all your strength"* (Deuteronomy 6:4-5). I shared this prayer with my students because Jesus prayed it daily his whole faithful Jewish life. Today, I too recited the prayer, more fervently than usual. A strong reminder to remain steadfast in my faith as Daniel had urged.

Proctoring a test usually provides an easier school day, a time-out, a come up for air kind of moment. It offers a respite from the marathon of teaching five classes a day. The only difficulty arises when the usual suspects show up with wandering eyes, scraps of paper, or writing on hands, shirt cuffs or desks. Oh, and the latest, cell phones between the legs. I hoped for no shenanigans today during testing time. I needed time to gather my thoughts and reflect on my encounter with Daniel.

On test days, anxious students find settling into a class prayer difficult. Instead of praying, I always direct their attention to the picture of my mother's brother, Uncle Jim, on my wall of saints. A Jesuit missionary in the Philippines, he spent forty years ministering in Quezon City, a slum area in the capital of Manila. The picture reminds them that taking the test pales in comparison to hungry and starving children, foraging for food in a garbage dump.

A game of Jeopardy before the start of the test. "The answer is Mandela... Frederick Douglass... Ida B. Wells..."

The crackle in the air startled me. Rhythmic waves surrounded me and bounced off me. What the...? I took a moment to catch my breath and then looked out at the students. No reaction there.

The motion came from familiar footsteps at the far end of the hallway. My brother Paddy in his well-worn shoes was making his way to my classroom. Super-hearing? What's that about? Hey, Daniel is this...?

Wearing his blue uniform, Paddy stepped into my doorway. His appearance set off a chain reaction in my room.

"Hey, Officer, arrest Mr. McCarthy," and "Officer, Mr. Mac hit me."

I turned the tables on the class. "He's here for Juan Santos. He's wanted for robbing people at Hunt's Point." First, dead silence, then howls as the students realized the joke. Juan is the nicest, politest kid in the class. He blushed but smiled.

"As most of you know, the officer here is my brother. I will cut you a break. If my brother, Mr. Notre Dame graduate, can answer a Black History question, I will give everyone five points." They hooted and whooped, pumping their arms in the air.

"Ready, Paddy. What woman is associated with the 'Ain't I A Woman' speech?"

My older brother's glare bore into me. He squirmed and finally blurted out, "Rosa Parks." Half the students, unsure if his answer was correct, waited for verification.

"The answer is Sojourner Truth. Mr. Notre Dame missed it by one hundred years." Laughter from the class but my brother's humor was missing in action today. I added, "Kwame, don't be angry at my white brother; you didn't know the answer either as a proud black man."

"You got that right, Mr. Mac," he responded. More laughter.

Paddy apologized to the students for costing them five points.

"Any of you mooks ever apologize for wrong answers?" I inquired. Sheepishly, they averted their eyes and went back to reviewing for the test.

"I'm glad you're okay. You're loved," said Paddy. He put his hand affectionately on my shoulder, caught my eyes, and smiled. "Mom knows and she's expecting to see you on Saturday after rugby for tea or dinner. She knows it's Lent so you can't use a rugby party as an excuse. She's worried. Mothers do that." He paused before adding with a smile, "There could be worse places to die than the scenic Bronx River." I chuckled.

He continued. "What chance do you think I'll use Sojourner Truth and 'Ain't I A Woman' in the projects today?" We laughed. Zero. Nada. No chance at all.

"An itinerant preacher in Jesus' name, she quieted unruly crowds with her powerful voice and strong convictions that Jesus is the truth," I told him as he headed toward the door. "You could probably use her help."

"Amen," we said in unison.

Take advantage of every available moment. That's a teacher's daily game plan. Less work to do at home. During my free period, however, I pushed aside a pile of tests. I needed to find Larry Schmidt, the head football coach. Like many Catholic school teachers, he works a part-time job outside of teaching. He moonlights as a tow truck man. No one gets rich teaching at a Catholic school. Well, I should say money rich. It's a richness of a different sort: love of job and kids, and making a difference. Priceless.

I strolled into Larry's athletic office by the gym. The place always has a bachelor pad feel to it. Clutter reigns everywhere: towels hanging on chairs, bags of balls, water coolers and bottles on the floor, scattered equipment in every available space. He jumped up to greet me with a hearty pounding on my back. He has a paunch, and always wears a colorful bandanna tied around a mostly bald head. His thick black glasses magnified his eyes, giving him a hint of madness. The mad eyes work well for a coach and a tow truck operator. He's been known to brandish a tire iron when other tow trucks try to take his business. Broken-down cars don't last long on Bronx roads. Stripped fast. Why lock it up when broken down? Be nice and leave the keys. You'll hear that in the Bronx.

"If it ain't my favorite Mick. What's up?"

"My German brother," I replied, "I need a tow of my deceased car on the Bronx River Parkway."

"What happened?"

"Black ice and a roll."

"Looks like no injuries. Luck of the Irish. Where's the car?"

"Between Gun Hill and E. 233rd, going south. Real close to the water."

"Close to having a cold bath, my friend. Glad you're okay," said the tough coach.

"Thanks, big guy." A verbal hug in a testosterone athletic office. "Larry, the car is totaled. A friendly reminder to take the plates. Whatever you get for parts and scrap metal, keep the money for your football slush fund. For the needy kids without cleats, equipment..."

"We really would have missed you." He smiled.

Walking back to class, I reflected on Larry, his love of the kids, and his do anything attitude for them. The only thing he refuses to do is recruit them: "Whoever comes to this school, I will coach and that's it."

"I didn't hang out in the rice paddies of Nam to kiss the ass of little grammar school kids. Not this grunt," he has said. "I saw kids in Nam die way too young. They got burned and they got broken. I refuse to hold the hand of some spoiled eighth grader and tell him he's special because he can play sports. No way. Insane."

It was insane. The focus on sports and winning has spun out of control at the college level, and the attitude has seeped into high schools, leading to an intensity of recruiting athletes. Some school administrators face pressure from parents and alumni for W's – wins, especially in football and basketball.

Sister Sam's an exception. Nurture the athletes, teach values and discipline. Forget recruiting, she has told the coaches. Work with whoever comes through the door. Her well-received message lessens stress in a jungle of many stresses for the coaches.

Larry's teams were always well-coached but often accompanied by a .500 mark; other schools recruit and skim off the talent. The administration at Dorothy Day has no problem with his record and realizes that Larry teaches a lot more than football to his players. The good coaches do.

The Reformation, a time of religious, political, and social upheaval that divided western Christendom in the 16th century, took up the rest of my school day. Martin Luther, a Catholic priest, broke away from the Church. His displeasure with the Catholic Church started with the practice of indulgences – a penitent offered a donation to the church for forgiveness of his sins or for the release of a soul from purgatory.

"Mr. Mac was this guy Martin Luther named after Dr. King?" asked a student at the beginning of class. A long pause. Some students realized the mistake and quiet smiles and mischievous eyes lit up their faces. Teaching can be a big chuckle, at times.

Many other causes led to the Reformation. Some included the worldliness of the Popes, the rise of political power, the use of the printing press to spread new ideas, and disgruntlement with the wealth and immorality of priests and monasteries. The result was the birth of Protestantism.

The Catholic Church realized the need to clean up its act. It renewed itself in the Counter Reformation, lasting from 1522 to roughly 1648. New religious orders, including the Jesuits, were established, and Catholic doctrine and piety were restored through the efforts of holy men and women, including St. Francis de Sales, St. Charles Borromeo, and St. Teresa of Avila.

Our Friday school day ended with a prayer over the loudspeaker, and then with Sister Sam's concluding words: "On Sunday, we go to church."

Daniel had hung out on the edge of my thought processes, but a full day of educating teenagers allowed no time to move him front and center.

After school, I straightened desks, and picked up scraps of paper, making cleaning easier for our competent maintenance staff. Maybe, this was my kingdom building.

Joseph, our hard-working Jamaican building manager, walked by and stuck his head in the door. He runs the building like he owns the place. Everybody agrees our school is safe and clean. Joseph often says in his thick Jamaican accent, "I'm no city boy from Kingston, man; I'm from the hills. My mom could make a dirt floor look good." He learned his lessons well.

"Friday afternoon, Irish. Are you headed to the staff gathering for some cold ones?" he asked. I nodded in response.

"When I was a boy, we would put Red Stripe beer in the mountain river to get it ice cold," he added. "You do that with Guinness?" He laughed. I just smiled.

"You Catholics are okay," added Joseph, a devout Episcopalian, as he walked out the door. Not exactly a ringing endorsement but Catholics have been called much worse. Sometimes, you're happy with an "okay."

I reflected on the day – typical, without a moment to spare. The familiarity of the routine comforted me. How long before my comfort zone vanished? I wondered.

I remembered Daniel's words from last night. "Most likely, as early as tomorrow you will be detected and put on their radar." Well, tomorrow was now today.

Nine

I'd like to thank the good Lord
for making me a Yankee.
Joe DiMaggio

Friday afternoon

I stepped out of school and pulled my jacket collar up against the cool air. The sun had fled behind the apartment building next to the school, and a pale yellow light slanted over the concrete jungle. The route to the local bar where the faculty was meeting took me along the Grand Concourse, a major thoroughfare, cutting north and south across the Bronx.

The Concourse was modeled after the Champs Elysees, the wide avenue through the heart of Paris. The Concourse is 180 feet in width and is separated into three roadways by median strips. It beats the French road in distance. The Champs Elysees runs barely over a mile, while the Concourse measures four miles in length. It runs from 138th Street up to Mosholu Park in the Bronx. I've never been to Paris but I'm pretty sure its avenue is not beaten down by poverty and grim like the Concourse. Graffiti on street signs, decaying storefronts, and a desolate look of having been forgotten. Slowly, however, it's trying for a comeback. Two new buildings have replaced boarded up ones, a coffee shop – no, not a Starbucks, something called Joltin' Joe – and a grocery store, which offers a pretty good selection of produce and meat.

I walked quickly along the sidewalk. A siren wailed in the distance. Buses rumbled by. Pieces of litter swirled in the wind. My guard was up as Daniel had cautioned me to be ready. For what, I wasn't entirely sure. Nothing threatening though – a woman walking her dog, a child holding tight to his father's hand, and a young couple snuggled close to each other on a front stoop.

I soon found myself at the Bar and Grille, the name written in block letters over the steel front door. The faculty just call it "The Local." Neon beer signs flashed in the barred window.

In the old days, owners locked up the alcohol behind a grill made of iron bars to prevent those who were so inclined from taking it. Inebriated customers thought nothing of vaulting over the wooden counter and grabbing what they wanted. The bar and grill protected the supply from the takers. Nowadays, bars on windows and doors in certain sections of the city serve a similar purpose. They are a deterrent to thieves.

I entered the bar warily, glancing around for any worrisome elements. Nothing out of the ordinary caught my eye – just familiar faces of faculty – and I let my guard down – at least a little.

"For Christ's sake, Mac, how did you walk away from that wreck?" Larry whispered to me. He stood immediately to the right of the door.

"You got it, Larry. It was all Christ."

Smiling, he saluted me with his cup. Tough vets don't faze easily.

"Mac, welcome. Give me a kiss, Irish boy," bellowed Mrs. J from behind the bar. A big-boned six foot two black woman, Mrs. J, aka Jackson, ran the joint. Manager and regular bartender. Maybe, the owner, too. She always said a cop, who had moved to the burbs, owned it. But no one had ever seen him. I suspected she put that tale out as a cautionary measure, hoping to ward off trouble with a capital T.

She handed me a cold one in a plastic cup. No chance it's a light beer. Don't even think about it. I don't do light. Mrs. J uses plastic cups, no glass in her bar. Beer bottles get poured into plastic cups as well as rail drinks – scotch, whiskey, rye, bourbon. No exceptions. She let us know that "glass can create trouble in a bar." Used as a weapon in a drunken brawl. Like a teacher, she anticipated and headed off trouble before it started. The bathrooms were clean and small. The men's room had a urinal and a toilet with no seat. "Some jackass broke it and I ain't replacing it." Mrs. J also locked the toilet paper dispenser. "They steal everything if you let them." Who "they" were, I wasn't entirely sure.

"How's it going, Mac?" inquired Mrs. J. "What have you been up to?"

Nothing much, I thought. Just a deadly accident. A face-to-face meeting with my guardian angel. And a new job: Mr. Angel. Oh, I could predict Mrs. J's response to that news – how many did you have before you walked into my joint?

"Same old, same old, Mrs. J," I responded. "Coaching starts up again soon, so my Fridays coming here after school will again be a thing of the past until the season ends."

"We'll be waiting for you."

"Hey, Mac, nice job zeroing in on your student Beth Anne." I turned to find Sister Chiara standing behind me. "You called that one right," she exclaimed. "Her parents' divorce is tearing her apart. Thanks for giving me a heads-up. I met with her and she shared her sadness about her family. She let me know that you noticed her sorrow."

Sister Chiara is an awesome social worker. A noble profession. As she says, "there are a million people in the Bronx and a million problems. I put band aids on them with love."

"Thanks for your good work. We couldn't do it without you," I told her. I moved on to mingle, and say hello to as many teachers as possible, especially the ones I usually don't see during the day or even the week. Although we're in the same building, teachers are often like passing ships as we speed to class or hallway duty or some other responsibility that calls our name. I always try to catch up with everyone at our gatherings and I usually succeed as I'm often the last one to leave. But no closing the bar tonight. I need alone time. A chance to ponder and sort through my jumbled thoughts.

"Here's to our last Friday off," said Brother Willie. He raised his beer to tap my cup as I walked by.

I headed to the area under the Elston Howard picture that hung on the wall. I knew I'd find Mrs. J's son sitting there. She named him Elston, after the first black Yankee, and a great one at that – a real class act. No Mets paraphernalia in this bar; it's Yankee territory.

I sat down with Elston after a hug and a kiss. He has multiple sclerosis and has been wheelchair bound for many years. Mrs. J loves that Dorothy Day High School has embraced her son; he is invited to all school functions and comes to many of them, including theatre productions and sporting events. He gets love and gives love back by sitting on the corner every morning to greet the students as they come to school. Elston has let it be known that "Dorothy Day is better than watching TV."

It's a toss-up which of us loved the Yanks more. We covered spring training and agreed the Yanks looked solid. In the sociology of sport, no one can ever overestimate how important the Yankees are to the mental well-being of Bronx residents. We live and breathe their performance. We expect to win. The Bronx borough, in reality and fiction, has been so beaten up that we need the Yankee outlet. We get to stick our chests out and be recognized around the metropolitan area, the nation, and the world with our Bronx bombers. Bleep the Red Sox!

Elston promised to come to one of my JV games. He always shows up. I asked if the small tremors in his hands, a recent development, were continuing.

"Yes and no," he responded. "I just started on a new med and it hasn't totally kicked in yet. If the tremors continue, I'll be using a straw with these beers," he said with a smile.

"Elston, atta boy. Who loves ya?"

"You do."

"Back atcha."

I bought a round for the faculty. It's easy to be generous with Mrs. J's prices. Besides, today felt like a celebration of life. First and foremost, I was alive. Add to that the wonderful staff and students at Dorothy Day.

I always feel comfortable at the local. It's my kind of place, a blue collar crowd – the working class of cops, firemen, transit workers, teachers, and hospital workers. Solid union workers. The salt of the earth!

In Lent, I always cut back on beer so the teachers gave me slack about my one beer limit. I used the round of beer to say hello to a spunky new teacher at our school, Annie Rose Ferber. She's always full of a vitality that radiates from her. A slim woman with loose curly shoulder length black hair, and liquid blue eyes. Her dimples are permanent fixtures on her face. She graduated from Cortland, one of the colleges in the State University of New York (SUNY) system. She would tell you that it's not necessary to spend $30,000 or more a year in college to follow your education dream. After graduation, she became a Volunteer in Service to America (VISTA) in one of those poor Jersey towns that are left off the Garden State's public relations list. Not done yet with volunteering, she left for Kenya, East Africa as a Peace Corps volunteer. She spent two years in a rural village, teaching secondary school and falling in love with the beauty of the place, the goodness and kindness of the people, and the slower lifestyle. They'd give the shirt off their backs, she has told us. Those who have the least give the most, it is often said.

Annie is the new service/volunteer coordinator at our school. She's on fire about peace, social justice, and women's history. I often see her at morning Mass. She refers to the Eucharist as her "soul food." Too cool. We have done polite chitchat but with coaching I rarely have time for a quality talk with her or anyone else.

"So, Rookie, what woman was at the heart of your lesson today?" I inquired.

"Florence Kelley! Ever hear of her? I bet not. Like most people, you learned HIStory and not HERS."

"I like that, rookie. Not bad! So, what did..."

"Thank her. Trust me! Just thank her. She fought tirelessly to end sweatshops, and for a minimum wage. Florence was on fire against child labor and promoted infant health and..."

"Whoa. Slow down. The floodgates are open!"

"And what woman entered your class lesson today, Bronx boy?"

"Now that you ask, Fannie Lou Hamer, Sojourner Truth, and Dorothy Haight. Anything else you want to know?"

"Yeah. How's your beer? Here's looking at you. From *Casablanca*, the movie, in case you're interested."

With a hoist of her glass, she turned back to a faculty member, immediately engaging in banter about her New York Mets. Never the Yanks. She was after all from "the Island."

I made my early Lenten good nights. Walking out of the bar, I heard Mrs. J barking "tell your problems to Jesus" to a regular customer, who always complains. The entire bar cracked up. A perfect meditation for night prayer.

My Bronx radar went off as I set off for home. The usual sixth sense for muggers or gangs had been replaced by a sense that someone or something was watching. The air throbbed and sent waves that hit my back. I moved into the shadow of a building and surveyed the street. A few cars, an old man walking a dog, and a group of three women across the street were the only action that I could see. The squeal of car wheels caught my attention. A cab barreled around the corner at the far end of the street and raced in my direction. Sweat broke out on my brow and the quaking air enveloped me. The cab came to a screeching halt opposite me.

"Hey, Mac, jump in. I'll take you home," called out Mr. Abdul, through the open passenger side window.

It took a moment for his voice to register and realize here was friend, not foe. I jumped in and quickly drew the door closed. I settled into the back seat and released a big sigh of relief. The vibrating air waves disappeared, replaced by a calmness to the night.

Tranquility and an oasis in a New York cab – who knew?

Ten

There is such things as guardian angels.
Dorothy Day

Saturday morning

Early morning found Daniel approaching Gracie's, a diner at Kingsbridge and Webster, just north of Fordham University. The local Bronx angels, nicknamed Heaven's Angels, gather weekly for updates and to plot strategy against the ancient enemy. This enemy, like New York City, according to Frank Sinatra, does not sleep.

Part way up the block, Daniel saw Mr. Abdul's cab sitting curbside in front of Gracie's. Each week, he picks up elderly Mrs. Epstein, a Jewish Holocaust survivor, and brings her to the meeting. Daniel spotted Pastor Sandy Pickering, a middle-aged Episcopalian minister, approaching from the other direction. Her Bronx parish, Epiphany, has become a sanctuary for struggling young women – single mothers, addicts, prostitutes, and victims of domestic abuse. One addict, who managed to get back on her feet with the aid of the parish, became a highly successful business woman. She has never forgotten Epiphany and keeps the parish financially afloat.

"Jesus loves you." Sandy offered her usual greeting.

"You got that right, Pick," responded a smiling Daniel.

Daniel pushed open the door with Sandy right on his heels. She paused a moment in the vestibule to touch and say a quick prayer at the sign on the wall: "Looking for Grace, Well Come on in."

Daniel gazed with pride at the angel crew gathered inside: Fireman Herb Palmer, Mr. Abdul, Mrs. Epstein, Sandy Pickering, and Mrs. Tilak, dressed in a purple sari. Angels come in all shapes and sizes and all walks of life. The common thread is that they all serve the light but in their own unique way.

"Daniel, are you the mook? Is it Mac? Or both of you?" asked Herb. "He's a loose cannon. Barely controlling his Bronx macho side at times."

"Nothing like cutting right to the chase, huh, Herb?" responded Daniel. "We'll get there soon enough. Right now, relax. Drink your coffee before it gets cold."

"Gotta love a diner," offered Mrs. Tilak. "Decent food for a fair price." She gazed fondly at her plate filled with scrambled eggs, hash browns, and two pieces of buttered rye toast.

Abdul with a mouthful of french fries managed to blurt out, "I'm eating french fries for breakfast. Obscene." He then reached for more.

"It's my Sabbath. So today your fries are kosher," added Mrs. Epstein with a twinkle in her eye.

The light-heartedness led to smiles and chuckles from the group.

"Our new angel, Kevin McCarthy, is barely twenty four hours old," began Daniel. "He needs time to figure it out and grow into his role. Meanwhile, the enemy lurks. We need to get the word out to the angel crews in Manhattan and Westchester. Kevin is parochial. He gets no further than that."

"I went by last night as you suggested, Daniel," said Abdul. "I chased off two formidable demons. They sniffed out Mac quickly, wasting no time. Mac was not ready for their level of evil."

"Did he sense their presence?" inquired Herb.

"You know, I think he did. Not bad in twenty four hours. Maybe, the kid will make it."

"My heart breaks when we lose a new angel," lamented Mrs. Tilak.

"Might not happen with this one," added Mrs. Epstein. "This

guy's on fire. He talked about the scourge of drugs to his classes yesterday."

"Even more reason I like this guy," said Abdul.

All nodded, knowing that Abdul had dedicated his life to stopping the evil of drugs.

"It's just one of his multiple battle cries," added Mrs. Epstein. "My granddaughter has him for a teacher. His topics lead to interesting conversations at our dinner table."

"His high school is aptly named. It models Dorothy's behavior, welcoming all to the school, regardless of religion," offered Mrs. Tilak.

"Sarah loves his class," said Mrs. Epstein. "She has related entire lessons that he has taught. He started one lesson by fiercely whispering to the class, 'They did not die, they are with us, with you, and with all humanity.' From a memorial at El Mozote in El Salvador for the one thousand people killed by soldiers in December, 1981 the largest massacre in modern Latin American history, he told the class. Sarah said he captured everyone's attention. He explained how the government used weapons to kill its own people. 'Who gave some of these weapons to the government?' he inquired of the class."

"Of course, your granddaughter knew the answer. How could she not?" stated Mrs. Tilak. "Look at the genes she inherited."

Mrs. Epstein gave a slight smile and then said "Mr. Mac informed students that the U.S. knew the government used the weapons against innocent people; we sold weapons to the country anyway. The saintly El Salvadorian Archbishop Oscar Romero ran afoul of his government by begging the U.S. to stop selling guns to his nation, and for crying out for the poor. His outcries cost him his life. He was martyred on the altar as he celebrated mass in 1980. Another dead prophet. Prophets are expendable but not profit! A non-communist country – we'll support it no matter what. Two American Catholic sisters and two lay missioners were killed by the El Salvadoran government. What were they guilty of? Helping the poor! Seven Jesuit priests and their housekeeper and her daughter were killed by Salvadoran troops. Again, guilty of supporting the poor."

Mrs. Epstein paused before continuing, "Wow, I've gone on. I got it all from my granddaughter. She can quote him verbatim. I'm thankful for his teaching. We need to stop all evil," stated Mrs. Epstein.

Mrs. Epstein has spent her life crying out against genocide: Rwanda, Cambodia, Bosnia. During World War Two, while in Auschwitz, Mrs. Epstein was an angel to the suffering prisoners, comforting them and sharing love amidst the darkness. A kind word here. A gentle touch there. Mopping a feverish brow. Sharing her piece of bread. She refused to let evil win. A beacon of hope in the darkness. As it says in Isaiah: "*You are my witnesses*" (Isaiah 43:10).

Herb broke the silence. "Maybe, not such a mook, after all."

"We're luckier this time," said Daniel. "By chance, we have an angel inside Dorothy Day."

The group nodded in agreement.

"I'm off this weekend as I just finished a long tour at the firehouse. Mac will be my project till Monday. I'll keep watch," offered Herb.

Herb, a holy angel as well as an earthly hero, was tall, broad-shouldered, muscular, with a square jaw and not an ounce of fat. His salt and pepper hair matched the colors of his walrus mustache. A legend in the fire department for his exploits as a front-line man – the first into a burning building – in the city's busiest firehouse and for his willingness to go the extra yard even if it meant saving a pet for a child. Herb never forgot the tears of joy and the hug of a young boy named Jonathan when he handed over Donovan, his pet rabbit. He gives credit to God's grace and daily mass for his earthly successes: "We are all instruments of His Grace." He was a pied piper in his firehouse, leading many of New York's bravest to daily mass and Blessed Sacrament visits.

"We'll work out next week when the time comes," added Daniel. "First, the weekend and its usual slew of problems."

"Tell me about it," said Abdul. "Some young immigrants are being targeted to use drugs down around All Hallows High School. Once I drop Mrs. Epstein at her home, I plan to head that way."

"If you could drop me off at the Zion nursing home instead that would be appreciated. A lonely patient will die this weekend. I'll be at her bedside so she doesn't die alone."

"At least my plan is a little more uplifting," said Pastor Sandy. "One of the women is celebrating her first anniversary without alcohol or drugs. For this prodigal daughter we will slaughter the fatted calf and celebrate her earthly resurrection from vice."

"I'm expecting my usual large crowd for the Saturday lunch special. It gives families an opportunity to eat out together," added Mrs. Tilak. "How about you, Daniel?"

"I've got a date with a fallen angel – quite the evil one at that – who's causing much havoc in the St. Raymond's area. Time for him to go."

"Careful, Daniel. Listen up, fellow wingmen and women. Break a wing!" concluded Mrs. Epstein.

*   *   *

One of the regular angel crew had missed out on the gathering that morning. Like her counterparts, she had responsibilities that sometimes overrode angelic commitments. For her, the day began with early morning pick-ups of food purchased at a steep discount from the food bank, and from donation boxes at local stores. The volunteer crew then packed bags of food: meat, canned goods of soups and vegetables, cereal, and bread. Individuals and families came by mid-afternoon for their "bags of hope." She knew each person by name and considered them her friends. Late afternoon found her on drop-off duty, taking bags to a family with three children, including a new-born. The mother thanked and blessed her profusely. "From my heart, from my heart," the mother whispered repeatedly, unaware she grasped the hands and gazed into the eyes of an earth angel.

As a result of the day's activities, strong feelings and thoughts flitted through the earth angel's mind and heart on her drive home:

Fourteen million hungry children in this country! How can this be with all the resources available in this country? Some people say that the U.S. is the greatest nation on earth. For me, greatness is measured in what a country does for the least of its brothers and sisters. "For I was hungry and you gave me food" (Matthew 25:35). Congress just cut money from the food stamp program. Again! How about making steep cuts in corporate tax write-offs? Never happen. Democrats and Republicans bow down to the mighty corporate powers. Most likely to garner campaign funds!

Liberal. I'm pinned with that label by people uncomfortable with my shout-outs about social injustice. If lending a hand to those in need is liberal, then bring on the label. But it's a disappointment; I want to be labeled radical. Then I'll have the satisfaction of knowing that I've been successful in living out the message of the Gospels – the clear blueprint as to how to live one's life as a Christian. "I will demonstrate my faith to you from my works" (James 2:18). Lead with love. Look not at my own feet but out at the world around me. Avoid the trap of materialism in society. Following the Gospels has helped me to sidestep that devilish snare.

My thoughts turned to my fellow angels, who had gathered without me at Gracie's, most likely, with a huge sigh of relief. They enjoyed their eggs and coffee without my usual sideshow of ranting, hooting, and hollering about society's injustices. My Dorothy Day classes are never as lucky.

Eleven

Nothing about my daughter is a mistake.
God does not make mistakes.
Ellen Armendariz Stumbo

Saturday afternoon

"You've changed."

"I wish I had but I came right from the rugby pitch, Brigid. I stink like ten men and need a shower."

"Not like that. Changed." She tapped my chest. "I'm sure."

"Brigid of the Bronx, he was a changed man today on the rugby field. Your slow brother flew like the wind," roared my friend Jack Leahy, coming up the walkway to the house. He had driven me from the rugby game and had been busy parking the car. Not an easy feat on Bronx streets, which suffer from a dearth of available spots.

"Jack," squealed Brigid. Then she wrapped her arms around him like a rugger in a scrum.

I looked at my older sibling, who has Down Syndrome. An extra copy of the 21st chromosome causes Down Syndrome, the most common chromosomal disorder. Mild to moderate intellectual challenges, short height, and a flattened face are typical characteristics. While some medical personnel suggested institutionalization for Brigid, the possibility wasn't even a blip on my parents' radar screen. They focused on ability, not disability, and can do, not can't. They treated all their children the same, with the same expectations and the same discipline. My parents cautioned family and friends to refrain from giving Brigid special breaks or favors. Give her a chance and more time and she can meet a challenge and succeed. Their children, especially, absorbed the message.

Brigid became the glue of our family, the love of my heart, of all our hearts. Always has been. Her heart is pure and an inner beauty radiates from her. Immeasurable joy she brings to our family and her presence has taught us the gifts of patience, tolerance, and appreciation.

The world needs more like her – loving, hugging, sweet Brigid. Yet, sadly, the majority of Down Syndrome fetuses are aborted. Unwanted. Maybe, the future parents should meet Brigid and other Down Syndrome babies. They are gifts from God. No doubt about that. Their presence reminds us of the gifts we have received and often take for granted. Life is the biggest gift of all. Amen.

"Kevin and Jack, you made it," my mom called out to us as she stood at the door. "The tea is waiting on you. Now what's this about changed?" said Mom as we filed through the door.

"You should have seen him, Mrs. Mac. He was everywhere on the rugby field, making tackles and sprinting up and down. Not his usual lead-footed self." Jack gave me a good-natured hit on my upper arm.

I smiled. I agreed. Definitely faster and stronger today in the rugby game. Compliments flowed from my teammates and good-natured teasing about "the juice" I was taking. Most likely, "angel juice," I thought at the time. Had my metamorphosis begun? Would it be fair to play rugby down the road? Questions for Daniel.

Mom looked at me closely and succeeded in biting her tongue, at least for the moment. She put before us steaming mugs of tea and a plate of oatmeal raisin cookies.

"Enjoy the quiet before the storm," Mom said to Jack.

"You got that right, Mrs. Mac."

Jack Leahy, the father of four daughters, Colleen, Fiona, Tara, and Grace Marie, would spend the rest of his day filled with the busyness of dance lessons, soccer and swimming. At the beginning of his teaching career, he and I taught in the same Catholic school but once his four daughters showed up, he moved to public school for the higher salary. A dean of discipline in a Bronx grammar school, he has dealt with serious behavior problems. Guns and knives have replaced chewing gum and running in the halls as discipline issues. You'd swear Jack Leahy was out of casting for the WWF, the World Wrestling Federation. Big and strong, he has a face that looks like it was cut from stone. Granite at that! A dean, a rugger, and a marine all rolled into one. He's a formidable presence in his school.

"Wanna play catch?" asked Brigid after Jack had left.

"Of course, sister. A little before dinner."

*   *   *

I love baseball and especially like being on a softball team. The season opens soon and I need to be ready. Some people think I cant play just because of my disability. As Kevin would say: "what do they know?" I pray for them.

My family and friends see me as Brigid, not Down Syndrome Brigid, not disabled Brigid. That's the way it should be. That's the way I see myself. I can learn and I have. I like reading, listening to music, and playing sports, including swimming, baseball, and softball. I'm good with a ball, especially throwing and catching. I try. Like everyone else. Can do!

*   *   *

"Fifteen minutes," Mom said as we went out the back door.

Brigid and I stood opposite each other, about twenty feet apart. Soft lobs as a warm-up before we moved into fielding grounders. I looked at my solidly built sister with hair so pale that it appeared white. "Angel hair," Mom always calls it. When the sunlight catches her hair just right, you'd swear a halo encircles her head. Angel hair, indeed. But it's her eyes that always mesmerize me. They have an innocence, which always disarms me. I become a child of God again when I gaze at them. Brigid loves unconditionally and in the moment. The source of her love is God. Can any spiritual master do better than love in the moment? As Mom says, "Heaven has touched that one indeed."

"Mom, Kevin's different," announced Brigid as we walked in the door.

"What do you mean?"

"I felt him. You try. Also his light is different."

"I just hugged him and I didn't feel anything different. Light? What light?" Mom turned to me. "What's going on?"

I shrugged. "Maybe, it's her imagination."

"Brigid is many things but imagination is not her strong point. I trust her instincts completely."

Mom would. She was born and raised in the Bronx but she had the immigrant experience. Her parents emigrated from Ireland – off the boat Irish, we call them. Like other immigrants, they brought wonderful superstitions and traditions with their brand of Catholicism. The saints, spirits, prophets, and the wee folk were constantly bantered about and had a strong presence in the home.

"Kevin, was it the accident?"

"Maybe."

"And?"

"Just a cat and a nine lives tale."

"Cat or God?" said Mom with an edge to her voice.

"You tell me."

"Your crash scared me."

"Mom, you knew nothing about it until after it happened."

"Don't use reason and your college diplomas on me, Kevin McCarthy. I was scared."

"Fair enough. But put your worries aside. I was down on my knees at morning mass in St. Nicholas of Tolentine. I'm in good hands." The church was a favorite of mine; my parents had met there.

"If you didn't play rugby, it wouldn't have happened."

"It wasn't the rugby.

"You get hurt too often in that sport." Mom added, "If your Uncle Eamon ever knew that you played a Protestant sport, he would have died."

Uncle Eamon, her Dad's younger brother, had been a member of the I.R.A. – Irish Republican Army, in a unit run out of County Tyrone in the north of Ireland in the 1970's. Many Irish considered the IRA a freedom fighting group against the occupying Brits. The British called them terrorists and treated them as such. The Irish lauded those who fought for freedom from British rule in song and drink. Numerous times at Irish bars, I sang along to "Kevin Barry," Clancy's and Makem's folk song:

Kevin Barry gave his young life for the cause of liberty...
another martyr for old Erin, another for the crown,
the British laws may crush the Irish
but they cannot keep our spirits down.

In the 1950's and 1960's, rugby was considered a Protestant sport. The Irish Catholics were expected to play Gaelic sports, such as hurling and Irish football. In *Trinity,* Leon Uris detailed the tension between Catholics and Protestants in the north of Ireland. Conor, the Catholic hero, became a great rugger and beat the Prots at their own game. When I was growing up in my neighborhood, the book was required reading.

"Enough, Mother. Good to see ya, lass. Pass the potatoes, Brigid of the Bronx."

I ladled the gravy over pot roast, which sat on a mound of potatoes on my plate. Creamed corn and biscuits added to my satisfaction. Cups of tea and rice pudding – my fave dessert – ended the meal. I patted my enlarged stomach and stretched out my legs. Mom's cooking always fills me up.

"Any word on Mickey?" Mom asked with a tremor in her voice.

Dad kicked Mickey, at 18, out of the house. Drugs and booze had taken over his life. He had even threatened Mom. No beating or words from me or my brothers could change the booze hound junkie.

"Mick, you can come back when you're sober and drug free," my father said at the door.

"Mickey, I love you but I don't like who you are anymore," cried Mom. The tears running down her face wet her collar.

Mickey has never returned. Neither has he gotten sober or drug free. He's a barfly, a skell – a human who has become a skeleton of his humanity because of drugs and alcohol. Mickey bops around the Bronx, Manhattan and lower Westchester, surviving the day. His address never lasts long and neither do his jobs.

"Mom, I heard he was up in Yonkers. Lake Avenue. Hanging out with a friend at The Emerald Isle gin mill last week. I'm unsure if he's working as I haven't heard anything. Sooner or later, one of my friends will bump into him, and relay any news."

She closed her eyes and offered a prayer. He was still alive. She lived in anticipation of the phone call announcing his death.

"I see him," Brigid interjected. Mickey would stop in to see Brigid at her adult education school in Bainbridge, Patrick's precinct.

His cops knew the score and kept an eye out for Mickey. They gave him space. Between Mickey and Paddy's cops, Brigid and her classmates were in good hands.

Brigid keeps Mickey alive. She saves his soul from turning completely dark. She's the only light in his life and he adores her. Her purity enables him to hold off the final victory of darkness. She's his lifeline and something in Mickey knows that, senses that. For Mick, it might only be a thread at the moment, but it hasn't frayed. Maybe, it will weave into something yet.

Looking at Brigid stirred the memory of Mickey going to jail for her. We obtained the police report from Paddy, who called in a favor to get it. The only witness was Marty, the bartender. He works at an old Irish haunt in the Bronx known as The Tinker. In Ireland, the tinkers were gypsies. Like gypsies everywhere, they had a bad rep. The skells in the bar owe the gypsies an apology. They had rap sheets and were going nowhere fast.

The report read:

I was bartending on an afternoon shift when some regular heavy hitters came in. About a dozen or so. Mickey McCarthy came in later by himself. He sat alone at the other end of the bar. It was normal for a while. Drinking all afternoon, commenting on the TV programs, playing pool and darts, listening to music... Then it got quiet as bars often do. One of the dozen, O'Leary, now high and bored, starts engaging McCarthy. "How ya doing, Mac? How's the clan? Where you living now?" Then one of the drunker ones, Fitzsimmons, starts making fun of McCarthy's sister who is handicapped. "Mac is your sister Brigid dating anybody? How about setting her up with Collin here. He's good looking and not too smart like her."

While they were laughing at McCarthy's expense, I saw Mac's reaction but they were unaware because of the booze. Mac got stone cold. Ice. He ordered another beer and two shots of whiskey.

The group continued to bait him. "Mac, I want to date her." "No me." The language got cruder and uglier. They were having fun with McCarthy. "Mac, let me be her first one." "Mickey, set me up." "Mick, she's kinda cute in a neanderthal way." "Mac, she's retarded but..."

Mickey took it all in. He drained the beer and hit back the two shots. He then stood up and headed to the bathroom. So far he had said nothing and as it turned out he said nothing the rest of the night. As he passed by the bar, the troublemakers continued to banter. "Mac, bring her to the bar. We'll show her a good time."

The last line froze Mac at the pool table. He picked up the cue, turned, and jabbed Curry, the last guy to speak, in his face. Curry screamed and went down, clutching his eye. McCarthy flipped the cue over and hit with the thick handle a man on his left and then one on his right. He kept hitting them back and forth. He pounded away. They went down but then the cue broke.

The rest went after McCarthy. One of them picked up Curry's knife, which fell out of his pocket when he went down. They backed Mickey up to the pool table. Nowhere to run. They were laughing jackals, anticipating an easy meal. McCarthy surprised them again. He grabbed some pool balls and threw them hard and accurately at those surrounding him. They stopped advancing.

Then McCarthy did a smart thing. He threw one ball through the big front window. Glass came tumbling down, and flew everywhere. I stopped watching and called 911.

The remaining guys rushed McCarthy but he surprised them again with one pool ball in each hand. He swung his hands and landed a fair amount of shots on faces. More went down. Some unable to get up.

Those still standing overwhelmed McCarthy. He was beaten and knifed up pretty good before the siren sent them running. The cops came and saw a half dozen broken bodies and a lot of blood. They called ambulances.

End of report: Marty, the bartender at Tinker, as told to the NYPD.

Mickey survived the fight. His broken bones knit back together, and several serious knife wounds, which thankfully missed major organs, healed during his time spent at Rikers Island, the main jail complex in the city. Today, only a missing tooth in the smile of my brother is a reminder of that night. Even that missing tooth gives him more of the roving rogue look. Only Mick.

The knife saved Mickey from a long prison stay. He swore (and lied) that Curry pulled the knife on him first and he was only defending himself. Curry's fingerprints were quite logically on the blade. All in the group had records of guilt for one crime or another. The judge gave the lot of them a few months in jail. Mick skirted more serious consequences since he was perceived as the white knight defending his sister's virtue.

Mom noted my pensive face.

"He's gone but he never leaves us," she said softly.

All the siblings, except Brigid, struggle with Mickey. He stole from and lied to all of us over and over growing up. Once he even put a stickball bat over my head and knocked me unconscious. He got lost for a few days till I cooled off. Mickey was a rascal but he was our rascal and we have trouble staying mad at him. The unconditional love of family members. His actions have united the McCarthy clan. He has taken money off the bar. We paid his bills and apologized, sometimes; other times not. Then we would be forced into a confrontation with people cursing Mickey out. Sometimes, it was words, other times, fists. Right or wrong, Mickey was family.

Sigmund Freud said "You can analyze anybody except the Irish." Freud got that right.

Before heading home, I helped Brigid put away the gloves and ball in her room. Her bedroom wall was a shrine to the Yankees: a jersey, numerous baseball caps, photos of the stadium, and a prized picture of her standing next to Derek Jeter, her favorite Yankee. Paddy, our brother, arranged for the picture when he was running the NYPD security detail at the stadium. Going to a game with Brigid means you might as well be there alone. She sits next to you but between watching the action on the field and filling out her scorecard, she has no time or desire to talk. She never wants to miss a pitch or a play on the field.

The women in my life walked me to the door.

"Mom, I know now," said Brigid. She had been studying me closely all evening.

"Tell me, darling."

"God touched him."

"Did He?" Mom was deadly serious. "Kevin!"

"I told you I don't know where Brigid is coming from."

"Hmmm... you do know. The accident, wasn't it? Paddy said the car was a total wreck."

"I told you. I used up one of my nine lives."

"You did. But I know my daughter and she knows God."

Brigid did, indeed. When she started to communicate, she told Mom and Dad how God talked to her before she was born. He still does but not as much now, she informed us. Every now and then. She rarely recalls what they talk about but she insists they do. God loves me, Brigid always tells the family. Just the way I am. All in the family believed she had a sixth sense about God and a mystical communion of saints and angels. It reminded me of St. Joan of Arc and the heavenly voices reaching out to her.

"Did God tell you, Brigid?"

"No. Not this time. I can just tell."

"Kevin, when God touches people He expects big things. You be careful and may the wee folk protect you." Then Mom and Brigid wrapped their arms around me like a boa constrictor in a squeeze. They finally ended their crushing hug and I breathed easily again.

As I stepped out on the front step, I stopped short.

"What the...? Again? Abdul, are you following me?" The honking of a horn and the calling of my name alerted me to a cab driving up the block and close to Mom's house.

"Mac, that would mean I'd have to go to your rugby games. I want no part of that. Now cricket would be a different story," said Abdul as he pulled up opposite me. "Jump in. I'm headed your way."

A thrust out hand and a "Hi, my name's Herb Palmer" greeted me as I slid into the back seat. As I glanced to the right, I took in a large man with a huge mustache. Cop or fireman, I reckoned.

"Kevin McCarthy," I responded.

"Cop family, right. I know your brother."

"Yeah. Yours?"

"Firemen," said Herb. "Me, my dad before me, and my grandfather before him."

"My family, too. A long line."

"The story of the Bronx," added Abdul.

The three of us chatted as we headed south on Webster Ave. As I gazed out the windows the Bronx slipped by: a Metro North train heading to Westchester; dog walkers; late night shoppers; groups of teenagers smoking in front of bodegas; mismatched apartment buildings; cluttered auto repair shops; moonlit statues and headstones in Woodlawn Cemetery.

"The way it's been going, I'll be seeing you tomorrow, Abdul." I added, "Herb, a pleasure to meet you."

At my front door, I turned and waved as Abdul drove off. In the comfort of my living room, I prepared my end-of-day routine. I lit my candle for night prayer and shut off the lights. I settled into my worn leather chair and focused on the crucifix on the table. The candle lit it up and sent its flickering shadow on the wall. Christ reached out from the shadowy space. A living, breathing Christ.

I started my breathing techniques by focusing on one that I've labeled Mystical Communion. Touch base with the heavens. I recited a litany of saints and prophets and asked for their help. I breathed in the Father and breathed out the poisons in my body. The poisons of sin and temptation... I breathed in the Son, out the poisons... in the Spirit, out the poisons... in Mother Mary, out the poisons... in Dorothy Day... in St. Thomas More and all the Saints, out the poisons... in John the Baptist... in John Paul II and all the prophets, out the poisons... in Daniel and all the angels, out the poisons.

In the still of the night, I moved deeper into prayer. My senses totally immersed in the risen Lord. I entered my prayer zone. I felt part of a celestial choir praising the Lord.

"What a consolation it is to know that as I sleep choirs of contemplative nuns and monks are chanting the Divine Office and that I as a member of the Mystical Body am sharing in their prayers" (Dorothy Day).

Twelve

The rosary is the weapon for these times.
St. Padre Pio

Sunday

Beads. Sixty wooden rosary beads clasped in my hand. Louisa, my Italian landlady, fingered her own set as we walked slowly side-by-side to mass. Both of us lost in the Gospels. That's what the rosary is – a retelling of the Gospel stories, such as the wedding at Cana, the Crucifixion, or the Resurrection. One meditates while caressing the beads.

I aspire to be like Dorothy, who not only managed daily mass but a daily rosary, also. My rosary meditation always begins with the joyful mystery of the Visitation. Pregnant Mary visited her cousin, Elizabeth, pregnant at the time with the future John the Baptist. I always recite Elizabeth's gospel words, *"And why is this granted me, that the mother of my Lord should come to me?"* (Luke 1:43). I then add my own, "Lord, I believe in you and welcome you into my presence."

Thoughts of school, the opposite sex, a ballgame, a beer usually slip away, replaced by wooden beads, Hail Marys, and an awareness of God's presence.

According to some Catholic traditions, the rosary goes back to St. Dominic, a Spanish priest. He started an order of preachers, the Dominicans, in the early 1200s. In 1214, Dominic grew frustrated at his inability to convert others to Catholicism, and went off alone to a forest to fast and weep. After three days, he fell into a coma. While in this state, Mother Mary appeared and told him that the best weapon to reform the world was the rosary. Empowered by Her words, he awoke and went on to encourage the praying of the rosary.

Once a month, Mt. Carmel parish has an Italian mass. A real

treat for Louisa and other aging Italians who refused to leave the neighborhood with white suburban flight. She has a rudimentary knowledge of English, a language she never bothered to learn as she and her family conversed in Italian. Her job had always been to take care of her three brothers. They were now deceased and she was alone.

Having me as an escort to mass relaxed Louisa. The new ethnic groups in the neighborhood frightened her with their mysterious ways. Her own ethnic group, the Italians, were misunderstood when they came to America. Papists! Followers of the Pope, not the President! Catholic, not Protestant! Their dark hair and olive complexion made them victims of slurs and discrimination. Time continues as different ethnic groups come and go, but the same problems remain.

I followed the Italian mass easily as Catholic mass is similar around the globe. Throughout the world, "Catholic calisthenics" involve the routine of standing, sitting, and kneeling. Rhythms of the ancient rite. Rhythms which are passed on in Catholic DNA.

My mind drifted during the homily, spoken in Italian. My knowledge of polite Italian words comes down to one: ciao. Thoughts that started my day returned. Daniel and angels twirled in my mind. A real head-scratcher – the unknown, the newness, the lack of a sense of normalcy. Did the whole ordeal cause me stress? No, not really. I was at peace about saying yes to God. I planned to stick with my usual routines until the road ahead was clearer.

My thoughts wrapped around Brigid, and Mom's comment that heaven has touched her. I recalled the remarkable day of her First Holy Communion. Her specialness, her purity, and her faith were apparent that day.

She had not attended the local Catholic grammar school so our local parish arranged for her to have her First Communion at a Sunday mass. She received the Communion host and the cup of the

Blood of Christ for the first time. Not satisfied and without hesitating, she proceeded to walk across to the opposite side and take from the other cup. She surprised the whole church. Brigid, with a beautiful smile, and radiating joy, announced "I wanted Jesus and more Jesus." The collective heart of the church was ready to burst. There wasn't a dry eye in the place. Unintentionally, she embarrassed those people who take the Eucharist for granted. Brigid – the teacher. Lesson learned. And yes, touched by heaven indeed.

At the end of mass, Louisa leaned on my arm, as we made our way home. I've learned to look at walking with elderly Louisa as a gift. The slow and measured pace leads me to notice the world around me. With Louisa, my head is always up and my take-it-all-in eyes sweep to the left and the right. Far different from my head down, I've got places-to-go attitude on many of my walks. Today, I took in the hint of yellow blossoms on bushes, a blue door with an Easter wreath, colorful plastic eggs hanging from a tree in a front yard, an American flag flapping in the wind, a squirrel scurrying up a tree. The colors appeared brighter, the air crisper, the sounds clearer, and the smells stronger than in past walks. My senses were on overdrive.

Louisa and I always have a cup of tea together after mass. Somehow we manage a conversation, with her broken English and my Bronxese. There's not any depth, mind you, but she looks forward to it and enjoys the company. Easy enough to do.

I spent the rest of the day preparing lessons and correcting homework. Teachers perform twelve months of work in nine. My two free nights are Friday and Saturday. Sunday afternoon starts up the work week again. The Peace Corps saying: "the toughest job you'll ever love" – yeah, I get that.

My work took longer than usual to finish. My senses continued to be heightened. Distractions from the outside world flooded my space: the noise of children playing ball at a nearby park, the scent of pepperoni pizza from the pizza joint a couple blocks away, freshly baked bagels at the local bakery, the sounds of squealing brakes, honking horns, and twittering birds.

"Ch-ch-ch-ch-changes," from a David Bowie song had played on a continuous loop in my mind all day. Is this the beginning of my angel identity? Daniel, where art thou?

Hours later, my head hit the pillow. My mom's warning about being careful had followed me throughout the day. But pretty much a routine Sunday of mass, Louisa, and schoolwork. No sense of someone or something lurking. Daniel had warned that trouble would find me quickly so the normalcy of the day surprised me.

I gazed intently at my rosary. It had been in-hand or close by all day. *"The rosary is the scourge of the devil"* (Pope Adrian VI). Add the Sabbath day and you have one powerful duo.

Thirteen

The Church's teaching is unambiguous with regard
to the pursuit of justice. Christianity is grotesque
when it turns its back on justice. It's not Christianity,
it's something else.
Father Niall O'Brien

Monday

"Hey, Mr. Mac, I'm a have-not."

"Me, too," chimed in Marcos. "I'm already hungry and I just finished lunch," he added.

"Yeah, a bowl of rice and beans ain't gonna cut it," sighed Robert.

"Oh, excuse me, let me bow down to one of the high and mighty," said Kathy to PK who had just walked into the classroom. PK grinned and patted his stomach.

"I'm stuffed," he said. "I really liked the dessert. Apple pie, my favorite!"

"ARRGH!" growled Marcos.

The student buzz increased my higher than a kite feeling by another ten feet. The feeling originated at morning mass, during the concluding rite, "Go and announce the Gospel of the Lord." I heard trumpets blare and God inviting me to spread the Word: "*Do not be afraid. I have fed you the Eucharist. I am with you.*" My enthusiastic response, "Thanks be to God," brought chuckles from our intimate school congregation. Sister Katherine shouted "Someone is rested after the weekend." I sang back the classic, "Sign me up for the Christian jubilee, write my name on the wall."

It was Hunger Day at our school. During the Lenten season,

all academic disciplines spend a week focused on poverty. For example, religion classes reviewed Scripture and Church teaching in regards to the poor; math classes compiled statistics of poverty in the world; and foreign language classes looked at poverty in other countries.

Today, at lunch, the students were randomly divided into the haves and the have-nots. Most of the tables were pushed to the side to open up floor space. Eighty percent of the students sat down on the floor. Their meal consisted of rice, a few beans, and a small glass of water. The remaining twenty percent sat at tables. Waiters served the top ten percent a hearty meal of chicken, vegetables, potatoes, and dessert. The other ten percent were offered turkey and cheese sandwiches with milk.

Hunger Day always ushers in my Christian Economics unit in Morality class. It's the hardest unit to teach. The students quickly grasp the other units, especially sexism and chastity, because they see all the brokenness and scar tissue from the sexual journey. As Americans, however, they often have trouble connecting the dots in Christian Economics. We, in the good ol' U. S. of A, are caught in a culture of narcissism. A culture that feeds an attitude that looks inward on our individual material needs and wants and not outward at the needs and wants of the larger community, both locally and globally. A culture that fuels a blindness to a responsibility to others. My job is to break down that attitude and get them to see how to serve and build the Kingdom of God.

We critique all historical economic models, pros and cons. We concentrate on capitalism because it dominates the world today. Even the supposedly communist Chinese government has jumped on the capitalistic bandwagon. In a more compassionate world, companies should make a profit but not by the blood, sweat and tears of the workers. Fair and decent treatment of the workers and of the earth needs to be our mantra.

My job in Jesus' name, the carpenter's son, is to free each student from the prison of a self-centered attitude. To widen their circle of compassion.

*   *   *

Mr. Mac's class was rocking as I went by on my free period. The word had gone out from my fellow angels to keep an eye on him; trouble was surely coming his way. His faith and prayer life will hopefully hold him in good stead for the battles ahead.

An interesting character, this Mac. His gregariousness – his loud booming Bronx voice – knows no bounds. He talks with everyone about anything and everything. Humility outmatches his gregarious nature. He never lets on as to the impact he's making on his students. He has to know. At Thanksgiving time, all the religion teachers encourage the students to fill out a hand-out that states: In this season of thanksgiving and gratitude, let us pause and say thank you to an adult at Dorothy Day. I would like to thank the following person... for these reasons...

The hand-out originated with Mr. Mac many years ago. You would never hear that from him. I found out the origin of this worthy activity from a staff member, who was at the school when Mac started here.

I've been privy to student comments about him: "You make God's words so appealing." "You continually challenge me to climb higher on my spiritual ladder." "You truly are a person of God." "You have inspired me to be a better person and have made me want to become accountable for my actions." "You are supportive of your students and are a positive role model

– actually living how you instruct us to act." The number of hand-outs he receives could fill a book. Again, you'd never know it from him.

I have no doubt as to why he was chosen to be an angel. It's perfectly clear. "Other seeds fell on good soil, and brought forth grain, some a hundredfold, some sixty, some thirty" *(Matthew 13:8).*

I vow to do everything and anything I can to protect him.

*   *   *

As usual, a daily quote was on my front board. My way of thinking is get students focused as soon as they come into the room. Today's quote was by Stephen Colbert, a comedian and political commentator:

If this is going to be a Christian nation that doesn't help the poor, either we have to pretend that Jesus was just as selfish as we are, or we have to acknowledge that He commanded us to love the poor and serve the needy without condition and then admit that we just do not want to.

The board quote is often a follow-up to the homework from the previous night. Colbert's comment was no exception. It complemented the homework assignment to research and find statistics on world poverty.

"Got it, Mr. Mac. It's like the homework assignment you gave us," said Doug.

"Me, too. I got it," added Donna, editor of the yearbook.

"Ah, my internet aficionados. You are the technology generation."

There are positives and negatives about technology. It brings information to student fingertips in the blink of an eye. Whether it's reliable or credible is another matter. One of the roles high schools must play is to teach students to evaluate sources and determine if the information is fact or opinion. There's no getting away from technology; it's pervasive, especially in the lives of young people. Smart phones, tweeting, and iPads consume their lives and dehumanize them, I believe. They learn to interface with machines rather than human beings, focusing on screens not faces. It's made cafeteria duty somewhat easier as many of them are often on some device during lunch. In my classroom, it has definitely cut down on social interaction with the students. Taking attendance, for example. I used to have casual conversations with the students as I walked the rows recording attendance. Now I look at a machine while marking attendance.

"Fourteen million hungry children in the United States," said Erin, our tallest volleyball player. "Did I get that right?"

"I found the same. And one out of three families at or below the poverty line," chimed in Les.

"And half the world's people live on two dollars or less a day," added Mike.

"Twenty percent on a buck a day. Not real," stated Vinnie.

"Real, Vinnie. With your buck, what would you buy? Mike, your two bucks are not enough for dating, my teenage Romeo." Snickers and cat calls in the room.

"Les, say good-bye to those stepping out shoes... Maybe, just maybe, you can buy a pair of flip-flops. And Erin, say farewell to school. You're female. Maybe, if you were a son. But you're needed to earn money for the family."

"Unfair! That sucks!" rang out in the classroom from students.

I gave an eye and raised an eyebrow. "In an academic setting, suck is not part of our vocabulary," I cautioned.

"Stinks. How about that?" asked Jake.

"Yeah, poverty stinks and it also kills," I responded. "Think

Madison Square Garden. The number of malnourished kids who die daily would fill Madison Square Garden."

Commonly known as The Garden or MSG, it's a big part of life in The Big Apple. Madison Square Garden, like Madison Square and Madison Avenue, bears the last name of James Madison, the country's fourth president. Madison Square, at East 26th St. and Madison Avenue, provided the original name for The Garden, which was located slightly north of it. The Garden stayed downtown from 1879 until 1925 when it moved uptown, first to 50th St. and then to its present location atop Pennsylvania Railroad Station in midtown Manhattan, between 7th and 8th Avenues, from 31st Street to 33rd. Concerts, pro and college sports, including hockey and basketball, national conventions, and dog shows all take place in the Garden.

"That's thousands of kids, Mr. Mac. That arena holds a lot. I've been there to watch the Rangers play," said Vinnie.

"You got it. Roughly, 18,000 a day."

I knew I had them. There are always exceptions; today, it came from Keane.

"I got my own problems. Why should I care?"

"That's what this class is about... caring. Compassion... it comes from the Hebrew word for womb. We're all from the same womb, the womb of God who calls on us to care for our brothers and sisters," I responded. "My job is to open your eyes. Look outside of yourselves – that 'fat American' side of contentment with our material goods, that part of us that leaves us complacent about others. Half the world is in complete survival mode."

"I understand where Keane is coming from," said Christine. "And it's the first I'm hearing about this. No one ever talked to us about this before or told us to think about it."

"That's why I'm here as your morality teacher. In Jesus' name, we must cry out for the poor. Dorothy Day spent her life fighting poverty in His name. Matt, be the voice for the millions without health-care. Eduardo, speak out against slum landlords. Isabel, take on lousy schools in poor neighborhoods, and you, Frank, shout out against unfair wages, demand a living wage."

"We're only sixteen years old. Cut us a break," yelled out Vinnie.

"Never too early to start. To focus on those who have less. To give to a food pantry. To volunteer at a homeless shelter. I could go on and on. But I'll leave you with one final thought. If capitalism is such a great system, why are so many humans on earth facing such challenges? The rich get richer and the poor poorer."

The intent look on their faces assured me that I had captured their interest. Like a fisherman, I had netted them with my introduction.

"Look at the side board. Think about it."

With more than 800 million people suffering from malnutrition, it is often difficult to find immediate solutions for improving these tragic situations. We must nevertheless seek them together so that we will no longer have, side by side, the starving and the wealthy, the very poor and the very rich, those who lack the necessary means and others who lavishly waste them. Such contrasts between poverty and wealth are intolerable for humanity. – Saint John Paul II, Go in Peace

"Peace and love" always end my class. The kids shout it back and today was no exception. This fine class left quickly as they knew my cafeteria duty loomed. No time for me to think about Daniel's angelic invitation. I'm a teacher. Bells ring, I move.

I greeted the kids at the cafeteria door with enthusiasm and interest. Andre, a humble Holy Cross brother at Notre Dame College in Montreal, and a recently canonized saint, guided my behavior. He had a small room next to the front door and chapel of the College. For forty years, Andre served as the college's doorkeeper. His prayer life graced him to see the face of Christ in all who entered. Grace continued to flow and he became a healer and a miracle worker. Unlike Saint Andre, I must check on uniforms and shaving regulations. "Tuck in your shirt" and "what's with the facial hair" are admonishments I say the most often.

Trouble. It came in the form of moving waves of air that hit my torso as I walked onto the floor of the cafeteria. The intensity grew as I made my way among the tables; it felt like baseballs bouncing off my chest. A peculiar scent also hung in the air. My nose twitched at the smell that was a combination of sweaty body odor and rotten food. Students said nothing; if they had smelled the foulness, they would have let me know loudly and strongly. I went on alert, scanning left and right, and quickening my pace. The strength of the odor and the force of the waves increased as I moved towards Rico Ponce, the same kid I sensed had bothered Manuel Navarros recently. He was egging on the football players in a taunting manner. No surprise there. Rico had transferred in this year, having been kicked out of two other schools. Sister Sam, unwilling to give up on a kid, was offering him a chance to succeed. But her soft heart only went so far; if she felt he was a detriment to the school, she would move him out. At this point, it definitely was not working. His bad attitude, out of place in this good school, frustrated teachers and even students. He had pushed the line but had not yet crossed it. He would. It was just a matter of when, not if.

A school spends the majority of its energy on ten percent of students who are troubled and angry. It's unfair to the decent kids as they get lost in the shuffle. It creates frustration for the vast majority of educators. Father Flanagan of Boys Town, who stated "There are no bad boys," was a holy exemption.

Joe Fox. Six feet seven and three hundred pounds. No little

boy fat on his hulking figure. He's our star football player. Coach Schmidt gets lucky occasionally, when a fine athlete shows up on campus. Big Joe, as he's fondly called by most everyone, is the son of a train conductor. His dad was always impressed with the Dorothy Day kids on his train – their dress, conduct, community spirit. He sent his daughter Amanda to our school. She thrived here. When the recruiters came for the 8th grade man-child, his father told them "my kid is going to Dorothy Day." Conversation over.

Big Joe anchors our offensive and defensive line. The recruiters say he is a sure thing Division One ballplayer, and has what it takes to get to the big show, the NFL. On the field he's relentless. He plays to the whistle. Off the field, he takes academics seriously, but doesn't go the extra yard. His older sister, an A student, spoiled us. Big Joe is content with B's, even though he's capable of all A's.

I always call him "Gentle Joe" because he is a tender giant off the field. His smile lights up his dark face and also the room. He befriends everybody. He's always polite to adults, addressing them as "sir" or "ma'am." His mom and dad keep him grounded with discipline and church. He attends St. Anne's, and serves as an altar boy. He knows God has blessed him and that he may get a ticket out of the Bronx. He also has articulated in class that he hopes football gives him the opportunity to help others. Number one on his list is his parents.

In the cafeteria, Rico continued to challenge the football players. Whatever he said was enough for Joe to no longer be gentle. Joe waded through the usual cafe chaos to get at Ponce. Everything and everybody, students, chairs, tables, moved in his wake. Rico's face only showed pleasure at having fired up Joe. What was Joe thinking? Obviously, he wasn't. I sprinted. Kids later told me I was "crazy fast." I wedged between the two; the one ready to pounce; the other enjoying the moment and showing no fear. Joe was beside himself. He muttered, "I'm going to kill him...He said bad things about my family, Mr. Mac." Joe's sheer bulk pushed me back, and he moved closer to the taunting Rico.

"No!" My booming voice carried to all corners of the cafeteria.

I moved quickly towards Joe and managed to get underneath him, pick him up, and slam his body on the table. No time to think about how this was possible. The table groaned and wobbled but held up under our combined weight. Joe's anger increased tenfold. He who bench presses almost four hundred pounds was about to put me on the cafe roof.

Putting my fingertips gently on his chest, I whispered, "Joe, no! You have too much to lose."

Zap! The air burst with energy and a spark passed from my fingers to Joe's chest. His eyes and mouth opened wide and a twitch passed through his body. He paused and lay still. I got up slowly but I kept my hands on his chest, realizing my fingertips had a taser-like quality. I removed my hands only when Joe nodded that he was okay and under control. The incident had taken less than a minute but it felt like hours.

"Get up to the Dean's office," I barked at Rico. My hard tone involved my eyes, voice, and emotion. Usually, I get the response I want. Not this time. Rico laughed at me. I glared at him, ready to take it up a notch. But his appearance stunned me and I paused. His eyes were cold. Icy was more like it. But even more unsettling was the ashen gray color that outlined his body. It wavered and flickered around his body. I shuddered from a sense of darkness and evil in the room.

"Later," Rico sneered as he sauntered his way across the cafeteria. The darkness surrounding him danced along with his movements. It was eerie. The beating air lessened as he walked away. A soft breeze took its place and brushed my cheek, circled behind my head and touched my other cheek before moving past me.

The eyes of Joe and I locked. Though surrounded by a sea of students, we were on a private island, all to ourselves. We both realized that we were privy to something but what that something was we had no idea. We started to walk up to the Dean. My hand rested lightly on his shoulder as the cafe cleared a path. We talked outside the Dean's office. Knowing I was a Jesus freak, he let me explain it supernaturally.

"Had to be, Sir. How else could your old rugby body slap me down?" We laughed.

"I had help. A legion of angels."

"Two legions, Mr. McCarthy. You got me pretty good."

"Because I care, Joe." He knew I was on his side. I taught him last year and we know each other well. I would present his case to the Dean. There were many witnesses to Rico deliberately calling him out and cursing his family.

"Sir, what does that punk want? It's not the first time. I have ignored him many times before."

"That I don't know, Joe. I do know, however, you don't walk alone."

We have two deans, a male and a female. Steve Holmes was an African American, ex-college ballplayer, in good shape, with a shaved head and goatee. His style was intimidating but the kids knew he cared about them. Nicki Espinosa was a Bronx girl, born and raised. Puerto Rican and proud. She received a diploma from Manhattan College and went straight into an education job. She had passion, and was never lukewarm about disciplining students. She held students accountable. Not there to be their friend, she often said; I'm here to listen, be fair-minded, and enforce the rules.

Mrs. Espinosa took down the story. She got witness statements.

All indicators had Gentle Joe in the right.

I worked my way to class. The cafe incident was the buzz of the building and definitely in my classroom. Comments flew around in the charged up atmosphere.

"Mr. Mac, you were crazy fast and strong." "Mr. McCarthy body-slammed Big Joe." "What's with the Hulk thing, Mr. Mac?"

Somehow, I settled them down and taught my lesson. What exactly, I can't say. I was too distracted. I made it to the bell and they filed out.

I sat down hard in my chair and rested my chin on my fist. What did happen? How did I manage to pick up Joe? I like to think of myself as strong but let's be real. We're talking about Big Joe here. My hands and Joe? What was that about? Who is this punk, Rico? No answers but plenty of thoughts and questions. Head-scratcher.

I followed up with the dean and the principal after school. Joe was off the hook while Rico was suspended in-house. A meeting with his parents was the next step. Joe's parents had been called and informed about what went down.

That afternoon was the first baseball practice of the season. Time to shift gears. The boys were stuck in first, however, and wanted to talk about the cafeteria incident. A warm-up of running, followed by infield drills in our rectangular shaped box field behind the school, took their attention elsewhere. No grass. Just dirt. A fence keeps neighbors safe from errant throws. More running followed long ball tossing. We moved inside to the gym and finished with batting practice at the cage. Practice ended with a huddle and announcements.

"Sit down," I urged them. "As you know today was different."

"Cafeteria, Coach."

"Yes. We all know Joe but who is this guy Rico Ponce?" I asked.

The Spanish guys started yelling out in English and Spanish.

"El Salvadoran. Gang member."

"Quiet!" I barked. The Spanish speaking players on my team are Dominicans and Puerto Ricans. "How do you know he's a gang member?"

"Coach, he's from El Salvador. A lot of them are."

"Is that true? Jose Casiano," I responded. "A lot of them? Then based on your ethnic background, you're a Shark gang member in *West Side Story* and your Irish, Italian, and Polish teammates are Jets." I pointed to McTague, Connelly, Hynes, Zmuda, Lanzano, Noonan, and DeStefano.

"Naw, it's true, Coach. He's a bad dude. A dealer. I hope Dorothy Day kicks him out. How did he get in here anyway?"

After they left, I hit the weight room to release my stress and to satisfy my curiosity about being stronger. Maybe, it was just an adrenaline rush in the cafeteria. I warmed up and then lifted my usual set of two plates, two hundred twenty five pounds. I had more in me so I added reps. Again success. Beast-like today, I told myself. Watch out brothers! I knew I could do more but I stopped to clear my head and reflect. Strength – was this part of the changes that Daniel had talked about?

I returned to my classroom and prepared for classes tomorrow. I wrote notes on the board, and placed my lesson plan at the ready on top of my desk. I stopped at the chapel on the way out of school. I always do. I consider it part of the salary in a Catholic school. Free and unlimited access to the Tabernacle. Priceless!

Fourteen

*Every economy should be judged by
the way it treats its workers.*
Saint John Paul II

Tuesday

After morning mass, Sister Sam and I spoke at the back of the chapel. My baseball team believed Rico Ponce was dealing drugs, I said. She nodded. The deans were on to him, she informed me, but had no hard evidence yet. She planned to share her concerns with his parents at their meeting.

In our modern world, schools often get a kid who thinks he's "smart enough" to deal drugs and get away with it. Eventually, schools step on the kid like a roach. Another roach will soon replace the first. The cycle repeats. It's often interrupted by a good kid whispering hints of someone dealing. Hinting technically allows them not to be a snitch. No teenager wants that label. Every kid on earth deserves a drug-free school. Education is a human right.

Education was humming in my first period class. Yesterday, I knew I hooked them with my introduction to Christian economics. It's often the first time that most students hear the message about the call of the Church for economic justice. Unfortunately, too many of them embrace the materialistic message of more rather than less in their lives – another pair of shoes, jeans, expensive watch. It's the rare kid who comes in with a defined sense of social justice, who sees he's one of "the haves" in society and marches to the different drummer of an awareness of conscience.

Maybe, Pope Francis will open their eyes: "*Today, consumerism determines what is important. Consuming relationships, consuming friendships, consuming religions, consuming, consuming... whatever the cost or consequences."*

"These encyclicals of the popes are radical stuff," said Liam, at the beginning of class. "My parents discussed them over dinner last night."

Liam came from working class union parents with a strong faith. Totally embracing the Gospel message of "reaching out to the least fortunate" and "we're all brothers and sisters," they used these guideposts to raise children with a social conscience. The whole family volunteers at a shelter the third Saturday of every month, preparing and serving the meal, and then cleaning up afterwards. Another day of the month finds the clan distributing food at a large food bank in the area. Liam runs the annual canned food drive at our school, and organized a fundraiser for a school in Africa last year.

"I tracked back the Church's economic teaching to the 19th century. Did I get that right?" asked Liam.

"Not counting, Jesus," I responded. Everyone smiled.

In 1891, Pope Leo XIII, in his classic encyclical, *Rerum Novarum (On the Condition of Workers)* defended workers and union rights as key in the evolution of human dignity. On the fortieth anniversary of *Rerum Novarum,* Pope Pius XI issued his encyclical, *Quadragesimo Anno: On the Reconstruction of the Social Order.* He wrote, *"The function of the State is to watch over the community and its parts; but in protecting private individual rights, chief consideration ought to be given to the weak and poor."*

"Let's bring it to present day. What did you find out about Pope Francis? What did he say?" I asked the class.

"This will surprise you but I got something," stated Chris.

I must admit to raising an eyebrow. Homework and Chris – usually not a twosome.

"You know I'm a believer in miracles," I responded. Chris smiled and so did the class.

"Pope Francis said '*Where there is no work there is no dignity.*'"

"You got that right, Chris. Nice job. According to Peter Maurin – Dorothy Day's partner in founding the Catholic Worker movement – our job is to make the encyclicals stick."

"I don't know about that. I can't even pronounce their names," said Victor.

"Focus on the message, my friend. That's the key."

Pointing to the quote on the board, Liam said, "This is the second time in less than a day that the name Gustavo Gutiérrez has come up. I had never heard of the guy before yesterday. First my parents last night and now you."

...The poor are a by-product of the system in which we live and for which we are responsible... They are the oppressed, exploited proletariat, robbed of the fruit of their labor and despoiled of their humanity. Hence the poverty of the poor is not a call to generous relief action, but a demand that we go and build a different social order. – Gustavo Gutiérrez

"A radical thinker, according to my parents," added Liam.

"Right they are. A Catholic priest in Peru, he's considered the father of Liberation Theology. He and a fellow priest, Father Leonard Boff, taught that in Jesus' name, we must liberate God's people from oppression of any kind: sin, economic inequality, racism, sexism..."

"Go Popes! Here's to Gustavo!" cheered Liam. I loved having this kid in class. A rare bird, for sure.

"Amen," I exclaimed. "Our culture defends the one thousand plus billionaires and not the billions who live on one or two bucks a day. We, as Christians, are called to do otherwise."

"Won't happen in this country," stated Joyce, her freckled face in a frown. "It's all about money, lots of it."

"What's wrong with a company making big profits?" chipped in Ethan.

"Is profit everything? And how much is reasonable? Take Walmart, the largest U.S. company, for example. The pay of its workers averages just above the minimum wage. Few get benefits and thus our taxes are used to take care of their food stamps, health care, and retirement. The individuals that make up the Walmart family have more wealth than over forty percent of the population combined in this country. That is roughly one hundred million people. Something is wrong with that. Would it be reasonable to suggest that the company should increase the pay and benefits of their workers instead of reaping huge profits?"

"So, we need to stand up for the poor. No standing on the sidelines," said Carlos.

"Definitely. The Church demands a preferential option for the poor. It says budgets are moral documents. The Church disagrees with Ayn Rand, the capitalist philosopher, and her disciples. They emphasize the individual while the Church stresses the community. Selfishness is not a virtue! A small amount of people control the majority of the world's wealth and resources. They have been called the one percent. Inequality in the U.S. is similar to that in Haiti or Africa."

"For real?" asked Meg, our track star.

"Real, Sister Meg."

"Religion and economics going together. What's with that?" asked Kenny G, our starting middle linebacker.

"The good Dr. King said 'any religion which professes to be concerned about the souls of men and is not concerned about the social and economic conditions that scar the soul, is a spiritually moribund religion only waiting for the day to be buried.' You go to Our Lady of Victory every Sunday, Kenny G. Religion is more than a Sunday game. We must cry out against all injustice, including economics, every day."

"I'm in."

"We need you, Kenny G."

"Why does Jesus allow this bad stuff to happen?" asked Alex.

"Jesus doesn't allow it. We do," said Mary, looking over at Alex. "That's been Mr. Mac's message from day one in the class."

"The absence of love – of neighbor, of fellow man," added Liam.

"And woman," Mary smiled with her teenage braces.

Mary Fierro was considered the brightest student in the school. Her parents were both professors at Fordham; her Filipino mom a professor of Eastern religions, her dad, born and raised in Brooklyn by Italian parents, teaches philosophy. Mary is a lovely combination of both of them – dark hair from her dad and soft brown skin from her mom – the present day all American child. Mary loves the ethnicity in the school. We have a bit of everything – a mini United Nations. I fall in love daily with our beautiful mix.

Her dad guest-lectured in my philosophy unit the past two years. He dropped philosopher names like I talk Yankee baseball – Ruth, DiMaggio, Mantle, and Jeter. He used a baseball context to present his dream team of philosophers. It includes the Greeks – Socrates, Plato, and Aristotle in the outfield; Kant batting cleanup and playing first; Spinoza at third; Confucius at second; Nietzsche at short. A Christian battery of St. Paul, pitching to St. Augustine, the catcher; St. Thomas Aquinas, the closer in the bullpen. Her dad's knowledge and enthusiasm for his subject and his baseball team concept snared the students. It's the rare New York kid – male or female – that can't relate to baseball or doesn't understand the game.

My education dream team would definitely be headed by Mary

and Liam. Their curiosity and motivation bring out the best in me. My energy increases, my passion as well. A teacher desires to impact every student in a positive immediate way. While I want all my students to be fired up on justice and peace, I've learned this is unrealistic and not to be expected. Be satisfied that I capture one, two, a few. And who knows what will happen down the road – what ideas heard by students in my class will really take hold later in their lives. Teachers are seed planters.

"The message of individual responsibility is getting through to you. Jesus gave us the how; it's up to us to do it. No one said being a Christian is easy, it involves faith and works. It's not just talk the talk. It involves walking the walk."

"Like Dorothy Day and her houses of hospitality," said Mary.

"Right you are."

"Peace and love, class." In unison, they respond "love and peace" before heading out the door.

A March rain led to indoor practice. I ran with my team. Time management. Only so many hours in a day and I needed the sprints for rugby readiness.

"Hey, you're flying," yelled Pedro.

Where did that come from? I raised an eyebrow. Faster? He was right. Faster, more energetic, and ready to go another mile. Not my usual tired after teaching self. This angel thing will be great for my rugby game, I chuckled.

All teams share the gym in bad weather, which always reduces practice time. Practice lasted only one hour, allowing me to head home early. I stopped at Fernandez, my local Spanish bodega, for takeout food. Mrs. Fernandez always makes sure this bachelor eats healthy. Barely a minute later, a prickling on the back of my neck alerted me to the evil that had come through the door. I continued to smile at

Mrs. Fernandez; when I turned, however, my face was serious. Two males, one burly, broad-shouldered, and squat, the other his opposite, tall and lanky, stood near the doorway. Both had massive arms, muscles my brothers and I would die for but never achieve, no matter how many hours spent working out in a gym. Their cold, angry stares heightened my sense of alertness.

Robbery was not their motive. I was. I sensed it in the foulness of the air that accompanied them through the door and in the feeling of pins and needles in my arms and legs. The first move came from Burly. He bumped into me as he made his way to the beer cooler, located at the back of the store.

"What's your problem?" said Lanky to distract me.

Meanwhile, Burly grabbed me from behind in a tight squeeze, pinning my arms at my side. Lanky advanced with raised fist to light up my face. Not gonna happen, I thought. I leaned into Burly's body, lifted both my feet and hit Lanky squarely in the chest. He went flying into a food display. Cans of Goya beans crashed to the floor and rolled in different directions.

My unexpected action left Burly unsure of his next move. I was clear about mine. I reversed a head butt on him, jamming the back of my head into his face. Stunned by the force of the blow, he loosened his grip on me. Reaching down, I grabbed two cans from the floor and used them to tattoo his face. His knees buckled and he slid to the floor.

I still had unfinished business. I grabbed his partner by the throat and hauled him to his feet. My iron grip throttled his larynx. His eyes watered and bulged; his face took on a bluish tinge.

"Take your pal and never come back," I warned him. "If you do, I will crush your throat as easily as a beer can."

Eyes wide with fear, he nodded. I released my grip and he sank to his knees. The air filled with the sounds of his harsh breathing. I waited a minute before dragging both to their feet and shoving them out the door. Fresh air replaced the horrid smell of their presence.

Mrs. Fernandez, speechless and motionless behind the counter throughout the incident, broke her silence with a flood of thanks to God and to me. I offered mine in silence. A roasted chicken, beans, broccoli, rice, and a beer – all compliments of Mrs. Fernandez – accompanied me out the door.

My New York radar on full alert sensed no one following me as I headed home. I stopped at a bench and sat down. My brain was on overdrive. Who were those guys? Were they sent by someone? Or was it spontaneous? Two guys used by God's enemies or everyday thugs?

I reflected and prayed. Violence had reared its ugly head. It can never be a given, I reminded myself. Pacifism – not an easy road to follow. Walk away. How does one do that? Is it possible to be a pacifist in all situations? Not sure about that.

Dorothy, for you, it was possible. In World War II, Dorothy Day believed that war was evil and one doesn't combat evil with evil. The headline "We Continue Our Christian Pacifist Stand" appeared in *The Catholic Worker* in 1942. Outrage soon followed. Subscriptions to the paper were canceled, many left the Catholic Worker movement, and fifteen houses of hospitality closed. Dorothy was buffeted by strong criticism for her pacifism but she held firmly to her belief.

Dorothy had been asked what she would do if her daughter was threatened by a maniac with a gun. "Restrain him, of course, but not kill him. Confine him, if necessary. But perfect love casts out fear and love overcomes hatred. All this sounds trite, I know, but experience is not trite."

God bless you, woman and your perfect love, I thought – me, the unsuccessful pacifist.

I came home to numerous phone messages inquiring about the car accident. Ancient history in my book. Felt like an eternity had passed. But I made sure to return the calls of my siblings, reassuring them that I was okay. Hugs over the phone. We all need them. I reached everyone but Paddy. I left a message to call me back. I needed information about gang behavior in the Bronx.

My last call was to my brother, Quinn. He's an interesting guy. A loud New Yorker, he loves to talk about everything, including God and politics. Two of my favorites, also. As a young man, Quinn ran hard. He excelled at partying and fighting. He got out of the Bronx by joining the Marines. His partying continued until tough love Sergeant Foster McTiemack took him under his wing and started him on the road to sobriety. After his Marine stint, he came home and made sure to attend Alcoholic Anonymous meetings daily. That awesome AA fraternity found him an apprenticeship in the Carpenters Union. He has worked his way up to becoming a talented carpenter.

Quinn works hard on the twelve steps of Alcoholics Anonymous, a program started by Bill W. (Wilson) and Dr. Bob (Smith). Bill had been a lawyer, a military officer, a millionaire and a drunk. Getting sober had been difficult for him. Treatment programs failed and Bill despaired of ever achieving sobriety. A friend, who became sober after turning to religion, encouraged Bill to do the same. The agnostic but desperate Bill gave it a try. Turning to God worked.

The guiding principle of AA is one drunk speaking to another. The twelve steps are a blueprint for sobriety. A few steps include admitting a powerlessness to alcohol, surrendering to a higher power (God), and developing a prayer regimen.

The AA concept has taken off and branched into scores of self-help groups, such as Narcotics Anonymous, and Gamblers Anonymous. I consider Bill W. and Dr. Bob to be modern prophets, similar to the ancient prophet Moses, leading people to God. They have guided millions of troubled souls to surrender to God and to talk to Him daily, to slay their demons or hold them off one day at a time. They led them out of the slavery of addiction and enabled them to resist the Prince of Lies and reject his falsehoods of alcohol, drugs, gambling. Bill W.'s army grows with people who are sick and tired of being sick and tired. They are transformed into instruments of light. God never stops sending angels, saints, and prophets to assist on our earthly journeys. Go Bill W. and Dr. Bob!

Was it easy for Quinn to fight off the urge for a drink, the buzz of alcohol? By no means. There were many steps backward before he strode forward forcefully and finally as a recovering alcoholic. He still craves a beer from time to time. He would be the first one to tell you he's unable to fight the alcohol urge alone. AA taught him to depend on God and to turn to the gifts and fruits of the Holy Spirit. Gifts such as wisdom, understanding, and love; fruits of faith, peace, and joy. His drunken stupors have given way to a cloak of contentment and love. He reaches out to others dealing with alcohol, patiently explains the power of faith to those who are scornful and roll their eyes at his belief in God, and always makes himself available to anyone in need.

Quinn and I usually begin our talks with the safe topic of sports. We root for the same teams, especially the Yankees and the Rangers. The conversation heats up when we enter the political realm. Quinn defends this country, no matter what. He barks at me and others, who he feels are unappreciative and unloving of America. Upset about detentions without trial in our democracy? Get over it, he'd say. Move out of the country if you don't like it. A love it or leave it mentality. We always go back and forth, exchanging opinions but keeping our cool.

A spiritual "check-in" always ends our conversation. Where are you in your prayer life? What are you reading? Anything new to share with a fellow pilgrim on the road?

Quinn with his strong faith and compassion always leaves me with hope. Yet thoughts of the violence that lurked around me and in me tempered my night prayer. Lord help me and guide me.

My prayer candle burned long into the night.

Fifteen

*I preached to gangs on the streets of Manhattan,
Brooklyn, and the Bronx – and miracles
began to happen.*
David Wilkerson

Wednesday

Not every day starts with the same prayer method. Last night, while I was meditating before the candle, I focused on my sacred reading for that day. This prayer method, known as *lectio divina*, involves taking a passage from Scripture, in my case "*This is what Yahweh asks of you, only this: to act justly, to love tenderly, and to walk humbly with your God*" (Micah 6:8), and meditating on it. Next, take a specific phrase for reflection. "*To act justly*" had been mine throughout Tuesday.

My morning prayer methods also include spiritual readings from saints and prophets. Today found me wrapped in *Thoughts in Solitude* by Thomas Merton, a Trappist monk:

My Lord God, I have no idea where I am going. I do not see the road ahead of me. I cannot know for certain where it will end. Nor do I really know myself, and the fact that I think that I am following your will does not mean that I am actually doing so. But I believe that the desire to please you does in fact please you. And I hope I have that desire in all that I am doing. I hope that I will never do anything apart from that desire. And I know that if I do this you will lead me by the right road though I may know nothing about it. Therefore will I trust you always though I may seem to be lost and in the shadow of death. I will not fear, for you are ever with me, and you will never leave me to face my perils alone.

Yeah, Merton, you got that right. I know nothing about the right road ahead of me. A good reminder that the Lord is ever with me and that I will not face my perils alone. An appropriate reading, considering I'm clueless about the future. Trust, no fear. Trust, no fear. My mantra for the day.

In homeroom, I called Maria Hernandez, the girlfriend of Manuel Navarros, into the hallway to talk privately. Maria is so gifted at soccer that Manuel is often referred to not by his own name but as "Maria's sidekick." The heart and soul of the team, she plays midfielder and controls the game. A natural leader. St. John's College, a soccer powerhouse in New York City, has expressed strong interest in her playing there. She's a wonderful story unfolding.

"What did I do, Mr. McCarthy?" inquired Maria. Typical of a good student, she was nervous she had messed up somehow.

"You're never a problem. I just wanted to share my concerns about Manuel."

Rigidity and fear replaced her nervousness. "You know?"

"I sense that he's being compromised."

She let out a sigh. "I'm scared," she responded. "It's cost me a lot of sleep."

"How can I help?"

"The truth is we talked about coming to you for help. We trust you. You care. We hope you can but we're not sure how."

"Share what you can."

"We never agreed on it. We've gone back and forth. Time is running out though. I need to tell someone."

"Go ahead."

"This is too much for me. Manuel's the love of my life and I know all his wonderful strengths. The gang, the Locos, sees him as a strong recruit because he is well respected and popular. His older brother joined the Locos and now they expect Manuel to follow. He's new blood, strong blood. There's no choice; they're waiting for when, not if. It's a gang thing."

Tears streamed down her cheeks and fell onto her blouse. She made no attempt to stop them; a dam of pent-up emotion was being released.

"What happens when you say no? Manuel's too good a man to hook up with those thugs."

"He can't refuse. Someone he loves will get hurt, his mom, dad, brothers, sisters, maybe even me, if he says no.

"You young people kept this to yourselves?"

"If he told anyone, they would surely hurt his loved ones. Just for fun." The tears kept flowing. "He only told me."

"Does he know who threatened him?"

"No, he never saw them before."

"Give me time to figure this out. My brother's a cop; I'll ask for help and advice. I'm truly sorry both of you are dealing with this. You're not alone. You hear me?" She nodded.

"It's been so hard. Our parents dealt with violence in their countries. That's why they came to the U.S. It would break their hearts if they knew they escaped violence in Central America and then their children found it here. They love America."

"Violence is a tired old universal human story. Unfortunately, it rears its head everywhere," I said.

Maria and Manuel share a similar immigrant story. Their parents were from Central America; hers from Guatemala, his El Salvador. Multiple jobs, a strong sense of family, and faith were their gifts to their children. The American story of immigration stretches back in time over hundreds of years. Latin America has replaced Europe as the main supplier of immigrants. What remains unchanged are the reasons for coming – opportunity, a better life, and a safe environment.

When I hear people complain about immigrants crossing the border into the United States, I gently remind them that Joseph, Mary, and baby Jesus were refugees. The Holy Family fled Bethlehem to escape King Herod and his slaughtering of the innocents. Jesus migrated not only from the Holy Land to Egypt but from the heavens to the earth. In the name of Jesus, a refugee, we are called to embrace immigrants. There's always room in our inn for the new face of Christ:

When a stranger sojourns with you in your land, you shall not do him wrong. The stranger who sojourns with you shall be to you as the native among you, and you shall love him as yourself... (Leviticus 19:33-34).

Suddenly, the energy around me shifted. I smelt him and felt him before I saw him. The familiar rotten food odor and pulsating air wafted down the hall. Rico Ponce escorted by the male dean came into view. His grayish aura was visible and outlined him.

"Morning, Dean Holmes. What brings you this way?" I inquired.

"Mr. Ponce needed an escort to the bathroom. He has a habit of disappearing. I wanted to make sure he made it back to the in-house suspension room."

The school had been unable to reach his parents. The number given by Rico rang and rang, not even a voice mail kicked in to leave a message.

"Buenos dias, Maria," said a cocky Rico. "May all your days be good."

A frightened Maria remained silent and turned away. Her body tensed and her hands balled into fists, which she held tightly against her sides. She clearly felt threatened by this no good kid. Harsh words from a teacher but I call it like it is. Redeemable – not this one.

The smell, the air waves, the aura – the devil himself or one of his minions. The road ahead was still uncertain but one thing I was sure of, my transformation was occurring – both my eyes and ears were developing abilities to sense evil.

"Do you think he is one of them?" asked Maria as Ponce walked away. "Is he in the Locos?" she continued. "Something is off with him. He likes causing trouble."

"I'm learning more and more. But no answers yet." I reassured her once again that I was there for her and Manuel. I would do all in my power to help.

The day resumed its normalcy. I tried to put Manuel's gang problem to the back of my mind but eventually, it crept forward. My heart sat heavy for Maria and Manuel. Rico Ponce had managed to bring the blues to our beloved kingdom of God here at Dorothy Day.

A hard rain led to indoor baseball practice. It's no accident that most American major league baseball players come from three states, Florida, Texas, and California. Warm weather allows them to play games pretty much year round, while we in the Northeast are often hampered by Mother Nature unleashing cold, rain, snow, and mud, sometimes, relentlessly. Lousy weather again made for a quick practice in a crowded gym.

After showering at home, I threw on faded jeans and my favorite hooded sweatshirt. I pulled up the hood as I headed out into a cool night. Streetlights threw a watery light in the soft mist. I decided to walk the mile and a half to the car dealer. Sometimes, hoofing it is quicker than waiting for the bus. Healthy urban hikers can save time and money by walking reasonable distances. I consider myself in that category. Plus prayer and walking go together. I think it's a pilgrimage thing.

I headed to Webster Avenue, an avenue that serves mainly as a thoroughfare for cars, buses, and trucks. Foot traffic is usually light. Numerous empty lots overgrown with weeds and littered with papers, broken beer and whiskey bottles, soda cans, and cigarette butts give an air of desolation to Webster Ave.

Lost in my rosary, I focused on the Mystery of the Annunciation. The angel Gabriel announced to Mary, "*And behold, you will conceive in your womb and bear a son, and you shall call his name Jesus. He will be great, and will be called the Son of the Most High*" (Luke 1:31-32).

Where did the angel appear to her? I wondered. In her house? In a dream? Laughing to myself, I ruled out the Bronx River Parkway. Instead, I embraced the image of Mary wrapped in a shawl, while receiving the message in her backyard under the stars. The mystery always leads me to the realization that God calls all of us, not just Mary. Do we listen? Are we too busy and not enough the listening Mary?

My New York radar alerted me to trouble ahead. When three young men moved to block my path, my prayer ended. Danger was imminent, yet oddly, my confidence level was high. I felt calm and at ease. Instinctively, I knew these social misfits were not the higher purpose I was destined for in the future.

"Hey, Mr. Hoodie, stop right there."

I slowly pushed back my hood. I wanted peripheral vision.

"Mr. Hoodie's a white boy."

"He sure is. And thanks," I said. I was relaxed and decided to be silly. "I hate when I'm called Anglo-Saxon. That's a British thing. And I'm anything but British. Do all white boys look alike? I'm Celtic. Irish but I could be Scot or Welsh."

"Shut your mouth, Celtic. Did I get that right?"

"Actually, no. You pronounced it like the hoop team, the Boston Celtics. That's the anglicized version. It's a hard K sound – Kel-tic."

"Shut up."

"Sure. You got it." I was enjoying myself. My banter kept them off guard.

"Where ya going?" asked the leader, who stood in front of the other two members of the rat pack. Robbing an innocent victim indicated they made a wrong turn somewhere in life.

"To buy a car."

"Ah, Keltic you got money – lots of it."

"Can't help you there. Bank transaction."

"Must be something in your pockets."

Game time. They stepped closer, ready to spring like tigers from an opened cage door. A cocoon of tranquility enveloped me. I braced in a martial art stance for battle. My left foot moved forward. As I planted my right leg behind me, it struck a bottle on the ground. Nudging it with my foot, I moved the bottle by my side. In a flash, I leaned over, picked it up, and gripped it tightly in my hand.

The broken bottle took on a life of its own, glowing bright green in the darkness, and emitting small flames from its rough edge. My startled expression went unnoticed as all eyes were glued on the bottle. I spun the bottle before them, put it against the neck of the leader of the pack, and drew blood. The leader went wide-eyed.

I felt part of a larger plan. A clear command to mark him permeated my being and I was unable to resist the force even if I had the desire. Like a man in front of a tidal wave or an avalanche, I felt powerless. The cut would be an invitation and a reminder to change for the good. I pressed the bottle harder against his neck.

"It's in all your best interests to stand still," I warned. The blood spilling onto the shirt of the leader pushed my message across. No one moved. It bought me a little time to collect my thoughts. These were not reasonable teenagers who would be responsive to a positive message: Go to school and work hard. Finish school and move forward in life. Naive, I was not. The comments would hit the brick wall of deaf ears.

Having decided on my next move, I spoke up. "Okay, my next trick is to make a bigger cut on this guy's neck. You two have one chance to run for it. Don't stop. Your leader goes later. Scram."

The two sprinted down Webster Avenue like bats out of hell. Well, maybe, not sprinted. It's difficult to run when your pants are halfway down your butt.

I focused intently on the leader, who remained still except for his eyes, which cast nervous downward glances at the bottle. I rested it on his shoulder. He flinched and then trembled as a pale ray came forth from the sharp edge and encircled his body. It quivered over his chest and came to rest over his heart. After a moment's hesitation, the beam brightened and then disappeared – dive-bombed, really – into the young man's body.

"What's your name?" I asked, breaking the silence.

"Aaron," he whispered.

His eyes narrowed, a quizzical look filled his face, and he appeared lost in thought. Finally, he pointed to his chest.

"The feeling. Here. It's different. Not sure what... hmmm... can someone feel quiet inside?" A serene demeanor and a soft voice had replaced his earlier menacing face and tone.

I gazed intently at the bottle. Talk to me, I thought, and then I smiled at my action. What was I thinking? A bottle answering my question... a dumb thought.

"An angel spared you," I responded.

Silence.

"An angel?" He looked confused and then repeated the word a few times.

"Yep, an angel." My firm response masked my own doubts.

I lowered the bottle and pressed a handkerchief against his neck to stop the flow of blood that reddened his shirt. Energy flowed from the hankie to Aaron's neck. He shuddered. He looked intently at me and then pressed his hand over mine.

"What's going on? It feels lighter." He tapped his chest. "That heavy weight that's always there. It's gone!"

"In all honesty, I'm unsure. This angel thing is new to me. My guess is grace. The hand of God touched you."

"Yeah, right... the hand of God. Me. A kid from the hood."

"God moves in mysterious ways. Trust me, I know."

"What now?"

"Not sure, in the long run, down the road. But now, you'll be left with a scar on your neck. A daily reminder of your encounter with the grace of the Lord. God has called you and all His children to great things."

"Ha, never been accused of doing anything even good."

His comment reminded me of a line from St. Jose Escrivá: "*Many live like angels in the middle of the world. You... why not you?*"

"The ray that circled your body sensed goodness in you; it sought it and found it," I said. "Time to become what you are truly meant to be. A strong role model lies somewhere in your life – who is that good person?"

"Yeah, my mom. I used to go to church with her. Not anymore."

"She prays for you, I'm sure."

"Like all the time... but look at what I am."

"Tell your mom her prayers were answered. Like St. Monica, a mother who prayed fervently for her son to have an awakening and embrace the Lord. He went on to become a saint in his own right, St. Augustine of Hippo. Also, tell her you're the prodigal son. She'll

Cooper Kalin

understand. Go to church with her."

Aaron listened closely and nodded his head. The ray of light had read him correctly. There was a human side of goodness in this kid caught up in the urban jungle where hope was in short supply.

"No time for this street thuggin' nonsense. You're going to school to get skills to fight injustice just like the good Dr. King, who was already in Morehouse College at your age."

"School. Right. It sucks. Leaks in the roof, fights in the halls, drugs, and thugs. Yeah, that's me, man."

"If public school isn't working, come to Dorothy Day High School. I have a connection there. Ask for Sister Sam, the principal. I'll give her a heads up."

Hope crossed his face for a fleeting second.

"Time to go. I'll wait to make sure a cabbie stops to pick you up." I put down the bottle. "Between a bottle held tightly in a hand and a street kid, no cabbie will stop."

"Here's cab money for a trip to Lincoln Hospital for stitches," I continued. "It has the city's medical experts on gun wounds and stab wounds because so many of those injuries come through the door. Tell them you got cut jumping a fence on a shortcut home. An urban conversation, huh, Aaron. Guns and stabbings."

I pointed my finger at him. "You still ended up getting money from me."

I put my hands on his chest. "Put your trust in God. Surrender daily to Him. Use your neck scar for strength. You've been marked by an angel. You won't walk alone," I said.

We grasped hands and shoulder bumped in that guy hugging way. He then looked me in the eye and said, "Thanks. I feel different. Is there really such a thing as hope?" He pointed at his chest. "Not sure as I ever felt it before. I can't explain it. Ya know, I wanna do good."

"We're born to be good. We're attracted to the Light. As Jesus said, avoid temptation."

A cab came and I watched him head off into the night. I was alone. I knelt on the sidewalk and completed the prayer I was reciting before Aaron and company showed up.

"I am the handmaid of the Lord," said Mary, *"let what you have said be done to me."* (Luke 1:38).

These words work for me. My fiat. I entered deeply into a prayer zone. Time passed.

Refreshed and confident, I stood up and walked home. No car buying tonight. Not much action on the street, except for a few cars passing by. The loudest noise by far was the sound of a snoring drunk, huddled under blankets in his cardboard shelter in a lot strewn with beer cans, styrofoam cups, plastic bottles, newspapers, broken glass and discarded household items – remnants of our throw-away society. His loud snores could have raised the dead.

Sixteen

...fierce wolves will come in among you,
not sparing the flock...
Acts 20:29

Thursday

In my dream, Aaron was sinking into quicksand. I stretched out my arm but inches separated our hands. The quicksand continued to suck him deeper, and his frightened eyes registered that the soft quivering mass engulfed him up to his chest. No hope, he mumbled, no hope... his voice faded away. I thrust out my arm one last time... I screamed.

I woke sweating and confused. Moments passed before I recognized the familiarity of my bedroom, dresser, and Celtic cross on the wall. I stayed in bed to calm myself and to collect my thoughts. I offered a prayer for Aaron – may you grow closer to God which will lead to a new hopeful life.

Blustery and wet weather greeted me from my kitchen window. Typical March weather but not a typical day. It was my dad's birthday. He died five years ago. Some days, it feels like yesterday; others, forever ago. His birthday always gives me a buzz. I looked forward to being one with him at morning mass which I would offer up for his soul. A special mass intention is a beloved Catholic tradition. It's a spiritual bouquet. My gift to him – none better.

Eucharist brings heaven and earth closer as we become one with the Father, Son, and Spirit, Mother Mary, the saints and prophets, angels, and our faithfully departed loved ones. Hence the name Mystical Communion. The thought accounted for the extra bounce in my walk to Dorothy Day.

The antithesis of the closeness brought by the Eucharist is the pagan tradition of Halloween. Many are unaware that Halloween came from Irish pagans and is the flip side of Mystical Communion. According to Druid priests, the veil between hell and earth was thinnest on Halloween night. Demons, witches, goblins, and warlocks escaped hell on October 31st to create havoc on earth. The early Celtic Church created All Saints Day on November 1st. The saints "come marching in" and put the demons back in place. Halloween means the eve of "All Holy." Hallow is holy (Hallow be thy name) and een is eve. Thus, eve of All Saints Day.

In medieval Christendom, the children dressed up as saints. In our ever increasing secular society, children and adults frequently dress up as witches and devils. A larger religious message or simply fun? I leave that up to the modern Druid scholars.

My thoughts turned back to dad. He was a local Bronx boy. He and my mother were high school sweethearts at St. Nicholas of Tolentine. His dad fought in World War II. My grandpa, a navy man, saw action at the battle of Okinawa. A quarter of a million people died, including twenty-five thousand Americans. The Japanese sent wave after wave of kamikazes, planes that flew into our naval fleet. Hell on earth. But that's the story of all war, hell. Grandpa, like so many of the "greatest Generation," never talked about his war experiences.

Before too long, war drums beat for Korea and then Vietnam. American Catholicism emphasized God and country. During the JFK era, Catholics were still viewed as an immigrant church. We felt we had to prove we were good Americans. My dad heard the war drums and signed up early for Vietnam duty. My parents married quickly and off he went. He saw action in two tours of duty before returning home for good. Like his father, Dad said nothing about the war. He was the complete opposite of Coach Schmidt. The coach's therapy was to talk about the war, while Dad's was booze and cigarettes, a two-pack a day man. When asked about Nam, he offered his standard reply, "You want to know tough. Try driving a bus in the Bronx."

"He came back a different man," Mom said. Dad became a functioning alcoholic. He abused his body, but never his wife or kids. Mornings always found him driving his bus route. He worked all the overtime offered to him. He earned respect in the parish neighborhood as a veteran, Little League coach, and union man. Union men were the good guys when I was growing up.

Strong memories of him sipping whiskey in a dark kitchen flooded my mind. He would chain smoke and when you first entered the kitchen for a snack, all you saw was the glowing end of his lit cigarette. The light from the open refrigerator let you see him in the shadows. He never saw you as his mind was elsewhere. When we were little, we'd say "Daddy's in the zone." We often felt he was reliving a firefight that he never talked about.

Halfway through the war, he told Mom, "The government lied to us about Vietnam." Later, when we all came of age, he warned us that our foreign policy served the economic interest of the few but not the American people. "Mark my words," he said. "There will be endless wars for profit." The bus driver got that right.

When my brother Quinn joined the Marines, Dad went deeper religiously. Between smokes, drinks, and work, he stopped into church daily. During the twenty minute break between bus runs, Dad, always with a cigarette in hand, walked to a church to pray for Quinn.

"Why do you bother to go to church?" Mom frustrated with his drinking once asked him.

"Because I'm a sinner," responded Dad. Conversation over. His theology was right on. That St. Nicholas of Tolentine High School diploma was looking impressive.

Cigarettes eventually killed him. During army boot camp, he started smoking the free cigarettes given to the soldiers by the tobacco industry. Previously, Dad had never touched a cigarette. I blame the tobacco companies that peddled an addicting product. Profit over the welfare of the soldier. A wave the flag to sell their product scam.

A few years ago, Dad entered the hospital two days after Christmas. He never stabilized; his heart and lungs gave out. His legal will allowed no extraordinary means of staying alive. It clearly spelled out no machines to assist him in breathing or living. I heard of his passing in a telephone call from my sister, Katie. My knees buckled, my back slid down along the wall, and my grief poured out on the floor in a pool of tears next to me.

The first mystical moment in my life occurred while I sat on the floor. These deepest of prayer episodes are very rare in the spiritual world. Yet some mystics, St. Faustina, St. John of the Cross, St. Julian of Norwich – all-star prayers – had been blessed with this spiritual gift.

I felt briefly the pain of the world. The story of labor – peasants, serfs, slaves, sweatshops... the hell of war with broken bodies, widows and orphans... The images rolled and rolled till they led to the cross. My moment ended with Jesus on the cross, suffering for us. How long did my mystical moment last? I have no idea but I know it was real.

At Dad's Irish wake, Mom joked between tears, "I will not be the merry widow." For fifty years, she had loved Dad, warts and all; now, five years later, she still missed him terribly. She had taken her love for Dad and poured it into her kids, grandkids, and her community of friends. Much healthier than booze and cigarettes.

Father Tim made today's morning mass special by mentioning

Dad's name a few times. After mass, the small congregation greeted me with "Happy Birthday to Dad." I smiled. We are resurrection people. Amen. I pictured Dad smoking a cigarette in heaven, waiting patiently for his bride and children. Thoughts of a merciful Lord and heaven offered comfort. No one says "damn it to heaven!"

The energy of the school hallways flowed around me as I made my way to class. Young people everywhere. Some stood or sat, others sprawled near their lockers, kids talked, slept, worked on homework, listened to music. Familiar daily vibes.

On my lunch duty rounds in the cafe, I stopped at the table where basketball players sat to talk about the merits of this year's New York Knicks hoop team. We all agreed the great reputation of the champion Knicks of old – Reed, Frazier, DeBusschre, Bradley, and Monroe – had nothing to fear from the present team.

"Will they ever win it all again, Mr. Mac?"

"It's been a long time, my young brothers."

Dean Espinoza entered the cafe and called me over.

"Lockdown," she whispered to me.

A tip about drugs in a locker needed to be checked out. The alert went out to every adult in the building. No one leaves the classrooms or cafeteria. In the cafe, I took the main door, while my partner, Matt Meehan, a Brooklyn boy, covered the side. No one would get by these two seasoned veterans.

Mrs. Espinoza returned fifteen minutes later. "Walk Rico Ponce up to Sister Sam's office," she informed me. "Give them five minutes to get ready." Ponce had been escorted to lunch from the in-school suspension room. He now would get an escort right out the cafeteria door and hopefully, out the school door.

I went over to Rico's table and stood across from him. He looked up and gave me a cold stare. He never disappoints. After I told him to accompany me to see the principal and the deans, he played the tough belligerent card – squared his shoulders, threw out angry words. Calmly and quietly, I waited him out and hoped this troubled kid would be leaving Dorothy Day soon. He was poison, taking kids down into his toxic well. It took more than five minutes for Rico to strut his way through the cafeteria and the hallways. Sister Sam waited at her office with the two deans. The door closed after them.

I walked over to the front office secretary, Susan Howell, and gave a big hello. Secretaries run the schools and they are the glue holding us all together. They keep administrators, teachers, parents, and kids all on the same page. Ponce's angry voice, cursing in both English and Spanish, interrupted our conversation. He stormed out of the office, slamming the door as he left. There was no reason for me to stop him. He cursed me out as he passed by and made threats against the school. His dark aura and smell stomped out of the building with him.

Dean Holmes alerted the cops about the treasure trove of drugs in Ponce's locker. This was no repentant "I'm sorry I made a mistake" kid. He would never set foot on campus again. Sister Sam tried the emergency numbers for Ponce's parents, but like her earlier attempts, no one picked up. I found out later a cop went to Ponce's address but she came up empty, also. No one lived there. Ponce was a mystery wrapped in an evil aura.

The school bells returned normalcy to our school day. My classes wrapped up and then my team had a decent indoor practice. We were slowly rounding into solid baseball form for next week's first scrimmage.

Rugby practice, usually a distraction from my mind chatter, was not tonight. My thoughts focused on talking to Paddy about the threat to Manuel. I hustled home after practice and showered before placing the call.

"Sorry I couldn't get back to you," he said. "What's up?"

"I need some advice." I walked him through the story of Manuel and Maria, Rico Ponce, our suspicions of gang activity, and drugs in our school.

"Your students said Ponce is in the Locos?"

"Yup. Kids usually know."

"This same gang wants Manuel to join?"

"Yes, again."

"You got a mess on your hands."

"I'm feeling that, Paddy. I think this may be too much for me to try and get right."

"The Locos are too much for anybody. No one takes them on solo. They're known nationally and even internationally. They instill fear wherever they go, living out their motto: kill and control."

"Oh, man."

"It's only part of their story. Throw in drugs, extortion, and prostitution."

"Does the high school have reason to fear them?"

"You bet. You do, too. Promise me you won't start playing Texas Ranger. Do you know the symbol of the Locos?"

"No clue."

"The machete, a peasant tool. I suspect Ponce was a plant, scouting your school and area. The Locos want to expand off Fordham Road. I betcha his parents were fake. Young punks like Ponce make thousands a week working for a gang. In their eyes, going to school is for chumps."

"I'm spoiled with good kids at school. I can be naïve at times."

"Tell me about it, altar boy."

"Is the gang running the Bronx?"

"Nah. The Bronx has always been too big for one outfit to control. But it is making inroads on the turf of some rivals."

"Break it down for me."

"Roughly, the Locos run the Fordham Road area from the University to the Harlem River. An Italian mob controls Pelham and all points east of the zoo; the Irish guys, you probably know some of them, the north Bronx, while the Albanians control the reservoir and its surrounding area. Blacks and Puerto Ricans split the south Bronx between them but they are facing a threat from Caribbeans, who are muscling in on their turf. Particularly, the Dominicans."

"Does the whole thing ever get to you?"

"Sometimes I sing the blues, especially when the problems of drugs, assaults, even murder overwhelm my day. Then I go home, kiss the wife, hug my kids and go back to work the next day and kick some ass for them, for your Dorothy Day kids, and for all the good people of the Bronx. It's a cycle in my life but it works for me."

"What about Manuel? What can you do? Anything, at all?"

"Problem is, he doesn't even know who threatened him." He paused and then said, "Tell you what. I know the commander of his precinct. Good man, Healy. I'll ask him to keep an eye out for Manuel and his family. It's not much but it's something."

"Will it work?"

"I won't lie to you. These are real desperados. If they want to hurt you, they'll find a way."

"Let's hurt them first."

"Careful. Stay out of it. Leave it to New York's Finest. Take it out on your rugby pitch. Who you playing on Saturday?"

"Old Blue on Randall's Island."

"Tough bastards on a tougher field. You might as well play on concrete."

"I'm hoping the rain keeps it soft."

"It stops tonight."

"Ouch."

Randall's Island lies under the Triborough Bridge, also known as the RFK Bridge, which links the Bronx, Queens, and Manhattan. Huge concrete arches crisscross overhead, carrying highways that connect the boroughs. The only grass on the island grows under the arches. None of the fields, cement-hard and peppered with rocks, is a field of dreams.

"Be careful," Paddy cautioned again before we hung up.

I contemplated the road forward, but no clear or definite plan came to mind. One thing, however, I knew for certain. I would *act justly* for the sake of my students.

Seventeen

God creates out of nothing, wonderful, you say: yes
to be sure, but He does what is still more wonderful:
He makes saints out of sinners.
Kierkegaard

Friday

The unmistakable aroma of coffee filled my nostrils. An unusual smell in my place as I'm a tea drinker. There's no Mr. Coffee in my humble abode. A dream... yeah, that's it, I'm dreaming. Nope, not possible, as I recognized the familiar sound of a morning garbage truck as it rumbled down the street in front of my home.

"To the rising of the sun," said Daniel. He sat on the corner of my bed, an extra-large cup of java in his hand.

My initial surprise quickly gave way to annoyance.

"Where ya been, Daniel?" I said crossly. "You left me hanging. It's been a week."

"Never, my dear friend. My cohorts and I have kept an eye on you. Kevin, you always tell your students 'you're not alone.' Well, neither are you."

"Really. How's that?"

Daniel snored loudly. My memory flashed back to the snores of the homeless guy last night.

"That was you? Why not just show yourself?"

"You have to learn on your own. To trust in your ability to fight evil."

"Daniel, this might be out of my league. My senses are heightening but so is my violent side. Violence by an angel. Wait, let me take that back. Angel-in-training. You know, I'm no St. Martin of

129

Tours. He said *'I am a soldier of Christ and it is not lawful for me to fight.'"*

"He was a soldier in the Roman army who turned to nonviolence. C'mon, homeboy, look elsewhere. Michael, the archangel," suggested Daniel.

"Hey, you're talking top gun. I'm a different story altogether."

"No. Same story. The righteousness of a cause. The fight against evil on any scale, to any degree. The fight for the Marias and Manuels of the world – at a school, in a grocery store, on a city street."

"Why me? This mook from the Bronx asks again."

"Why Daniel?"

"Huh, what's with that – whadda ya mean?"

"Of all the names you could have picked for a guardian angel, you chose Daniel. Why not Peter? Or Paul? Or any number of different names?"

"The lion story. I fell in love with it. Daniel and his faith in God triumphed. *'My God sent his angel who sealed the lions jaws, they did me no harm...'* (Daniel 6:23). Lions, an angel, strong faith. I ate it up as a kid."

"You bear the fruit of the Spirit – joy, peace, kindness, faithfulness, love of God, and love of neighbor. You realize the gift you've been given. You educate teenagers in the way of the Lord, lead them to the Light, and away from the Darkness. Your job's unfinished."

"Wow, Daniel. What a morning wake-up. Where do I go with that?"

"How about to the kitchen to make yourself a cup of tea? Then settle in front of your burning candle. Live in the Spirit and follow the Spirit. It will continue to guide you on your way. I gotta run... fly," he said with a twinkle in his eye.

"Hold on. I've got questions." They teemed in my mind,

jumbled up and tripping over each other. None of them came clearly to mind.

"Trust in the Spirit. You always have."

The aroma of coffee in the room lingered longer than he did.

*   *   *

"Did you hear about your buddy, Elston?" A shake of my head gave my negative response to Diane Dragotto, a fellow teacher, who came up to me outside the chapel. I had just left morning mass with the dismissal, "Go in peace, glorifying the Lord by your life," still ringing in my ears.

"Gang members flipped his wheelchair over with him in it. He was on the corner near the school."

"Where's he now?"

"Nurse's office," said Diane.

As I hustled to the nurse's office, students in the crowded hallway, parted like the Red Sea in biblical times, clearing a path. I flew in the door and saw Margie Ann McDermott, the school nurse, leaning over Elston. Big Joe, who carried Elston to the health room, sat by the door, alert and ready to protect Elston if need arose. It would take a strong force to get by Joe's massive frame.

"He's okay, Kevin. Some abrasions," said the nurse.

"Thanks for letting me interrupt." I said. I hugged Elston. "What happened?"

"Relax. I'm fine. I was at my usual corner greeting kids. It was early. Mass time. So not many students yet. Two guys sauntered up, and stopped in front of me. One of them said, 'Hey, friend of Dorothy Day,' and slapped my face a few times. 'Tell Dorothy Day we're thinking of her,' he added. Right then, Big Joe turned the corner, shouted, and ran toward me. They saw him but no panic as far as I could tell. Two cool customers. They casually turned over my chair before walking into the street, without a concern for the moving traffic. Big Joe wanted to pursue them but he stopped to help me. Thanks again, Joe."

"No prob... and I still want to get them," he responded.

"I second that, Joe. Go and get ready for class. I'll stay with Elston a bit longer."

"Got it, Mr. McCarthy."

The nurse walked out with Joe to get a cup of coffee. "You two talk; I'll be back soon," she called out over her shoulder.

"You sure you're okay?" I inquired.

"Mac, I've fallen worse going into the shower and getting on and off the toilet. This was nothing. It wasn't about me. They were sending a message. Dorothy Day has a Locos problem. Today was the opening act."

"You're right, my friend, the intro." I filled him in on Rico Ponce and Manuel.

"Elston, my brother, this is going to escalate. Why don't you lay low?"

"I know you care but it's tough to scare a guy in a wheelchair. What are the gangsters going to do? Break my legs?"

We both laughed but I knew it could be much worse. They're not called "crazies" for nothing; the name Locos has been earned.

"Time to get back to my spot and greet the kids who show up at the buzzer and the late ones," said Elston. I knew he also wanted to show those who might be observing that he and Dorothy Day, as well, would not be scared off.

"They're on my radar," I informed him.

"Usually, you're too nice. Today, you got ice in your veins.

What's with that?"

"Righteous anger."

"Channel it, Mac."

"Promise, bro. You'll let your mom know what happened?"

"Yeah. She would hear anyway. Now that's someone the gang should fear." We both laughed again, this time heartily.

"Who loves ya!?!"

"Back at ya," he responded. Smiling, he propelled his wheelchair out the health room door and we both headed down the hallway to the front door of the school. Students greeted and high-fived Elston, happy to see him, a Dorothy Day fixture for many years.

I returned to the chapel to focus and center before class. In any school environment, news spreads like wildfire so the kids would know of the incident by class time. I needed to be ready to respond to their questions. Remind them in a world of too many bad guys that they needed to be like Big Joe, who was courteous and kind to everyone. Most of all, I needed to remind myself. Anger boiled and bubbled inside of me. Down on my knees, I gazed at the cross, then the tabernacle. "Jesus pray for me, Father pray for me, Mother Mary pray for me, Dorothy Day pray for me."

Saints and Prophets, the topic of the day in my Church History class, provided an opportunity to fight off the blues. I smiled at the thought of the Holy Spirit sending saints and prophets to my aid at my time of crisis.

"Open your notebooks. Let's review. During the Reformation, the Catholic revival was led by a strong pontiff. Name him."

"Yeah, that's it, Christina. St. Pius V. Who led the Jesuits? Who's that you said, Eduardo? Loyola? You got it. St. Ignatius Loyola gave us an army of spiritual warriors."

"Who led the Council of Trent? St. Charles Borromeo. Right

on, Eugene. St. Francis de Sales added his voice and pen to the Council. He was aided by... whoa, that's it, Judy, St. Jane de Chantel. What saintly woman led Spain's reform?"

"St. Teresa of Avila," responded Bianca.

Students enjoy the story of Teresa of Avila. It took the saint over twenty years to define her direction in religious life. Through many obstacles, the Church being the biggest one, she persevered in the reformation of religious life and made it less dependent on personal comforts and attachments to the world, and more focused on simplicity of lifestyle and an intimate personal prayer life with God. I believe students embrace her story for two reasons: the lengthy time it took her to get her act together and her clear admission that she was a sinner, that she messed up.

"Saints and prophets then, what about now? We need saints here at Dorothy Day, and in the Bronx."

"You're kidding, right? Saints here and now. This ain't the Middle Ages."

"Luke, yes, here and now. We're on holy ground right now. This is sacred space because we're children of God."

"Huh? This is the Bronx. And look at this motley crew."

We all laughed. "Luke, motley works. It's said that God writes straight with crooked lines. My brothers and sisters, we're the crooked lines."

"I got it. A crooked line isn't perfect so, we don't have to be perfect to be saintly," said Karen, a star on the field hockey team.

"Right on, Ms. Field Hockey. Perfect is Jesus and Mother Mary. The rest of us sin. What's a saint? 'A saint is a sinner who keeps trying,' according to author Robert Louis Stevenson. The great St. Francis of Assisi said, '*I have been all things unholy. If God can work through me, he can work through anyone.*'"

"Anyone?" piped Danny incredulously.

"Anyone. Saints and prophets are in the building right now. Brother Willie and the holy nuns, Sisters Sam, Katherine, and Chiara. Father Tim's a prophet. What about Mrs. Kistinger in the cafeteria? She's the epitome of a holy church lady. Ms. Cullen, the sign language teacher."

"You forget this holy of holies here," said Danny, pointing to Lenny, the class clown. The class broke up howling.

"Being holy, I refuse to respond to his finger pointing. I, of course, will take the higher road," pontificated Lenny. Sophomore humor. "I'll be Jesus and forgive him." More laughs.

"Joking aside," said Danny. "Anyone can be a saint? What about Hitler?"

"Hitler achieved historical infamy," I responded. "He could have achieved sainthood or been famous in a positive way, but he abused his freedom. Freedom is the choice of how to serve, be it cop, fireman, doctor, nurse, teacher, professor, mother, father. There's happiness in serving. Lead with love. Then we'll reject the lure of selfishness, 'sex, drugs and rock and roll' and the devil himself. We'll avoid descending into a world of sin. Real freedom is centered in God."

"Deep, like that's really deep. I'm only a sophomore. A kid," said Danny.

"Age has nothing to do with it. It's not a variable. Mother Church canonized eleven-year old Maria Goretti, who was martyred shortly after her First Communion. She fought off a lustful man. For the first time in church history, a mother watched her child's canonization. Tell me, Danny, will your mom see yours?" Everybody laughed but none harder than Danny.

"St. Augustine of Hippo was called by God to serve but he kept answering 'not yet.' His greatness came when he finally said yes to the Lord. So young people forget the response 'not yet.' Say yes and become great in His name."

"Not yet, I get, Mr. Mac. Party now and have fun. Maybe, later," said Peter.

"Who are you, kidding," yelled out Bobby, Peter's best friend. "Not now, not later." The class roared once again.

"Like most of us don't have a clue as to what we want to be later," said Julie, one of our cheerleaders.

"The great St. John of God was a fool for Christ, stumbling along in many different jobs until he started an order of Hospitalers. You'll figure it out but we must always be saintly on the journey."

"Messed up is the norm in my housing project," said Lenny, seriously. "The journey's rough."

"Lenny, there are good people everywhere. Take your mom and dad, for instance."

"Can one study or train to be a saint?' asked Jess, the class scholar.

"Of course, you can. Many saints started on the road to saint-hood by reading the lives of saints, case histories in salvation. Go for it, Scholar. Start with Dorothy Day. There's only one unhappiness in life, not being a saint."

"All that reading. The rest of us ain't as smart as Jess," commented Tony.

"Then let one word guide you. LOVE. Love of God. Love of neighbor."

"Do we have a choice about sainthood? That's a lot of pressure," said Betty. "I have enough to deal with right now."

"According to saintly Mother Teresa: *'Holiness is not the luxury of the few. It is simple duty for you and me.'*"

They heard me. I saw it in their faces. Mission accomplished.

Teachers need to call students to their better selves, to expect them to strive for and to achieve it. Talk about it. Show them the way. We disservice them if we leave them unguided, if we avoid the topic. They will rise to the occasion and be thankful for the direction. I often hear from students that no one ever discussed this with them. They are open to the message; we just need to pass it along.

"Homework tonight – in the Good Book. Matthew 5, lines 1-12: *'Blessed are the peacemakers, for they will be called children of God.'* There are eight more *Blessed are...*"

"No chance of that, street fighting man," said Tony as he looked over at Doug.

"Street fighting?" I asked.

"My parents are Rolling Stones fans," Tony blurted out.

"Me, too." I broke into song: 'Say a prayer for the hard-working people, say a prayer for the salt of the earth.' My favorite line from my favorite Stones song, 'Salt of the Earth.'"

"My father's favorite, also," said Courtney Marie, who sits in the first row, near my desk. "He's a big Mick Jagger fan. Cracks me up, an old man like Jagger running around the stage, kinda like you running around the classroom every day."

"Old? Did I hear old? Moses and Methuselah were old. Me. I'm still young enough to ruck and maul with the brothers in this room."

The class howled. Fun was in the air. Class aim achieved.

*   *   *

I heard him before I saw him. "Oh, let the saints go marching out, oh, let the saints go marching out," bellowed Mac. Two holy nuns in the school refer to him as John the Baptist, who paved the way for the

Lord. He's paving the way for teenagers with Gospel teachings and his emphasis on turning to and relying on God.

I check on him every day to see how he's holding up. He has been his normal boisterous, demonstrative, loving self. Daniel checked on him today; the angel wire service passed along the news. His doubts are normal, so is his uncertainty as to the road ahead. Trust me, I know. Been there, done that. He's definitely on the devil's radar. It starts out as small encounters at first but the intensity will build. The bell is ringing, time for class, break is over. Mac's right; we answer to bells.

*   *   *

The scent of roses tickled my nostrils. A gentle breeze caressed my cheek and wrapped a feeling of tranquility around me. I relished the pleasures of scent and air at the end of the class and looked around to determine the source. I shrugged... no answer. It just was.

After the kids left, I straightened desks, one of the many small tasks a teacher performs daily. My thoughts turned to St. John Chrysostom, *"What is nobler than to mold the character of the young?"*

The rest of the day hummed. The feeling of love in the air affirmed my vocation as teacher. You pour out love and it comes back. Maybe, here at Dorothy Day, we were unconsciously trying to love more to counter the negativity of gangs.

After school, I stopped in the cafeteria to embrace the school community before the weekend. Close to two hundred kids show up every afternoon in the cafe to hang out, flirt, and work on homework in a safe, clean environment. They delay going home to their mean neighborhood streets. Two moderators cover the cafe after school. An investment of time and money, but priceless. The students leave at 5 pm, a time when many of the parents are making their way home from their jobs. I worked the crowd, greeting and bantering with many of the students, and then headed to the ball field.

A cold crisp day made for an efficient baseball practice. When it's cold, practice moves quickly. Work them hard and get them home. Two of my players swore some Locos members were eying the team. They spoke excitedly in Spanish and I suddenly realized I understood their speech. Ah, Daniel, those French mademoiselles that I talked about earlier are not far behind, I chuckled to myself.

The Bronx with one million people always has a lot of foot activity. People pass by the field, sometimes, even stopping to watch the young lads hit and field. Occasionally, bystanders offer positive comments or shout out a cheer when a good play is made. My eyes saw nothing unusual but the air quivered and the wind picked up. I gripped my bat like a weapon. Saw no evil, heard no evil, but felt evil. I called it a day and headed home.

Eighteen

The Lord loves those who hate evil
Psalm 97:10

Friday night

Showered and toweled off, I slipped my solid green Murphy's Irish Pub polo shirt over a long-sleeve black shirt. I work part-time as a bartender and a bouncer at Murphy's, a Woodlawn bar, one of twenty in my old neighborhood. Extra cash for this Catholic school teacher. A bouncer spends time outside the bar – hence my layers of two shirts – controlling the crowd, dealing with drunks, calling a cab, helping someone who's sick, or simply, for a breath of fresh air.

I sat down to my usual Friday meal of two grilled cheese sand-wiches and a bowl of tomato soup. No meat, of course. Not on Fridays in Lent. The bishops ask Catholics to fast on Fridays all year. No longer a rule, just a spiritual suggestion. An act of self-denial to remind us of the poverty of the world and the Good Friday sacrifice of Jesus on the cross.

I called Mrs. J, Elston's mom, while I sat over a cup of steaming tea.

"Mac, thanks for reaching out. Elston is a tough kid. Abrasions are nothing, compared to the many stitch jobs he's had over the years. The poor guy kept trying to walk even though his mobility was dimin-ishing. It led to many emergency room visits where the nurses knew him by name."

"Is he there, Mrs. J? May I speak to him?"

"He surprised me and said he wasn't coming by today. Some of the Dorothy Day crowd is here, however. Sister Chiara's holding court. She's a pistol."

"You got that right. Incredible stories. She loves her job as a social worker but she needs to laugh at the Byzantine bureaucracy that she deals with every day. Otherwise, she would go nuts. It's her release, her safety valve. Please tell Elston, I called."

"Will do, Mac. In all honesty, Elston's a bit down. Not for himself but for Dorothy Day. He's worried that today's incident will escalate. I'm on his page, from what he told me. Do I need to worry?"

"Not going to lie to you. I'm worried, too, but I've learned while worrying is normal and human, it achieves nothing. Before the kiss of peace at Mass, the priest says, 'Deliver us, Lord from every evil and protect us from all anxiety.' Trust in Him. Focus on that. Be yourself. Strong as always."

"You got that. There's no alternative. A mother has to watch out for and take care of her kid."

"You always do that and more! Not only Elston, but the Dorothy Day community, as well."

"We're family."

"Amen, good woman. Peace and love."

Like her son, she responded, "Back at you."

Gazing out the kitchen window at the final rays of the sun, I sipped the remainder of my tea. The last of many in the day. To get spiritually centered, I breathed in and out slowly to enter a quiet zone. Strengthened and invigorated, I headed out the door.

I arrived at work with time to spare. Murphy's has a long wooden bar, which takes up two thirds of one side of the room. Numerous beers are on tap, including the Irish brews, Smithwick's and Guinness, and bottles of Irish whiskey, scotch, bourbon, and vodka, line the three shelves behind the bar. On the wall to the right of the shelves is a stained glass Celtic cross, a bright green shamrock to the left. Three dart boards hang in an alcove past the bar on the right. The area is always active, attested to by the pockmarked dart boards and surrounding walls. The eight by ten foot stage area stands opposite the bar. Tables and chairs, packed so tightly that it's difficult for the wait staff to maneuver at times, fill the rest of the room. Pen and ink drawings of Irish literary figures, such as James Joyce and W.B. Yeats, hang on the walls. Gab and the pen – gifts given to the Irish.

Settled on the sturdy wooden bar stools or on chairs at the tables, a noisy crowd filled the joint for Celtic heritage night. Tonight's performer, Maureen Ivins, a Woodlawn girl, had practiced her way into an international reputation by winning world championships in fiddling. Local girl makes good. She married a neighborhood guy, Kieran Culligan, whose dark hair, blue eyes, and chiseled jaw turned many a female head. While growing up, he invested his time in music, not sports. Presently, he and Maureen travel the world, riding her fiddle, bringing joy and foot-stomping, wherever they go. Though Maureen and her group have performed at New York's Lincoln Center and the Kennedy Center in Washington, D.C., she has never forgotten her Bronx roots. She usually plays "surprise" sessions in the neighborhood around St. Patrick's Day. The whispered secret had the place crowded and humming by the time I walked in the door.

"Work the crowd," said Murph, the owner. "Keep eyes and ears open. Grab empty bottles and glasses but for Christ's sake let nothing happen on this special night. Nip anything, immediately."

I made the rounds, basking in neighborhood friendships and shooting the breeze, especially about sports, and families. Guys flirted with the colleens. Colleen is an Irish first name but it's also used generally to refer to females.

The smell of pot signaled the first sign of trouble. Not in the air but the residue smell left on clothes. Looking around, I noticed the two Byrne brothers sitting at the end of the bar. In their thirties, they had left the neighborhood for lives with wives, kids, and houses with mortgages in the suburbs. They still partied regularly, however, in the neighborhood.

There was no love between us. They had run-ins with my family and friends over the years. Boisterous, belligerent, and just downright nasty, especially when fueled with alcohol, summed them up. I heard them talking but I went unnoticed for the moment.

"The Bronx sucks."

"It's getting dirtier and more violent every day. It's a dump."

"Yeah, who would wanna live here?"

Why come here? was the obvious question. But I knew the answer; these guys buy their pot and coke in the Bronx. What little patience I had for drugs just got thinner. Time to speak to them and I moved in their direction.

"McCarthy, I see no date again," shouted Buck O'Connor. "Friday night and your celibate monk self is hiding behind bouncing at Murphy's. Cut to the chase, man, and admit no one wants your sorry ass."

Buck O'Connor is a dear friend. That said he offers no breaks. His MO is to make fun of everybody and to keep firing away with non-stop barbs and comments. His steady girlfriend was by his side.

"Elizabeth Jean, what do you see in this burly man with thinning hair?"

"Burly man with thinning hair. I like that," interjected Buck. "Not fat, not bald." He patted his head. "Grass doesn't grow on a busy street."

Elizabeth chuckled. "He makes me laugh." Not a bad reason in an often difficult world.

Buck took his Irish music seriously. He was a bagpiper in the Sanitation Department's Emerald Society. "It's simple, Mac, pipers and kilts are sexy. Join a band and even you could get a date."

Buck mentioned a recent piping gig in Inwood, an old Irish neighborhood, but now multi-ethnic. It sits on the northern tip of Manhattan, bordered by water and a wooded park, which we city folks call a forest. The Cloisters, a medieval art museum, sits at the southern end of Inwood.

While in the neighborhood, Buck had run into my brother Mickey. He let me know that Mick was now a bartender at the Galway Bay. Located on 216th St, the bar is close to the waters of the mighty Hudson.

The river, named after Henry Hudson, an Englishman, who sailed it in 1609, travels 315 miles, officially starting north of Albany, the capital of New York, in the Adirondack Mountains. It forms the border between New York and New Jersey before emptying into New York Bay. In the early nineteenth century, the river inspired author Washington Irving to write of river valley inhabitants in his classic short stories, *Rip Van Winkle,* and *The Legend of Sleepy Hollow.* The Hudson River school artists glorified the river in paintings in the latter half of the century. Today, it's a vibrant artery of the New York area, plied by pleasure craft, ferries, freighters, and sightseeing boats filled with tourists. The river keeps on rolling along. It's New York's Mississippi.

The bar buzzed as Maureen warmed up. The Byrne brothers drew my attention as they headed to the bathroom. Guys don't powder their noses together; their powder goes up the nose. I followed them. Opening the door, I found the brothers leaning over the sink, snorting lines of coke.

"Suburban boys, time to take your show on the road to Westchester."

"You're kidding, McCarthy. This is the Bronx or have you forgotten where you are?"

"I never forget. I live and work here. Your clothes reek of pot, and now your noses are lined with cocaine. I also heard you trash the Bronx after you just bought your drugs here. Do you get the irony? Well, it's time to head back to Westchester. Stay there and buy your drugs in your own backyard."

"What are ya gonna do about it?"

"This teacher likes multiple choices. A, we get physical – very tempting; B, I tell the half dozen Bronx cops here about your drug stash; C, you're outta here. Tell it walking."

Both glared at me, huffed with an attitude, and then puffed out their chests. I was ready to blow their house down. Even the Byrne brothers, however, had enough sense to take their show on the road. They slammed open the bathroom door, grabbed their jackets from the bar stools, and quickly left the premises.

Maureen started her magic, her bow humming across the fiddle strings. On fast songs, the rosin powder rose up from the bow like smoke over a fire.

I saddled up next to Roger Larkin, who sat at one end of the bar, nursing a whiskey. His carrot top hair led to his nickname, Red, and his freckles added to the Irish look of this gentle, friendly, and harmless guy. A barfly, alcoholism had its grip on him. A shame since he's brilliant and knowledgeable about politics, sports, religion, all things Irish, and any other topic someone wants to discuss. Oftentimes, he breaks into Irish song as he's quite the crooner. His singing, especially "Danny Boy," earns him plenty of beer. Yeah, we know he has a problem with "the drink" but we do it anyway. Go figure.

Roger and I have chats that often center on God, an appealing topic for two former altar boys. Red is drawn to God and partakes in the sacraments, even when hungover, which is frequent.

"I'm a sinful man. We're all lepers in need of healing," he says.

Red actually intensified the God in me. He knew lightness and darkness. Booze never vanquished his yearning for God.

"Mac, I finished *The Long Loneliness* that you gave me. In the book, Dorothy Day wrote that nothing can fill the void for God on earth. Not booze, sex, or materialism. On that note, tomorrow I get sober." He drained his glass, stood up, steadied himself and left the bar.

So far tomorrow has never come. Red proclaims Christ but demonic booze holds him tightly in its grasp. He's a daily reminder that "there but for the grace of God go I."

The crowd clapped and stomped as Maureen made her fiddle sing. She wrapped up her set with a haunting "Immigrant Soul," a crowd favorite. Kieran ended the session by reciting a tear-jerker poem about an Irish wake, not for the dead, but for someone emigrating to the United States and leaving beloved Ireland and family behind. Everyone raised their glasses to toast St. Patrick, other saints, Irish freedom fighters, martyrs, and the homeland.

In Woodlawn, St. Patrick's Day is really a month, a season. The first two weeks of March are a warm-up to the big day. The St. Patrick's Day Parade marches along Fifth Avenue, the center line of the street painted green. The sound of bagpipes fill the air, Irish flags fly from buildings and lampposts, and crowds pack the sidelines, yelling out to friends and family members marching in the parade and just cheering in general. For two weeks after the parade, we Irish bask in the glow of our moment in the sun. In March, we own NYC and the world, or so we think.

Maureen's set left the crowd charged up. As the night was still young, most stayed to hear a neighborhood band.

Stationed at the door, I leaned against the frame. A survey of the bar revealed smiling customers content with the Irish tunes and their companions. My brief respite ended when John Murray, a retired dock worker, came through the door.

"Red's being hassled in the alley," he said. "Sorry, Mac, my days of fighting are long over."

I flew out the door and quickly turned the corner. Red lay on the ground and bled from his lips and his nose. A lowlife named Mugs and his boys, neighborhood punks, stood over him, laughing and guzzling beer from cans. Alcohol fueled their bravado.

"Hey, back off!" I snapped.

"What are you gonna do, religion teacher? Say a prayer? Give us a speech?" Mugs laughed along with his lackeys. He continued. "Why don't you give us detention? Or better yet, make us go to confession?" More hard laughter followed his comments.

Mugs thought of himself as one bad dude. Most people believed differently; a neighborhood bully enclosed in a six foot four, two hundred and fifty pound body with not an ounce of muscle. He and his boys, all in their early twenties, were losers and banned from most of the bars in the neighborhood. Mugs earned his nickname from frequent police mug shots for petty crimes.

"No, Mugs. No speeches. I taught good kids earlier today and you're not one of them. Today, I'm especially tired of bullies; I'm in no mood to talk."

Coleman, one of the punks, shifted behind me and another, Clifford, edged up on my right. Mugs moved in front of me. They were trying to box me up against the wall on my left by attacking from three directions. My alert senses picked up their movements. A peacefulness wrapped around me, preparing me for the coming storm.

Stepping forward toward Mugs, I quickly backed up, landing a right elbow smack into Coleman's nose. Crack! Hit my mark! Down for the count, his bullying night was over. A left-handed two fingers in the eyes of Clifford caused him to howl out in pain, loud enough for residents in the neighborhood to turn on lights.

Glaring at Mugs, I offered some advice. "One chance. Just one," I warned. "Go. Now. If you fight, I'm going to hurt you. Not a matter of if but how bad. You put your punk hands on my friend and I'm not happy. Call it righteous anger."

Red stirred at my feet and I reached out to lend a hand. Mugs took advantage of the moment and lunged at me. The large man moved slowly, giving the heel of my boot plenty of time to hit his knee before he touched me. Down he went, screaming and clutching his leg. He tried to get up but his knee collapsed under him. My fury continued and I grabbed his hair.

"I gave you a chance to walk away, now you won't walk for a while. Maybe, a limp forever. A reminder of your evil ways."

"Superman, that's what I'll call you from now on," said Red, still on the ground. "I never knew you could move so fast. And how many pairs of eyes do you have? It's gotta be more than one."

"Let's go." I pulled him up and kept a sure grip on his arm. He tottered at first but then he gained his balance.

"Hey, you get to tell everybody how you beat up three no good jerks by yourself," I said.

Red flashed a drunken smile. "Well, Kevin McCarthy, you helped a wee bit. We made a friggin' great team though."

"That we were."

"After all this, I could use a drink."

"On the house. Clean up first. I'll have my one Lenten beer with you, my friend." A limit of a single beer, by no means easy. Where I grew up, nobody drank just one. In the past, I gave up all beer for Lent but this is more difficult. The taste and coldness of the beer hit the spot and I always want another.

"*Abstinence is easier than moderation*," wrote St. Augustine.

The Bronx boys have nothing on Augustine. In *Confessions*, his autobiography, he shared his reputation as a party boy and a womanizer, having a child out of wedlock. He held off God's invitation for a long time with "not yet." Between God and his mother Monica, who shed copious tears over his sins and prayed for his salvation for years, Augustine didn't have a chance. Eventually, he came full circle. He was baptized in 387, ordained, and later, he ministered as bishop of Hippo, for thirty five years.

"Deal," said Red. We walked into the bar, leaving the punks to fend for themselves.

"A new Irish rebel song about you and tonight's battle between good and evil should be written," I said. "Standing up to bullies. It will be right up there with the legendary songs, including 'Kevin Barry,' 'Boys of the Old Brigade,' 'Heffo's Army' and 'God Save Ireland.'"

"And the title?" asked Red.

"Hmmm... Let's go with 'The Legend of Red from County Bronx.'"

"Works for me. We kicked some butt tonight."

"Indeed, we did," I responded.

"Maureen Ivins and a good fight. A grand evening." A mile-wide smile crossed Red's face.

The rest of the evening proved uneventful and routine. A few sloppy drunks and raucous outbursts but all controllable. Last call went out and then cleanup. I finally worked my way home in the early morning hours of a new day. My radar was on alert but no one tailed me in the shadowy streets. The quiet before the next storm.

I settled into my armchair in front of my lit candle for my night prayer.

"Blest be the Lord, my rock, who trains my hands for battle" (Psalm 144:1).

Violence in the name of the Lord? How does that fit together? I found myself pleased that I kicked losers out of the bar and fought punks in defense of the innocent. Am I to clean up the Bronx by fighting in bars? I wondered. Not exactly the same as Jesus throwing the money lenders out of the temple.

I conjured up images of Jesus in encounters with bullies. I saw Him as a five year old, playing in a desert sandbox with other children. One of them tormented a lizard by twirling it over his head. Jesus said "enough." The kid kept on so he temporarily blinded the youngster in a sandstorm directed only at him. I then saw Jesus, as a teenager, putting the fear of God into a pack of male teens harassing females. He pulled a strong as Samson strength number, picking up mighty boulders and hurling them at the feet of the boys. They ran like lightning, frightened out of their wits. I started to drift asleep, but not before one more scenario of Jesus danced in my thoughts. He prevented scabs from crossing His carpenter union picket line on strike for a living wage.

Go Jesus.

Nineteen

The Lord is near to all who call upon him
Psalm 145:18

Saturday

"You're green," announced Brigid as I walked in the door.

"Like the leprechauns, little buddy. You know it's my favorite color. That's why this shirt."

"Not your shirt. It's around you," she stated matter of fact.

As I turned to my sweet sister, the aura that surrounded her body took me aback. A flickering blue-greenish color outlined her body and danced around her. How long had that been there? I answered my own question. Most likely since birth, I thought. Holiness beamed from Brigid. Her white hair and aura gave her a radiant beauty.

In the family, Mom's a blond, dad, was a red head. The hair color of the nine kids range from the pure white of Brigid to the carrot top of Seamus, with all kinds of shades of blond and red in-between.

"Green? Brigid, what's going on? Those are black shorts and a red shirt your brother's wearing," stated Mom as she walked into the room.

"It's around him," Brigid responded. Her hands outlined my body. "But I have more colors."

"Blue and green," I responded.

"Jesus, Mary, and Joseph. What's gotten into you two? Your own special code?" asked Mom.

I shrugged; Brigid smiled.

We sat down for an early evening meal. Ah, home cooking! Mom fed me, like many moms, with plenty of food. I demolished a full plate of ham, pineapple chunks, sweet potatoes, and applesauce.

Seconds followed. My big breakfast at a local diner was long gone. Eggs, rye toast, bacon, hash browns, juice, and tea – all for $7.95. Not sure how the diner makes out at that price but it sure fits my budget. I'm not one to cook and have no desire to learn. What with Mom's home-cooked meals, diner food, Chinese take-out, and pizza, I make out alright in the food department.

Mom wanted to talk about the incident at Murphy's. Through the Bronx grapevine, information had already found its way into the neighborhood. Downplaying it earned me a disturbed mother look – tight-lips, furrowed brow, squinted eyes that looked directly at me, and tried to bore inside. Though not satisfied, she moved on to the upcoming feast of St. Patrick. Clan members attend mass and the parade on their own. Afterwards, in the early evening, we all gather at Mom's for a family celebration of our Irish roots. Most years, everybody makes it but Mickey, although the celebration of St. Patrick has created other AWOL casualties every now and then. The drink or a pretty colleen can twist the best laid plans. The opposite has also proven true. Sometimes, siblings bring home strays from bars and the parade to meet Mom and join in the festivities. None of us feel any pressure to celebrate at Mom's. We come because we want to see each other.

Every year, Mom sends a verbal invitation to Mickey through one of us. She gave me the assignment this year.

"Make an effort and let Mickey know he's invited, Kevin."

"Will do, Mom."

My huge hug enveloped Brigid and she snuggled close to my chest.

"Who loves ya, little sister."

"You do," she crowed.

"Big time."

*   *   *

Kevin has always been my favorite. He's always smiling, and makes time to hang out and listen to me. He treats me the same as he does everyone else. He learned my parents lesson well and sees my abilities, not my disability. I know I have Down Syndrome. God made me this way and that's okay. Kevin has always seen the inside of me and tells me I have my own special strengths. He lets me know I'm a gift to the family, bringing a lot of love and happiness. Mom worries about me, but she shouldnt. I'm happy. I have family, friends, and a job as a teacher's aide. I have a life. Mom also needs to stop worrying about Kevin. As long as I can remember, he's had a close relationship to God. My skin often tingles when he's nearby. No tingling today, just his green color. Not surprised because green is his favorite color. Green is also an angel color. Is Kevin an angel? I dont know. All I know is I love him, always have, and always will.

*   *   *

Night prayer involved an examination of conscience to take a close look at my past twenty four hours. To reflect on my actions and feelings, and to ask for God's help in understanding them.

Anger, anger, and more anger on my part. Plenty of violence at the bar last night, and on the rugby pitch at today's game when I hard-tackled a guy numerous times for taking cheap shots at my team members. I was beginning to realize how much this theme of violence was part of my life.

My anger was on behalf of others. Does that make it defensible? Does my response fit into the category of righteous anger?

"Blessed are those who hunger and thirst for righteousness" (Matthew 5:6). St. Thomas Aquinas, a giant of a theologian, believed there was no sin in righteous wrath provided there was no undue desire for revenge.

Does righteous anger apply to the use of violence to combat violence? Is it possible to stop bodily harm from fists and beatings through non-violence? I'm certainly not in Dorothy's league. Her writings and speeches, not her fists, expressed her anger at the "filthy rotten system" in the United States that produced so many poor, homeless, unemployed, and hungry people. She had national and international exposure and left an awesome reputation as a dedicated and committed fighter against injustice. In his September 2015 speech to Congress, Pope Francis mentioned Dorothy as one of four Americans who truly inspired him.

Find your own path, be true to yourself, Daniel had cautioned me. Perhaps, I was born to be a warrior angel. Maybe, I'm meant to fight the filth and rot of bullies and gangs, be it in a bar or on a rugby pitch or in school. Me, yeah, me, a mook from the Bronx.

My examination also led me to be grateful for Brigid, to see God's presence in her purity and love. Some spiritual writers have speculated that beautiful souls like Brigid may have volunteered in heaven to come down to earth and witness the light in a challenged state, mentally or physically. Once here, they don't remember volunteering, but God's grace makes their light shine.

May I be aware of God's presence in my daily life. And at the end of my life, may I voice a sentiment similar to Dorothy's: "...happy to have had our good Lord on my mind all these years."

Twenty

With God among us, we shall fight like heroes,
He will trample our enemies
Psalm 108

Sunday

I woke early, no need for an alarm. Lying in bed, I slowly moved my arms and legs, and checked for soreness. All systems were go. Like NASA, I chuckled. No post-rugby problems from yesterday's game. Unusual after a game to wake up the next morning without numerous aches and pains.

I always stay close to home for Sunday mass. Tonight, I planned to attend mass at Fordham University. Saturday mornings usually find me in different parishes. Yesterday, I went to Blessed Sacrament on Tremont Avenue with Father O'Connell presiding at mass. A well-respected and wise man, he loves being a retired priest because he works fewer hours, now only twenty to thirty a week, plus no meetings. He focuses on the priestly duties of praying, listening to and counseling parishioners, and performing the sacraments. He's a curve ball in Lent because he looks like the image of St. Nick with white hair and beard, and a burly physique. He reminds me of Advent, the time in the church calendar that leads into Christmas.

During my morning prayer today, I reflected on yesterday's Lenten reading. Prophet Isaiah takes us places like few others:

...Is not this the sort of fast that pleases me – it is the Lord Yahweh who speaks – to let the oppressed go free, and break every yoke, to share your bread with the hungry, and shelter the homeless poor, to clothe the man you see to be naked...(Isaiah 58:6-8).

Here I am, my Lord. I want to be in deep communion with

155

Thou. Let me be your light.

Yesterday, Father O reinforced the scripture with a five minute homily at the thirty minute mass. Observe the holy season with devotion to the message of the Lord. Build up your spiritual muscles, through prayer and by attending mass, to wage battles for the downtrodden in society and with the demons of sin, which come in many forms. Make church your gym.

On Sunday mornings, I treat myself to two newspapers, *The New York Times* and *The Daily News*. Quite a difference in the quality of the papers and the depth of coverage. I read the various sections of *The Times* thoroughly, especially the main one; sports coverage is my only reason to buy *The News*. It's all about those Yankees. I devour the stats of the individual players and the stories about the Bombers. Tea and a bagel loaded with cream cheese add to my morning contentment.

Schoolwork always beckons by late morning. I took on my grading piles, while James Galway, a renowned Irish flutist, played in the background. In my school routine, grading comes first as it's my least favorite activity. Planning and setting up weekly lessons always follow. Four hours on Sunday, typical for this school teacher. People have no idea that teachers work sixty plus hours a week, including after school and on weekends. Adding up all the extra hours – the way I figure it every hour of our summer break is well deserved and earned.

A spiritual reading to contemplate and provide guidance always accompanies me on my Sunday afternoon jogs. "The point of this life is to make our story fit into the story of Jesus," wrote Dan Berrigan, a Jesuit priest. How would I fit my angel invitation into the Jesus story? The tension of using violence vs. non-violence?

I went to the track near the new Yankee Stadium, a shrine to Yankee history, a mini Cooperstown Hall of Fame. It was built across the street from the old stadium, which was torn down. The baseball field was kept, however, and now local kids play on the same field that saw the likes of Babe Ruth, Joe DiMaggio, Lou Gehrig, Yogi Berra, and Mariano Rivera. Cool! A park and a track finish off the refurbished area.

I cranked out laps as I meditated. Loud shouting intruded on my spiritual zone. At the far end of the track, I saw young people surrounding a teenager dressed in a long sleeve shirt and khakis. As my lap drew me closer, I heard them threatening the young man, who remained silent. I walked over just as one of the horde smacked the well-dressed teen in the face, followed by a punch to the ribs, knocking the air out of him. A hard blow to his head followed and he went down, flat on his face.

"Enough!" I bellowed.

The group turned on me and a punk asked, "What's it to you?"

Their breath stank of booze, their clothes of pot. Bloodshot eyes and bottles of quart-sized malt liquor in their hands indicated a long Saturday party evening that was continuing into today.

"You talkin' to me?" I said. I love that line spoken by Robert DeNiro in the movie, *Taxi Driver*. "What am I going to do? I'm going to recommend you follow Jesus. How's that?"

"Screw you," said the guy closest to me as he stabbed an index finger in my face. I grabbed his pointed finger and twisted his arm up and behind him. He doubled over and fell down on his knees. I quickly grabbed his malt liquor bottle with my other hand, and squared off against the others. One of them continued to advance, throwing punches at my face, so I smashed the bottle over his head. Not only did he go down but he was out. Clock rung! The broken, ragged edge of the bottle plus the two bodies on the ground stopped the movement of the other two thugs.

"Gentlemen, you can take your friends and leave or I'll keep going. Who's next?"

They hesitated and took a step back.

"What's it gonna be?" I asked.

Keeping their eyes on the bottle, they slowly bent over and seized the arms of their fallen crew members, half dragging, half carrying them away.

I looked down at the fallen teen and realized I knew him. The mark on his neck made verification easy – Aaron, the teenage mugger from the other night.

"Are you all right?"

He groaned. I knelt down and gently rolled him over. He blinked his eyes a few times before he completely opened them. I helped him to his feet and we walked slowly to the bleachers, where he sat down.

"Who are you?" he asked.

A question for Daniel was answered in that inquiry. I had wondered if someone would recognize me if we had met earlier in my angel state.

"You don't know me," I responded, "but we have a mutual acquaintance."

"Yeah? ... Like who?"

"An angel friend. He asked me to keep an eye on you."

"I mighta met one the other day," he said hesitantly, "but that's a wild idea, huh? An angel spending time with a kid from the hood. And a messed up one at that."

"I get what you mean... Trust me. I completely get it."

"Are you one? ... Forget I asked. Two angels meeting up with me... no way."

"I'd like to be. Maybe, an archangel, fighting for justice and righteousness. But I'm just a guy, Kevin McCarthy, from the Bronx.

How's it going?

"Man, oh man, it's hard. Really hard."

"Bruce Springsteen sang, 'It's hard to be a saint in the city.'"

"Never listened to him but he's got that right. Drugs and booze in my life as long as I can remember. Staying away from them... I'm trying but it was my life. And treating girls with respect after years of treating them like dirt... not easy."

"And how about your buds?"

"Can't figure me out. I can't figure me out. But I know I need to stay away from them."

"I can't figure myself out, at times, either. Especially now."

"You? You just busted up some bros. You didn't seem confused."

"Easy. They were partying all night. I'm puzzled about what's next, where I'm headed in life." Or death, I thought.

"That angel, the one I mentioned, gave me an order. Follow the Gospels. He zapped me – like a taser. It was strange... a different feeling – I thought it felt like hope, maybe... I guess... but I'm not too sure. It's like nothing I ever felt before. I want to move forward." He looked down at his clothes. "I went to church with my mom," he added.

"Your light of witnessing Jesus attracted the darkness of those sorry losers. The devil attacks light and wants to snuff it out. Stand tall."

He offered a soft smile while straightening his shoulders.

"How are things at school?" The teacher in me made me ask.

"Don't go there. You know that hopeful feeling I was talking about, well, talk of school will kill it."

"Listen, I teach at Dorothy Day H.S. I'll help get you in there next year."

"Yeah... and there are no rats or roaches in the projects."

"Scholarship, my man."

Silence. He stared at me with eyes narrowed before he shook his head from side to side.

"No way," he finally said.

"I'm serious, dead serious. Two rugby friends, Ted and John L, who work on Wall Street, always offer to pay for a scholarship for a deserving kid. You fit the bill."

"Me? ... Yeah, right... a bro from the Bronx."

"God works in mysterious ways. Trust me on that." I chuckled before continuing. "You're trying to do good. Keep trying to be the light, my young brother. Don't fall for the false brotherhood of gangs."

We shook hands. His grip was firm and a smile lit up his face.

"Remember, I'm Mr. McCarthy. Come to Dorothy Day during Holy Week. I'll introduce you to Sister Sam, the principal. We'll set you up for September. How about Spy Wednesday?"

"Spy? What the heck is that?"

"You heard right. It's the Wednesday of Holy Week. Judas betrayed Jesus on that day. Come by about four o'clock."

"Not sure I believe you... my mom won't believe it, either."

"Sure, she will. Church ladies believe in miracles."

"Mom will cry," he said with his head down. He was ahead of his mom in the tear department.

"Should I tell the coaches we may have another ballplayer next year?" His athletic build, muscular arms and legs, and his height gave notice he might play sports.

"Hell, yeah. Football and hoops."

"The only rule for the scholarship is for you to keep trying to be Christ-like. Not perfection, my young brother. Just try."

We fist bumped and parted ways. I finished my laps with a grin on my face.

Night mass at Fordham University. The Jesuits and the college students pumped me up. The Jesuits, founded by St. Ignatius Loyola, are premier educators, who run schools around the globe; Fordham is one of them. In my mind, the university is one of the seven wonders of the Bronx, along with Yankee Stadium, the Botanical Gardens, the Bronx Zoo, Bronx High School of Science, the mighty Hudson River, and Long Island Sound. Quite possibly, the Bronx has eight world wonders. Woodlawn Cemetery with its illustrious "residents" would be a worthy addition to my list. Yeah, the Bronx can hang and has bragging rights.

I scanned the church crowd. Hundreds of college kids on Sunday night giving praise to the Lord. Maybe, like Aaron, each person needs to be invited to fulfill his glory. Too often we concentrate on "we are sinners." A reminder to this teacher to emphasize that we are the reflection of God and that is our destiny. I settled into a state of joy. I felt one with God and His people.

Twenty-One

Cast the burden of thy cares upon the Lord,
and He will sustain thee
Psalm 54

Monday

"We need to talk," said Sister Sam outside the school chapel. Worry creased her face and her brow.

She told me of the savage beating of Maria Hernandez last night. Her assailants left her for dead, a block from her home. She had run out to the neighborhood bodega at her mother's request to get milk for the family. Now, attached to machines in a hospital, and comatose, Maria was fighting for her life. Damage unknown. The doctors were not optimistic.

The Locos had made their move. Sister Sam was blaming herself for bringing Ponce into the school. A street smart nun, Sam realized this time her usual redeemable kid radar had failed. Instead of a hopeful convert, she had invited evil into our community.

In every homeroom, the first order of business was prayers for Maria. They would flow throughout the day, in the prayers offered at the start of every class, and in the chapel where people would stop in and get down on their knees throughout the day. It was announced that a healing mass would take place the next day. As a Christian community, we believe in the power of prayer as well as grace to deal with the situation.

I returned a phone call left by Maria's parents. They asked me to stop by the hospital and pray with them. They said Maria would have wanted me there. "She trusts you and believes in you," the father informed me. Trust? How was that? She's fighting for her life and I had failed to do anything in regard to the Locos. Had I been naive enough to believe nothing would happen? The parents reassured me no one was to blame except the ones who beat her up. They surprised me with their request to bring Brigid. Maria had told them of my classroom tales of Brigid and her special grace. I called Mom to relay their request. I heard her speaking to Brigid in the background. She'll be there for Maria's family, Mom assured me.

My school day blurred except for a visit with Manuel in the counseling office. He was beyond lost. He wanted to kill, cry, and run out the door all at the same time. Revenge was foremost on his mind. Sputtering and raging, he shouted out, "I'll kill them, I'll kill them all." His rage carried him from one side of the room to the other. He banged on the walls, pounding his fists so hard that bruises appeared on his hands. His rantings, threats, and expletives thickened the air of the room. And then he broke. Moans and tears escaped from him. Time to hold onto him, to murmur soft words. "Maria needs you more than ever. Stay strong and smart for her." The thugs would leave him a martyr at best if he went after them.

He calmed down by taking deep breaths and by walking slowly around the room. He shared a chilling message delivered by gang members. They gave Manuel until Saturday "or they will hurt again." I pleaded with him for patience and promised by Saturday, I would deal with it. Time to act and stop this evil. Whatever "angel juice" I had would be put to use.

"Right now, we need to focus on Maria. Let's meet at the hospital this afternoon." Manuel grasped my hand, and nodded yes.

I shot to Woodlawn right after school in the used car I purchased over the weekend. Brother Willie would cover my practice. NY traffic cooperated – a rarity – and I made record time. An anxious Brigid was waiting at the door, ready to go. We chatted on the way, especially about St. Patrick's Day, which was fast approaching. She made me smile when she reminded me that she is named after St. Brigid, the Mary of the Gael.

"Brigid of the Bronx, how did St. Brigid describe heaven?"

"A lake of beer," she responded. We both giggled. You gotta love the Irish saints!

No need to circle the parking lot at the hospital as we snagged a spot on the first pass. Hand-in-hand, we walked into the hospital through sliding glass doors. Brigid was quiet as she looked around at the surroundings. People moved to and from the elevators. Others sat in the blue chairs, some reading, others talking. A mother cradled a baby while her son played with a truck on the floor. A man standing spoke on his cell phone. We were second in line at the information desk in the middle of the room.

The information volunteer directed us to the third floor. Brigid laughed and tapped her stomach as the elevator moved upward. A left and four doors down brought us to Maria's drab green room. Machines hummed and dominated the room with frequent beeps and fluctuating numbers and lines. Maria lay still, her face marked by bruises, one cheek swollen to the size of a baseball, and her arms full of IVs. Her inert form was tucked in a white blanket except for her hands and arms, which lay outside the cocoon.

Maria's parents stood by the window, holding hands and talking softly to each other. They noticed us standing in the doorway, came over, and hugged us. Small smiles crossed their otherwise worn-looking faces. Maria's aunt was on her knees, praying her wooden rosary beads at Maria's bedside. We all knelt down with her, lining up in a row on the hard floor.

Brigid was the first to stand. She went to Maria's bedside and clasped her hand tightly. At first, I thought it was my imagination but then realized a change had definitely occurred in the room. It was warmer and brighter. A glow outlining Brigid flickered and gained strength. I was the only one privileged to see it.

"Angels are here," she said softly. "There are four of them. Two there." She pointed to the foot of the bed. "And two by the window."

"To protect Maria or take her?"

Brigid was unsure.

"What do they look like?" I asked.

"Two are like me." She tapped her hair. "The others have dark hair and brown skin like Maria's mom and dad. Three women and one man. Not old, not young. They're good angels," she informed us.

"How do you know?" I inquired.

"Their blue and green colors and their smell. Like roses," she told us.

Roses and angels. I recalled the smell of roses at my classroom door the other day. What was that about? Angels in Dorothy Day?

Maria's holy parents and aunt took great comfort in Brigid's words. They pulled her close, and enveloped her in a sea of arms. Maria's aunt read aloud the scripture passage she had chosen for this afternoon:

See that you never despise one of these little ones, for I tell you that their angels in heaven are continually in the presence of my Father in heaven (Matthew 18:10).

A subdued Manuel entered the room, shoulders slumped and feet dragging. He found comfort when told of the heavenly guests that Brigid had seen.

Brigid took a small plastic bag out of her pocket. It contained cinnamon. She sprinkled a small amount on each of Maria's hands and around the feet of the bed before placing a cupful on the bedside table.

"Angels like the smell of it," she told the parents. Brigid does this in our family home so I was used to it.

"The bad ones don't like it," she continued. "It smells too nice."

I was unsure how the nurses would handle cinnamon in the room. Maybe, like me, it would bring back delightful childhood memories of toast with melted butter and a sprinkling of cinnamon on top.

We hugged Manuel and the Hernandez family and began our trip home. Brigid chatted the whole way.

Arriving at the house, I walked Brigid to the door and gave a holler for Mom. She came out of the kitchen, wiping her hands on a dish towel.

"There were four angels," Brigid offered.

"I'm glad you went. Your words were a great comfort to the parents, I'm sure."

"I can go again. Maybe, next time, I'll talk with the angels," she responded.

"Thanks, buddy for your help. I'll let you know," I said.

"Prayers, Mom. You and the ladies," I requested.

"Already started. We're way ahead of you."

A kiss planted on Mom's cheek and I went out the door. I worked my way to Mickey's bar in Inwood. My mission was two-fold: pass along the invite to St. Pat's and ask him what he knew about the Locos in Fordham. The afternoon at the hospital had brought some comfort but I found my anger rising. People who hurt kids were ticking me off. I pondered Jesus' words: *Let the little children come to me; do not stop them* (Mark 10).

Someone had threatened Maria, a religious young woman who lived her faith. Someone was going to pay. So be it.

I parked the car and walked a short distance to the Harlem

River. Coincidently, this spot on Manhattan Island where the Hudson River meets the Harlem River is called Spuyten Duyvil, from the original Dutch settlers. It loosely means Spitting Devil. And I was sick of devils and bad guys.

Rage that had built up since the morning, I unleashed with a howling scream as a subway thundered on the tracks overhead. My hands clinched in fists, I screamed again, letting out "Not Maria. Not the innocent ones."

I took some minutes to regroup, before heading to the bar. Peeking in the window of the Galway Bay, I saw Mickey wiping the bar and talking to a customer. I walked to the corner to order Chinese. Dinner would be on me.

My presence in the bar surprised Mick. A few customers. U2 played at low volume on the sound system. The Knick game was muted on the TV.

"Well brother, teaching isn't working out and you now work delivering Chinese takeout? Catholic schools need to pay you more."

"Not bad. Here's the deal. I buy you dinner and you treat me to a cold beer."

"Done." He poured two glasses, handing me one. We clinked glasses.

"Quiet day, Mick?"

"Yeah, pretty typical. Mondays are quiet in most joints. Recovery day after the weekend for drinkers. But the Galway does okay. A Daddy crowd. We get a fair share. Remember Dad used to say, 'I'm not here for the conversation.' I fill the drinks of that crowd and leave 'em alone. We all got demons."

"True enough. As always, Mom wants to bury demons and invite you to the St. Pat's celebration."

"As always, tell her I'll see."

"Fair enough, Mick. You've said it before."

"I have and mean it."

"But you never come."

"Kevin. I never say never. That by itself is a victory. I've kept the door open."

"Logical answer but not logical if you never come."

"Family has nothing to do with logic."

"Agreed, little brother. But this can't be what life is about." I panned the drinkers at the bar.

"It's my world."

"I respect you and your world but our world is small compared to the bigger picture."

"Which is?"

"God."

"Should I be born again?"

"I know you well enough. You are cut off from formal family but you've never cut yourself off from God. If you surrender to God daily..."

"Who said I surrender? I dance with God." He laughed and then quoted his favorite poem, "The Hound of Heaven" by Francis Thompson. "I fled Him, down the labyrinth ways, of my own mind; and in the midst of tears I hid from Him..."

"Like an Irish bard, Mick. A minstrel poet indeed."

We both ate bites of food. Decent food for a cheap price. Tasted good.

"Hey, Mr. Dance with God. Dance over here and give me a drink." A customer, midway down the bar, shouted good-naturedly, catching Mick's attention.

"On my way, Otis." Mick poured a glass of beer and a shot of whiskey for the retired fireman.

"Mick, my patron saint Dorothy Day would listen to the writer Eugene O'Neill, her buddy, recite 'The Hound' in a saloon in Greenwich Village called The Golden Swan. Then she would put his inebriated self to bed."

"Well, I'm not inebriated." Pause. "Yet. But I like being in the company of O'Neill. Both of us reciting poetry in Manhattan. Great minds think alike, I guess."

"To quote your poem: 'I fled Him, down the nights and days.' Our God pursues us. Time to surrender."

"What answers you got, teacher of religion."

"'Do not go gentle into that good night. Old age should burn and rage at close of day; rage, rage against the dying of the light.' Dylan Thomas. Our Welsh Celtic cousin."

"Hey bro, what's that about? You think of an answer as I fill some drinks." Mick moved down the bar.

Easy enough. Teachers rarely have time to dwell on an answer in a classroom. It's usually more of a bang-bang.

Mick came back, sat down, and settled into his food. "Go ahead. I'm all ears."

"Maybe, the wisdom of Dylan Thomas is that fighting and partying to the end of life serves nothing. Dylan died a drunk. Perhaps, he's telling us there's more to life. Even your author, Thompson, said in his poem, 'my mangled youth lies dead beneath the heap.' He, who was addicted to opium and was homeless, knew what he was talking about."

"OK, Teach. I hear you. And we're back to square one. How about the knight in Chaucer's *Canterbury Tales*? He said that the world is but a thoroughfare of woe, and that we are pilgrims passing to and fro."

"Fair enough. My Dorothy said that God has brought us together to be instruments of each other's salvation. Pilgrims together."

"Are we?"

"The clan needs you."

"Really? They didn't need me before. I was asked to go."

"And you freakin' deserved it. You were out of control, druggin' and drinkin' and scaring Mom. But that was then and times change."

"How's that?"

"First, we are not partying kids anymore. Second, we are a family, for better or for worse, and there's a hole without you. We need you for our healing and you need us for your journey."

"Again, I hear you. I'll think about it. One more time, I'll see."

He extended his hand and I shook it. He offered me a second beer but I refused. We moved to a safe topic, the Knicks, who were having a dismal season again. My friends and I were quickly losing interest as the team game we loved was becoming obsolete. An all about me attitude, one on one, has replaced the beauty of team play and crisp passing.

"Mick, I need your help."

"How so?"

"A young female student of mine has been badly beaten by the Locos and her boyfriend is being seriously threatened. I need to knock on their door and tell them to back off."

"You serious? Knock on their door? Are you nuts?"

"Have you been there?"

"Yes. The headquarters on Fordham, right?"

"French Riviera mansion."

"The same. I've done business there. Drugs. A lot of business. I repeat, are you nuts? They're bad boys and kill easily."

"I know."

"Are you sure you know? Then why go there?"

"Life and death."

"Yours!"

"Maybe, so. But the lives of my students are at stake."

"Why not Paddy and the cops? Get off your shining white horse and let them take care of it."

"Nothing to go on. Their hands would be tied. What's on the inside?"

"A lot of technology, cameras, security, weapons. Plus a dozen bad hombres. You won't surprise 'em. You can get in but you won't get out alive."

"Maybe, bro. That's why I want you to reconsider about St. Pat's. Life is short."

"Do not go gently, huh, bro?"

"Exactly."

He then walked me through everything he knew about the layout of the building – doors, staircases, windows, men, and firepower.

Our brotherly good night embrace lasted longer than usual. I was at peace. Not so Mick. He knew what I was up against.

Twenty-Two

The heavens open and multitudes of angels
come to assist in the Holy Sacrifice
of the mass.
St. Gregory

Tuesday

Heaviness hung in my homeroom. I felt that I could reach out, grab it in my hand, and wrap my fingers around it. No change in Maria's condition.

My spiritual ladder on the front board was simple today. Next to the ladder, I wrote a big red D and in smaller black letters – evil. Together, they spelled Devil.

The school community slowly worked its way to the auditorium for a school-wide mass. A time for healing and prayer, which we all needed as the shadow of Maria fell on all of us. The seriousness of the situation matured the students, at least for today.

Strings from the music department, led by music teacher Laura Emerson, a skilled violinist in her own right, played as the students filed to their seats. A beautiful piece of music but also an effective quieting technique.

Our large gospel choir, clothed in scarlet and gray robes, stood on three tiers on the stage. Made up mostly of African-American students, it had a smattering of our school-wide ethnicity, and two faculty members, including Annie Ferber. That female could rock with the best. The liturgy started with the choir swaying and clapping, and the horns blaring. Slowly, at first, but then faster, the grieving community flowed into song.

"The house where they were assembled ROCKED and they were

filled with the Holy Spirit" (Acts of the Apostles 4:31).

The well-chosen readings for the mass told of Jesus overcoming evil and sin in the world. Father Tim brought the message home with a fine homily.

"Recently, we had Black History month," he said. "Frederick Douglass, a former slave and great prophet of the 1800s, was in great despair and feeling the blues. Obstacles appeared insurmountable, hope was in short supply. It took Sojourner Truth, an itinerant preacher and women's rights activist, to renew his fighting soul. 'Is our God dead?' she asked Douglass."

Father Tim paused, waited, and then repeated the question.

"Is our God dead?" The students' faces started to shine.

"One more time, I ask you, is our God dead? And now you Dorothy Day high school say..." He cupped his ear.

"No," said the students.

"One more time, Dorothy Day."

"NO!" roared the students.

Father Tim paused and the auditorium stilled.

"Our God is not dead and neither is Maria," he said. "Let's beat back the blues, despair, and darkness. Let's rekindle hope. Let Maria feel our prayers, our energy, and our collective spirit. Let's sit in silence for a few minutes and pass all of it forward to Maria."

Silence and high school students are usually incompatible. Not today. Students reflected and opened themselves up for one of their own. Love, friendship, and community flowed together as one body.

Father Tim broke the silence. He reminded us that in the Our Father we pray "this day."

"So Dorothy Day high school, Jesus gave us this prayer and today he gives us all we need. Not tomorrow. Now. Our living God takes care of all of us. Trust. In His way. We will praise God 'hallowed be thy name' and conclude with 'lead us not into temptation.' We cannot do it alone and neither can Maria. So let everyone link hands in the glorious Our Father. The prayer of our Savior. He told us whenever two or three gather in His name, He is there. We are much more than two or three. We are a school and a family. Let Maria know our God is with her. Do you have someone's hand?"

"Yes," came the community response.

"Did I hear you?"

"Yes," they shouted louder.

"Can Maria hear you?"

"Yes," they yelled.

"Can God hear you?"

"Yes." The auditorium rocked, just like the words stated in Scripture.

"All right, Dorothy Day, slow and easy as we pray as one family the words of Jesus, 'Our Father, who art in heaven...'" The auditorium was ablaze with God's love.

A mystical moment occurred at Communion. With tears streaming down her face, Karla, Maria's best friend, waited on the communion line of Annie Ferber, who was serving as a Eucharistic minister. Two soccer teammates supported her, one on either side, as the last forty eight hours had been an emotional roller coaster. Before receiving communion, Karla suddenly hugged Annie and hung on for dear life. Flustered momentarily, Annie quickly regained her equilibrium. With a Eucharist in one hand and the paten, the plate filled with Eucharist, in the other, she wrapped her arms around Karla and gently cradled her. It appeared that Karla was being caressed by the body of Christ.

The clarity and sharpness of witnessing in God's name faded by afternoon. I was on my own roller coaster. At practice, I became lost in my thoughts while hitting fungoes to my infielders and out-fielders. It's usually a favorite part of coaching. The ball reaches an apex in the air. Stops. Drops. Timeless. The complaints of my infielders penetrated my fog. You're hitting too hard, they informed me. They were right. Dangerous. On the other hand, the outfielders loved going full speed after the balls. To quote them, I was hitting "crazy far."

I apologized, chalking it up to the distraction of Maria. They heard me but they still wondered about my new strength. Cirilli, an outfielder, said "it has to be steroids." They laughed as I mumbled something about super strength in a crisis.

My shower at home never felt better. The warmth of the water eased the knot between my shoulders and soothed the ache in my back. I let the water cascade for a long time. So much for conserving water – usually, but not today.

Two months ago, my Woodlawn friends made a date to watch the Rangers in a bar near Madison Square Garden. A beer and burger night. A chance to catch up but now also a welcome distraction from the Locos. Season ticket holders, wearing their New York Ranger jerseys, would add an extra buzz of excitement at the bar before and after the game. They are always pumped up and ready to rock and roll.

I left the train at Columbus and 59th Street, located at the southern end of Central Park West. Some of the finest apartments and hotels in the city line the streets. My sister Molly lives and works a few blocks west of the subway station. We have a rule that I try to stop by, even if only for a quick hello, when I'm in Manhattan. She often works late and justifies the extra time in the office by her lack of commuting time, home being just a ten minute walk away. Her efforts have paid off; she's a highly successful publisher for a major company. Always a lover of books, she majored in English at Boston College. We thought she would become a librarian, writer, teacher or even a college professor. Her book journey brought her to the publishing world, where she met her future husband, David Basile.

Molly helped raise us in many ways. When we were growing up, Mom was always busy with managing the household, shopping for food, dealing with the nine of us, addressing any child issue or problem that cropped up, and taking care of Dad. Molly stepped in and introduced her siblings to books and words. Even my brother, Mickey, who loved partying, found another addiction in books. All of us became ravenous readers. And what Irishman is not fond of words, blarney or not!

Molly always knew the appropriate book for your age and interest. She hooked Mary Claire on *Little Women* by Louisa May Alcott. For me it was J.R.R. Tolkien's *Lord of the Rings*. I shared the story with my friends after pick-up hoop games, stickball or touch football, or over an egg cream, a delicious carbonated chocolate Bronx soda drink (no egg involved) or while eating Carvel ice cream. They teased me about my reading habits but I noticed they always asked for updates. I enchanted them with hobbits, orcs, wizards, elves, dwarfs, and Strider, destined to be king. Tolkien once said of his classic, "Of course it is a Catholic Christian story." Good versus evil – a never-ending battle.

My friends learned of the world of rabbits with human traits in *Watership Down* by Richard Adams. The toughest rabbit, Bigwig, led the fight for freedom in the quest for utopia. Sherlock Holmes and Doctor Watson gave them mystery under the writing hand of Sir Arthur Conan Doyle. King Arthur and Lancelot provided legend while Jack London gave us dogs and wolves.

Molly insisted that the entire family read *A Tree Grows in Brooklyn* by Betty Smith – a story of a family with an alcoholic father. Brigid and I read the book together and then watched the movie. It's her favorite film and she watches it often.

My storytelling skills improved with every book I read. I became quite the raconteur, which has served me well in my five thespian acts a day in school. Classrooms are great places for stories. Every kid in my class has a unique story and it's my job to learn it. Then real learning can take place as I try to connect the dots between their stories and the Jesus story.

Kyle, a smart kid, once asked, "Mr. McCarthy, Jesus can't always be the answer. What about evil?"

"The absence of Jesus," I answered.

I found Molly in her cramped office. Her stacks of books filled every nook and cranny in her office; her priceless view of Central Park, however, was left unobstructed.

"Good to see ya, lass," I said as we exchanged hugs.

She boiled water for two cups of tea in a hot pot, which sat on the window sill. The Irish in us. We discussed the upcoming feast of St. Pat's and wondered if Mickey would make an appearance. I shared with her his usual comment, "I'll see."

"Maybe, we should appeal to his Catholic guilt? Nephews and nieces are being raised who don't know him. Do you think that angle has a chance?"

"Nothing else has worked. It might be worth a try."

"Is he still reading?" Molly placed a lot of faith in books, not only for providing a solid foundation but also for serving as a catalyst for change and growth.

"I have hope for him if he's still reading. I really think it keeps him alive."

"Yeah, his addiction to books continues. I don't know what he's reading now as we never made it past his favorite poem, 'The Hound of Heaven.'"

"I wish that hound would catch him. How about you, Kevin?

What are you reading?"

"*A Persistent Peace*, by Father John Dear, a Jesuit priest. The book relates his struggle to build a non-violent world."

"How's your own dance with pacifism?"

"Still dancing. I am, as always, a reluctant pacifist. The temptation to be the sword of God is very alluring. Righteous anger. Like King Arthur and his Roundtable that you turned me onto."

"Fighting injustice in any form has a romantic edge to it."

We soon exchanged goodbyes. I headed south to Madison Square, billed as the most famous arena in the world. Billed by whom – had to be New Yorkers. People walking by kept me busy contemplating a cast of characters in all shapes, sizes and colors. I chuckled at the variety of clothing – someone in a charcoal gray business suit next to a young person wearing cowboy boots, a short denim skirt, and a yellow jacket with a colorful scarf wrapped around her neck, a well-dressed woman in a fur coat, walking her white poodle, who was decked out in a red knit coat and a rhinestone collar, a guy in a brown cape that billowed around him in the wind, and a woman in black spandex pants and hiking boots, a yoga mat rolled up under her arm. It's always refreshing to see people comfortable in their own style. Also, people watching is free entertainment.

A twenty minute walk in the cool night air brought me to McGinns. Located near the Garden, the bar's clean and classy with wooden walls that glisten and shine. Touches of Irish paraphernalia – a stained glass shamrock, and photos of Ireland, including people, landscape, doors of Dublin, and Irish pubs, hang on the walls.

My Woodlawn boys stood at the marble-topped bar, with pints in front of them. Marvin Kalinowski, a fire lieutenant, and our most avid hockey fan, was chatting with the bartender about the Ranger players and their individual stats. His dad, a big hockey fan, named him Marvin because the Hockey Hall of Fame Chicago Blackhawk Bobby Hull's middle name was Marvin. Why not Bobby? He already had given the name to his older son. Sports fans can be crazy at times. Duane York, our beer connoisseur, was smiling as he sipped his beer and listened to TJ Kavanagh, our telephone man, regaling him with a story.

High fives and chest bumps were exchanged as I greeted everyone. We shared updates on families, wives, and girlfriends. My lack of a girlfriend was once again noted.

"Hey, Mac, what fun book are you reading now?" inquired TJ.

"Notice he said fun. We don't want to hear about your latest spiritual book. Some monk from the 12th century or whatever," interrupted Marv.

"*The Dresden Files*, by Jim Butcher. A series of books about Dresden, a modern wizard, in Chicago. He keeps evil at bay."

"We could use him here in NY," chipped in Duane.

While ordering a round, I felt someone's penetrating gaze on my back. Turning around slowly, I set eyes on a gigantic man. Well-dressed and good-looking, he stood inches taller than my own six foot three inch frame. His muscular body looked like he should be playing tight end for a team in the National Football League. His fitted shirt barely contained his bulging muscles and looked ready to pop at the seams and buttons. Even more alarming was the dark aura that surrounded his body. It struck me then that I, too, wished we had Dresden, the good wizard, here in New York rather than in Chicago.

We settled into the game, Rangers vs. Flyers, the Broad Street bullies of Philadelphia. Our big scorer, Rick Nash, led with his usual hustle, giving the Rangers momentum, and control of the puck.

The giant pushed his way past me to get to the bar. "I'm sorry, little man." My spilled beer fanned out across the bar counter. "Did your drink get knocked over? Can I get you one?" His words dripped sarcasm.

"No drink needed, big man. Few have called me little man. Maybe, in an age of steroids, looks can be deceptive."

"What are you saying, little man?" He stood taller. Mountain-like. He was unhappy with my response.

"Maybe, you're not what you appear to be," I retorted.

His aura grew darker as he stepped toward me. Fortunately, a couple of sexy bimbo types with necklines down to their navels, pants so tight it's a wonder they're able to sit down or take deep breaths, and skyscraper heeled shoes that caused them to wobble as they walked, came over and hugged him at that moment and oohed and aahed over his redwood biceps. His focus turned to them and he moved away with one babe glued to each arm. My well-being remained intact.

My streetwise boys knew that I had just dodged a bullet.

"Next time, Mac, spill your beer on his expensive clothes rather than the bar. That will show him," said TJ. We all laughed but there was an edge to the levity.

A Rangers win wrapped up the game. Gotta love the boys in red, white, and blue. What should have been a total fun night, however, had instead become a guarded one. The giant's gaze had drilled into me all night, tempering my joy. Preoccupied with hockey, my buddies had not noticed.

We said our goodbyes and headed in different directions. I made my way to the nearest subway that would take me north to the Bronx. A deserted platform, except for two homeless women huddled together, one passed out and the other kneeling next to her, guarding her vulnerable companion.

The first warning of trouble came with a foul smell in the air, followed by beating air waves. The giant from the bar, fast approaching on the platform, came as no surprise. He strode confidently and without fear. This guy was no lightweight but the real deal. It oozed out of him.

"Do I know you?" I asked.

"You're too much a newbie at this angel thing to get it. Well, virgin angel, it's going to cost you. You've no time to learn by experience."

"Stop right there!"

The loud authoritative voice slowed his forward movement. We both turned in the direction of the sound. The kneeling homeless woman was rising up and grew to a height as tall as the ogre. A white mist outlined her form. In her left hand, she held two broken off branches twined together to form a wooden cross. Fireballs exploded from her upraised right hand and fell at the feet of beastly evil.

"Begone," she bellowed, "or pay the price and fight."

Her stare momentarily froze the brute before he howled in rage. Meanwhile, his human form gave way to a reptilian type creature with a covering of horny plates. Hatred burned from his red eyes.

"He's mine!" he screamed.

"Not tonight." She quickly moved over and stood in front of me. "You know you can't defeat me so go back into the darkness from whence you came. That or death. Your choice."

He hesitated and then turned to me. "Careful in the Bronx tonight," he hissed. "Humans are the least of your problems."

He jumped on the tracks and screaming with fury, he vanished into the tunnel. A strong cold wind came whistling out of the passage, casting papers, dirt, and debris into the air.

When I turned to look at my rescuer, the homeless woman stood there. My thanks were profuse.

"You and that evil, are not faithful to your appearances," I noted.

"I suspect the man you called 'the giant' changes more frequently than I."

"How did you know I called him that?" I inquired.

"You're easy to read. You haven't learned to cloak yourself yet. He called you a virgin angel and that you are. Virgin angels often fail to survive long enough to acquire experience. Word went out to be ready to assist."

"Daniel?"

"It started with him but the word came from someone else."

"And you're...?"

"Agnes. Please call me Agnes."

"A warrior angel?"

"Yes and no," she responded. "I spend most of my time protecting the homeless. Particularly women." She pointed to the passed out homeless lady. "Her name's Elaine. Our enemy, the devil and his minions, don't always go for quick victories like your intended death tonight. More often the process is a slow ruin of the human soul. They sense weakness for alcohol, drugs, sex, anger, gambling and then they attack this human flaw and corrupt the purity of man and snuff out God's light." She pointed to Elaine again and commented, "Her light is not yet extinguished. Her memories of growing up in a loving home, and a daughter she gave up for adoption keep her going."

"Your warrior side?"

"I fight, if the occasion warrants," answered Agnes. "Tonight, I was ready. We need angels to combat the ever increasing darkness and shadows. Women are especially exposed and vulnerable in a world of too much violence and abuse. Women, children, and the elderly are the easy victims."

"You saved me. Was it luck that brought you here?"

"The word got passed that you'd be in Manhattan tonight. The Garden. A calculated guess had you coming home by this Bronx bound train. Elaine didn't care where she slept." Agnes leaned over to stroke her face. "Late at night, the platform for the D train is pretty empty, thus a good place to attack. My calculated guess paid off. Mac, you have allies and you're unaware of them. You also have enemies and don't entirely see their intense evil. Like tonight. Time to take it up a notch."

"Yeah, I hear you but..."

"Embrace the change and speed up your transformation. You made your choice when you decided to live and fight in God's name after your accident. You know the road ahead; you weighed your options. You chose warrior angel. Accept it," she urged.

"I'm struggling with the warrior part."

"Bring peace to yourself by abandoning everything into God's hands. Time now to climb a rung on your own spiritual ladder."

"I'm trying... doubt consumes me at times... most of the time."

"Mac, trust in Him. Depend on Him. To worry about your chosen path or to doubt draws you away from Him."

"Tell me about it. I'm spinning wheels about this angel thing."

She nodded. "I know and understand – violence in the name of Christ."

"Yep. You hit the nail on the head. Saying yes to the Big Guy, no problem. It's the how that is troubling me... you were ready to use violence tonight." It was a statement not a question.

"Indeed. When I said yes to the angel invitation, I never gave up the option of using force to defend the innocent. We're no longer humans called to be non-violent in Jesus' name. Angels use force to defend. The beast on the platform knew that he would be defeated."

"You sure of that?"

"Oh, dear. Of course, yes," replied Agnes. "The good warrior belongs to the Trinity of Father, Son, and Spirit. We'll win this earthly battle because Jesus showed us the way; however, evil continues to roam, cause harm, and wreak havoc. Our job is to protect the innocent to the best of our abilities. Today, tomorrow, and until judgment day."

"You recognized that he was demonic. How's that?"

"Angel insight – it's the beginning of many lessons you need to learn from me and others. Elaine's not going anywhere." We both glanced at her gently snoring figure huddled under blankets on the platform.

"I need all the help I can get. Thanks."

"Part of an angel's job. Evil possesses many forms. Humans have no idea the number of spirits, good and bad, that walk and battle in this tired but wonderful world."

"I'm finding out," I said.

"Let's begin. First of all, you need to decrease..."

"Decrease? You're all of five feet nothing with your shoes on... you increased to the size of the gigantic demon. What do you mean decrease?"

"Easy, Mac, easy. You need to make room for the fullness of the Lord. '*He must increase, but I must decrease*' (John 3:30). You occupy an interior space as a human and a sinner. Decrease and empty thyself. Let your darkness be consumed by the light of the Lord. Let the light occupy your emptied space. The increase in the Spirit allows you to fulfill the tasks the Lord has set out for you."

"I'm hearing you but..."

"The first step is concentration. Breathe the air deep into your lungs, and I mean deep – your lungs need to entirely fill."

There, on a New York subway platform, I performed deep breathing exercises. My chest heaved in and out. Agnes encouraged me to slow down and relax: "*Be still and know that I am God*" (Psalm 46:10).

I gradually achieved an unhurried rhythm, pulling air deeply and fully into my lungs.

"Next step is to unlock the angel in you," said Agnes. "Our good God offers angels increased powers of speed, strength, and enhanced senses to fight evil. You'll stay in man form but you'll be able to tap into your angel self at a moment's notice."

Agnes paused as a train rumbled in and out of the station. She moved over to Elaine and gestured to me to follow.

"Elaine is part of God's creation. He loves Elaine as much as any saint. He adores her as much as His glorious cosmic Milky Way. And trust me, the Old Man has a lot of pride in his Milky Way."

I cracked up. "You call God the Old Man?"

"Sure, why not? Sometimes, I call him Old Lady. How about that? God has a great sense of humor."

"Yeah, He must. He picked me – a shmuck from the Bronx."

"God is all things to all people. Tall or short, old or young, beautiful or ugly, a rainbow of color, male or female... He delights in His many images."

"Delights? Is that so?"

"Certainly," she responded. "He Himself told me. Back to the teaching."

Agnes knelt down beside Elaine and laid a loving hand on the face of her companion.

"God's creative energy is in her. Let us call it love – the love that is in all created things. Search for it with your fingertips, Mac. You never knew to probe for it before this moment. This source of God's energy may be the difference between life and death. Good angels draw on it, while evil ones are unable to tap into the energy because they turned away from the love of God. It gives you an advantage against the formidable devilish forces."

I knelt beside Elaine, opposite Agnes. I gently moved my fingers over her dirty hair but I felt nothing unusual. I tried again. Again, nothing. I paused, prayed, and regrouped. Lead with love, I reminded myself. Like Agnes, I lovingly stroked Elaine's cheeks. I brushed her hair with affection. My fingertips quivered and stirred with something akin to a pulse. I continued my actions and the pulse gained strength, feeling like a heartbeat, which soon gave way to a consistent stream of energy out of Elaine and into my fingers. A tickling, tangible feeling of goodness. I nodded to Agnes.

"Thy strength will come by running your hands over thyself," she directed.

With my fingers, I touched my hair, face, arms, chest, and legs. My energy level exceeded what I felt with Elaine.

"Angels have more loving energy than humans," said Agnes. "Lay your hands on me."

Her high octane energy, overwhelmingly strong but pain-free, flooded into my fingertips.

"Let's practice drawing out more energy. Once mastered, you won't need your hands to tap into your internal source of God's creation. You'll draw it up from your own loving source. Decrease. Increase. Empty yourself completely for God's limitless, loving energy."

No sense of time – a minute? Ten? Thirty? Time flew by like the trains that came and went in and out of the station. Lost in a zone, I felt blissful with contentment and joy. Taps on my shoulder brought me back to the reality of the subway platform. The few people who waited for a train paid no attention to us. Anything goes in New York City.

"Through love and mercy, He is offering you to call on the God in you at a moment's notice," said Agnes. "Few are offered. Use it wisely. His help will come in unexpected ways. And keep practicing to totally master the gift," she urged.

"What's with Daniel? He never offered this kind of help."

"No one's ready in the beginning. It's somewhat like your beloved teenagers. We learn from trial and error. We take a few steps, then walk, and finish by running. Some even learn to fly." She smiled. "Daniel has not left you unaided. Our ancient enemy knows the weakness and vulnerability of new angels. Daniel has watchers ready to assist. The enemy outnumbers us but we are more powerful. A balance is kept."

"Devils are fallen angels, right?"

"Of course, Mac, the theologian. '*Pride changed the angels into devils; it's humility that makes new angels,*' according to St. Augustine. Keep being humble. We angels think you might survive because your prayer life invites and welcomes humility. Go deeper in prayer because evil will try and take you down in any way possible."

"Just pride?"

"All seven deadly sins. Pride is just the first sin from which all else flows. Some of the early angels wondered why God loved man so much. Their pride led to envy and weakened their relationship with God. They grew angry that He loved others; they wanted the love just for themselves. They vowed to destroy man, to bring him down. Greed became their norm. They lusted for food, drink, money, and sex. Sloth was the final blow. They grew lazy and stopped praying; they were no longer one with God. The last link was cut and they were alone, isolated, and easy pickings for evil. Stay centered in prayer, keep lighting your candles."

We joined hands and prayed together, accompanied by Elaine's background hymn of snores.

"Be on guard tonight, Mac. The demon warned you about the

Bronx. To survive, remember '*He must increase...*'"

"*But I must decrease.*" I gave a thumbs up.

"Peace be with you."

Seconds later, a D train pulled into the station, the doors clattered open and I hastened into the car. It was an unwritten rule to stand up on late night Bronx trains even if seats were available. You're more vulnerable sitting than standing if bad boys show up. Those who haunt the trains look for easy marks. Tonight, standing was a no-brainer. No less than a devil had warned me.

The ride home went without a hitch. At the Tremont Avenue station, I flew down the stairs and hit the streets for the walk home. At a fast pace, I headed north toward Fordham Road and covered a couple of blocks before my senses alerted to evil. Eyes peered out from the darkness of side streets and low growls rumbled around me. My Jack London books with memories of the Yukon came back to me. I sensed animals circling, not in the Yukon, but here in the Bronx.

Half a block later, a pack of stray dogs, a dozen growling hell-hounds, emerged from the darkness, bared their teeth, and advanced on me. They formed a half circle and trapped me against a parked car. Instinctively, I jumped onto the roof of the car. The dogs snapped, barked, and circled the car. Some managed to get on the hood and the trunk but most had trouble staying there, sliding off the smooth slopes. I kicked off the remaining ones.

I recalled my conversation with Agnes and I turned inward, focusing on help from God. Deep breathing... "*He must increase, but I must decrease.*" I tapped into the energy of creation.

Agnes had taught me well. A surge of energy pulsed from within and I felt jacked and ready to rumble. A sword appeared in my right hand. No time to think about it or study its appearance. Time to defend.

I met the next attack of dogs with a broad sweeping stroke of the sword that cleared two dogs off the car hood. My sudden turn in the direction of the trunk led to a thrust through the red eye of another beast. The others stayed off the car but continued to circle, snarling and shaking their huge shaggy heads from side to side. Drool catapulted out of their massive jaws and the thick yellowish goo fell like big drops of rain, covering me, the car and the ground. Going on the offensive, I lunged with the sword. My long wingspan enabled me to pierce the back of one of the fiends. The remaining pack edged away but still menaced and threatened.

Evil came in the form of these hounds; however, I was a hound of heaven. I jumped off the hood and with a swift movement my blade came down and sliced a dog in half. The broad range of my sword picked off the two closest to me. I flung their carcasses at the rest of the pack and then by jabbing, sticking, and ramming with my blazing fast weapon, all went down except the pack leader, a large German shepherd junkyard type dog with a mangy coat, bared teeth, and glowering eyes. He stood opposite me, three feet away. A filthy breath and smell emanated from his body. With gnashing of teeth, he sprang at me. My arm propelled the blade upward through his open mouth and out the back of his head. He hung on my sword. Skewered!

Wounded dogs whimpered on the ground around the car and near my feet. I put them out of their misery with quick stabs of my sword. I thought of saying a prayer for them but my theological education had me hesitate. Dogs are soulless. Spirits? Maybe. I abandoned my diploma thinking and reached out to our good God, who is the creator of all. I asked the Lord to bless these animals who were innocent before being possessed. Then for good measure, I asked St. Francis, the patron saint of animals, to take care of them.

I studied closely the blood-splattered sword in my hand. It was extremely light with a razor sharp three foot silver blade. Celtic art covered the entire length of the kelly green handle. A shamrock stood out in the center. Actually, my shamrock. Dark green. In my Irish neighborhood of Woodlawn, it's common for guys to get tattooed at age 18. A rite of passage. We get inked, often choosing Irish symbols – harp, shamrock, four-leaf clovers, the tri-color flag of Ireland, the Notre Dame fighting Irish symbol. The shamrock on my shoulder was replicated on the handle of the sword. A designer sword for me? A question for Daniel down the road.

Once again, a Bronx street became my pew as I knelt down. *"There stood by me this night the angel of God"* (Acts of the Apostles 27:23). Thanks, Agnes. Also, thanks Old Man, Old Lady. I laughed. Then I tightly gripped my weapon in front of my chest and lifted it over my head. I offered the sword and myself to the Lord. When I stood up, refreshed and confident, it disappeared. I knew it would. Not sure how I knew but I did.

At home, I showered and cleaned off the drool and blood clinging to my body. The fresh pine smell of soap replaced the polluting stink of the dogs.

For tonight's prayer or I should say early morning as the clock had ticked past one, I turned to St. Faustina, a Polish nun and mystic. She became the first official saint of the 21st century, canonized by Pope John Paul II. She brought the news of the Lord's Divine Mercy to the world. I reflected on a passage in her diary:

After Adoration, halfway to my cell, I was surrounded by a pack of huge black dogs who were jumping and howling and trying to tear me to pieces. I realized they were not dogs but demons... I said if this is the will of the most merciful God, tear me to pieces... To these words the demons answered as one, let us flee, for she is not alone; the Almighty is with her.

My few hours of sleep were tranquil and dreamless. Comfort came in knowing the Almighty was with me.

Twenty-Three

The Lord is my helper
and I will not be afraid.
What can man do to me?
Letter to the Hebrews 13:6

Wednesday

Maria was out of intensive care. If walls can move, then they vibrated in the school with the news in morning homeroom. A deafening roar erupted out of the classrooms, raced down the hallways and back again. The place rocked.

Father Tim's words at morning mass came back to me. "Our God does not abandon us and if we call out He is there." Eucharist, which means thanksgiving, had truly become it.

Manuel barreled into my room, and wrapped his muscular arms around me in a tight squeeze. His tension flowed out with his tears.

"I don't care what happens to me. I can face whatever goes down as long as Maria is okay. I'd even join 'em so no one else gets hurt," said Manuel with downcast eyes.

"You mean well, my brother," I responded. "But that's not how it works. No one gets hurt until the gang asks you to hurt someone. You're not allowed to refuse. Forget about it. You're not joining the Locos. Give me time. That was our agreement. Let's just celebrate life. Scott Peck, a Christian writer, pointed out that the word evil spelled backwards is l-i-v-e. Right now we live. Celebrate. You visit Maria in the hospital and I'll take care of the rest. Peace."

Manuel walked out of the room in a healthy state, both body and soul. The whole school mirrored his mood with a sense of jubilation settling in for teachers and students alike.

After school, we had our last baseball scrimmage at Iona Prep, a Westchester County school run by Brother Willie's order, the Congregation of Christian Brothers, founded by Blessed Edmund Rice. The Prep, as it's familiarly known, has a top-notch baseball field. Located on the private New Rochelle campus, the field is free of the "leftovers" – burnt out cars, beer bottles, needles – that are often found on the public fields in New York City.

Carlin pitched well for us and Phillips supplied the offense for an 8-2 win. I felt confident about the team and thought we'd meet with success during the season. Our schedule opened up against two previous New York City champs, Cardinal Hayes and Cardinal Spellman. Two great Bronx schools, academically and athletically. Supreme Court Justice Sonia Sotomayor is an alumna of Cardinal Spellman. Yet the school doesn't "own her" as the entire Bronx brags about one of its own making it.

The kids joked and laughed on the way back to Dorothy Day. Their moods reflected their baseball win and their happiness about Maria. Their upbeat spirits carried out the door as I sent them home.

I corrected a quiz, made copies of handouts, and tied up loose ends from today's lesson. Loose ends are normal; a teacher never knows what might need further clarification or where a lesson might finish. We aim for a specific conclusion daily but sometimes, things come up in class, for example, an unplanned discussion that is lively and engaging. If it's worthy of class time and on topic, I let it flow and then adjust my next day's lesson plan.

I hit the weight room for a work-out. Chin-ups and weights are my usual routine. Today I would be in and out in fifteen minutes as I needed time to reflect on the dire situation of Manuel and consider a plan of action.

On the way out of school, I stopped at the chapel to visit God in the Tabernacle. I picked up a Bible lying in a pew and opened it for a spontaneous message. My eyes fell on *"And so we will not be outwitted by Satan – we know enough what his intentions are"* (2 Corinthians 2:11). Message loud and clear! God speaks to us through Scripture. I always remind myself to be open and listen to Him.

I left school with darkness already having thrown its mantle over the day. I zipped up my jacket and pulled on my cap in the crisp March air before walking swiftly along the pavement in front of the school. My senses started to tingle and I shivered, realizing that the cold air was not the cause. Two hard-looking guys, standing on the corner across the street, had replaced the threat of the canines from the night before. Robbery or a beating was not the goal; good riddance to me was more like it. I definitely had bugged someone.

I've walked this route home a thousand times and know it well. The choice of battle ground would be mine. A large abandoned lot overtaken by trees and shrubbery lies two blocks from the school. The bordering sidewalk would be in darkness and shadows at this time of night. I flew down the street and my two companions had trouble keeping up with me. I slowed down near the lot while the duo sped up, perhaps figuring this was an ideal spot to take me down.

I calmed myself with my newly acquired breathing techniques. Decrease so the Lord increases. Decrease... increase. I tapped my inner energy zone and was able to call up my sword. A split second later, the first man rushed me from behind. I turned and held the blade straight out from my waist. The man never saw it coming and impaled himself by the forward movement of his body. His brown eyes bug-eyed in surprise. As blood gushed out of his wound, his hand went limp and let go of his knife.

The second man quickly followed his pal. Seeing the impalement of his partner, he took out a gun and fired. The dead body on my weapon became a human shield, taking the bullets meant for me. Thrusting the sword forward, I shoved the body of the dead man into his buddy. Though bullets continued to fly, the thug was thrown off-balance and missed his mark – me! With a mighty heave, I plunged the blade through the dead man and into the gunman's chest. Deja vu – bug eyes and a look of surprise. Clank went his gun as it dropped to the sidewalk.

As I pulled out my sword, blood dripped onto the ground and pooled in a deep red puddle. I breathed in the cold night air and closed my eyes in an effort to still myself. My sword vanished with the demise of the evil at my feet.

I propped both men into sitting positions against the fence. With my gloves on, I grabbed a few empty beer bottles and put them next to and in the hands of the dead men. I took one of their cell phones and dialed 911. The dead deserve dignity and should not be left alone on a Bronx street. Covering my mouth with my scarf to muffle my voice, I spoke to an operator. "Help! 188 St. off the Concourse, east side."

The cops would try to come up with some plausible scenario. Good luck with that, I thought. I placed the phone, gun, and knife in their laps. I said a prayer for their souls and for those who called them friend or family. I genuflected and made the sign of the cross before leaving.

On the way home, I recalled the chapel reading: *"And so you will not be outwitted by Satan – we know enough what his intentions are."* His intentions were clear – a gun and a knife to kill.

I lit a candle, and settled in for a night of reflection on a powerful day. Tonight, two men were dead due to my violent actions. I had killed humans for the first time. I slaughtered dogs last night.

The impact was now resonating with me. Violence in the name of defense to avoid violence against me. I had chosen my path as a warrior angel; accept it and be at peace, Agnes had cautioned me.

My eyes were closed but I realized the room was brighter. I opened my eyes to Daniel, standing in front of me with his hands behind his back. I greeted him with a soft smile. A good night to show up; I could use an advocate.

I saw him differently this time. A golden hue surrounded his body. His blue eyes glowed with the fierce determination of a warrior willing to serve the light, not dominate it. He glorifies the Father, Son, and Spirit. He serves only one master.

"Little grasshopper," said Daniel, "you're really seeing me. Agnes taught you well. She's darn good."

"I killed..." My voice broke and tears ran down my face.

Silence.

"I never killed anything before," I said at last. "Dogs last night and now men."

"That's why I'm here."

"Guardian angel, where have you been? I needed help." I wiped my tears.

"People more vulnerable than you would have perished if I left them. Down the road you too will have to make difficult decisions to protect the weakest and hope the strong can survive on their own. Sometimes, they do and sometimes, they don't. We're gifted but it's impossible for us to be in two places at once."

"Then God needs to send more angels?"

"He sends more than you and even I know. Although not enough for the numerous earthly battles of today."

Quiet again. Daniel broke it.

"You had your first kill tonight. You're unsure that this is for you. You hesitate. You want to follow your saintly, Christ-like, and paci-fist hero, Dorothy Day. Except there's a difference. She was human and you no longer are. You have to write your own story. Forge your own journey. It's your own unique spiritual ladder now, not Dorothy's."

"Agnes gave me the same message. To climb a rung on my own ladder."

"She also shared that she turns to violence when necessary. When? Against the devil... that's when."

"Like me against the dogs and the two thugs."

"Yeah, you got it. You've been up against the devil. Satan, Lucifer, Beelzebub or whatever name this generation calls him is active and preying on souls. He and his minions are an evil force attempting to disrupt the designs of God. Every day they snare new victims and followers. The greatest deception of the Prince of Lies is to convince us he does NOT exist.

"It's only been a short time and I've already faced a few battles..."

"Mac, there's a war going on with epic battles ahead. The world is blind to the devilish battles in our homes, churches, commu-nities, and nations. In our own hearts and souls. If people do not see – they will not battle. You? Me? We see and must battle for them as Jesus did. He asks us to fight for his children. Individual souls. *'Your enemy the devil prowls around like a roaring lion looking for someone to devour. Resist him'*" (1 Peter 5:8-9).

"Like in my school."

"Lucifer has been very busy. The world is shifting to secularism. We need people like you, religion teacher, to provide students with an awareness of the evil that lurks, in their school, neighborhood, and world."

"I'm trying."

"More than trying. You're shouting from the mountaintop, my

Bronx friend."

"Will I need to kill again?" I murmured.

"Most likely, in order to survive. You're being hunted. You're part of the light and you'll attract light but your beacon will also attract darkness. There's work to be done in His name."

Then with a twinkle, a smile, and with an Irish brogue, he said "I need to be elsewhere soon. Are you in?"

I hesitated a moment before a slow smile crossed my face. "Indeed I am," responding with my own version of a brogue.

We both laughed.

"A few quick questions before you go."

"Fire away."

"My sword – designed for me?"

"Most definitely."

"I named it Shamrock."

"I know. Well chosen. The symbol of the Trinity – the Father, Son, and Holy Spirit – created by St. Patrick himself."

"In following my chosen path, will I leave the pacifist path behind?"

"You're no longer on the earthly plane. You must defend life in all stages. Womb to tomb. The seamless garment. Never may you start violence. Respond like Agnes in the subway. When a threat arises, square off against it. Defend yourself and others."

"I want the comfort of the Sacrament of Confession."

"Angel priests. We have them. Go to Father Bonaventure, a Dominican priest in the south Bronx. Sacred Heart parish in Highbridge. Shakespeare Avenue. Make an appointment and tell him Daniel sent you... I've got to go."

Questions teemed in my mind but Daniel's time was in short supply.

"You're a work in progress. Unfortunately, you've been shoved to the front lines early on because of Manuel's situation. Trust in God and yourself. You were picked for a reason. God speed."

"Thanks."

"One last thing. The Devil sends demon after demon to take people down. There's no timeout as they are relentless. Angels see clearly the contrast between good and evil and have the burden of riding the tension between holiness and war. Be careful, stay centered in the Prince of Peace."

"Amen, Daniel."

He disappeared in a blink of my eye. Hmmm... I gotta learn that trick.

I called for my sword and it appeared in my right hand. I ran my hand gently over its length and then touched the floor with the tip of the blade. Down on one knee, I grasped the top of the hilt and wrapped my other hand around the dark green shamrock on the handle.

"Shamrock, we need to be one," I whispered.

Twenty-Four

...give me this day my work to do,
no, not my work, but Thine.
Florence Nightingale

Thursday

"*Which commandment is the first of all? Jesus answered, 'The first is... and you shall love the Lord with all your heart, with all your soul, and with all your mind and with all your strength...'*" (Mark 12: 28-30).

"Copy the passage off the board and then let's talk."

This technique settles students down and focuses them as soon as they enter the class.

"God said that loving God is the greatest commandment. Why?" I asked.

"Jealousy?" said Benjamin, the unofficial kickball specialist of the school. Kickball in gym class. What's up with that?

"Not our God. He's not a jealous guy."

"Maybe, we need to love God first before we can love anyone else," said Gaby. "Love of God leads us to love of parents, siblings, friends, even strangers. God tells us to walk with them, love them, and even forgive them."

The class clapped at Gaby's response.

"Looking good with that answer, my young scholar. I know I need to love God before I try to love my messy teenage students."

Laughs and smiles throughout the class.

"'They say they want the Kingdom but they don't want God in it,'" I sang. The line comes from a song written by Bono, the lead singer for U2, an Irish band. Johnny Cash, not Bono, sang it on one of the band's albums. I played the song for them. Can't go wrong with music and teenagers.

"The song, the line, and the Gospel reading. Connect the dots."

"Easy enough," said Adam Ruxton, a talented guitarist and a thoughtful student. "Like Jesus is telling us you can't have or build the Kingdom without loving Him."

"Amen. You want to build the Kingdom – get centered, get Jesus, hit the chapel, go to church and pray. The kingdom is in you. Roll up your sleeves and get to work."

A rousing amen from the students ended the class.

A typical day with teenagers demanding my full attention and concentration in the classroom. Baseball practice and work at a homeless shelter afterwards would also allow no time to dwell on dogs, thugs, sword, and the evil that surely awaited me.

Once a month after school, Dorothy Day HS sends six students to the Franciscan shelter called Christ House. We bring the ingredients for a meal, cook it for the men at the shelter, and clean up afterwards. The volunteer coordinator from Dorothy Day, Annie Ferber, had the supplies and kids ready when I jumped in the van after baseball practice.

Students volunteer one hundred twenty hours before graduation. They work at shelters, soup kitchens, nursing homes, hospitals, food pantries, and elementary schools. It's a win-win for the volunteers and for those they serve. Hopefully, seeds take root and students will spend their lives serving in some way, shape or form. Critics say you shouldn't force a student to volunteer. A head scratcher. A Catholic school is the perfect place to teach young people how to follow in the footsteps of the Lord. Teach them the importance of serving their communities. Let them find out the gratification that comes from helping others. Yes, we need to teach that community service is the vehicle to fulfill the second greatest commandment, Love thy neighbor.

St. Elizabeth Seton parish provides the space for the shelter. The first American born saint, St. Elizabeth, started an order of teaching nuns, the Sisters of Charity of St. Joseph. She is considered the Mother of Catholic Schools in the United States. Seton Hall University in New Jersey is named for her.

In the large basement of the parish hall, thirty beds lined up in six rows of five are on one side of the room, six round tables on the other. At the back of the room, a doorway on the left leads to the kitchen, one on the right to toilets, showers, and a washer and a dryer.

The clean and safe shelter offers a respite from the dirty and chaotic city streets. If a guest is found with alcohol or drugs or is high or drunk, he loses his space. The homeless men know they have a good thing going and collectively are thankful guests.

Brother Tyrone, a tall black Franciscan with a scraggly salt and pepper beard, always greets us at the shelter door. He would spend the night being brother to everybody.

"That's why I became a religious," he once explained.

The Franciscans oversaw the shelter but Margaret, the only paid worker, ran it. You need at least one full-time person to direct a volunteer organization; otherwise, it falls apart from lack of coordination. Like all religious, the Franciscans were stretched thin, working as chaplains, nurses at free health clinics, and administering parish churches.

Everyone falls in love with Margaret. Originally from Kenya, East Africa, this holy woman always smiles and the whiteness of her teeth contrasts with her beautiful dark skin. She wanted to become a nun; she had heard the call growing up. Her father had another idea, marrying her off to a man quite older than she. No choice involved.

A form of slavery that happens to millions of young girls in the world. Sad. Makes me angry to think about it.

After her husband died, Margaret left Africa with her three children and came to the United States. She worked long hours and two jobs in a typical immigrant story. Her kids excelled at school, the value of an education instilled in them by their mom. They all have jobs now and two married and started their own families. Margaret lives in a small apartment, simply and frugally. She sends back every spare dollar to her poor Kenyan village. Her donations have funded water and housing projects. She thought of returning to Kenya to live after her kids were raised but she is a daily communicant and in small Kenyan villages, it's difficult to attend daily mass. No parish. The Eucharist is her daily nourishment so she stayed here. What a testimony to faith and the Eucharist.

Our group prepared pizza casserole, consisting of pasta, cheese, mushrooms, peppers, ground meat, and pepperoni baked in tomato sauce. The guys love the change from chicken, the usual fare served by many volunteer cooking groups. A bell rang to signal the start of the dinner hour. Everyone who was able stood for grace; some were not, being wheelchair bound due to having lost limbs to gangrene or fire. Margaret always asks for a volunteer to lead the prayer. Henry, a long-time guest, answered the call. He concluded with "we ask this and all things in God's name."

Margaret shouted out, "He has a name and it's Jesus!" Smiles around the basement.

"What's wrong with saying God?" whispered Ellen, a student volunteer, standing next to me.

"Nothing. But the use of God can be abstract. Jesus is more personal and concrete. He walked this earth."

"Got it. Thanks."

"Thank Jesus." We both smiled.

Students brought the food to the tables, sat down, and ate with the men. One kid per table. New student volunteers are always nervous but not the repeat volunteers. In most cases, the men are very polite and willing to relate their stories. The young people are usually surprised when they learn that some of the homeless have never abused alcohol or drugs. Some are the working poor, with a full time job but a minimum wage. A minimum wage is not a living wage. Not in this country. They can afford rent but not food or vice versa. One of the guests has a full-time minimum wage job and also attends school part-time. His money funds his tuition. He has permission to study in the kitchen when the shelter lights turn off at ten.

I introduced myself to a new face. An older man in a wheel-chair, he was missing both legs below the knee. A victim of war or the war on the streets? Many guests come in beat up in body and spirit from living on harsh city streets. Margaret makes healthy drinks in a blender for those who have their jaws busted up. They manage to drink through a straw. She changes the dressings on the limbs of those who stood too close to a trash can fire when they were high or cold. She also distributes the daily medications. Some men are not mentally reliable enough to remember. Margaret plays many roles – mother, sister, friend, nurse, cook, and cleaner. She is the feminine face of God here for men who know hard streets.

Felix, a large middle-aged Puerto Rican with a ponytail of long black silky hair, takes over at dinner clean-up time. He works as a full-time worker, like Margaret, but unlike her, he's a volunteer. Once homeless, he now lives at the shelter full-time. The guests come in at 5pm and leave after breakfast at 8am. Felix coordinates the needs of the guests when they arrive, organizing a shower schedule, doing the laundry, and putting the clean clothes into bags marked with the guest's name. He has a small room but often gives it up when an extra bed is needed. A mystic, he spends most of the night in front of the Tabernacle, anyway. My heightened skills, acquired from my work with Agnes, alerted me to the soft glow gently vibrating around his entire body.

Felix is the unofficial cop when Margaret leaves after dinner. His story is only partially known. Embarrassed by his sins, he told us that drugs, alcohol, and women led him into trouble. The Big Three. Prison followed. He offered no other details and we never asked for more.

For Felix, sin became an agent of change and bettered his humanity. His is not sin management but sin transformation. He repented and asked forgiveness from the Lord. He says he will spend his life making amends. He has access to the shelter during the day but he's rarely there as he's often on the street, offering a sandwich, a hot cup of coffee, or a listening ear to those in need.

I would canonize him tomorrow. St. Felix of Christ House. Along with Margaret and Brother Tyrone, too. The world needs saints. They give us hope of the Light and become the living face of God. Goodness triumphs over evil.

Before heading out, we gathered in the kitchen to pray in a circle. Students, teachers, Brother Tyrone, Margaret, and Felix held hands. Dynamic Annie Ferber addressed our group, sharing a quote from Dorothy Day: "Christ remains with us not only through the mass, but in the 'distressing disguise' of the poor. To live with the poor is a contemplative vocation, for it is to live in the constant presence of God."

"Tonight," Annie said, "when you go home, get on your knees at bedtime. Go over how you saw the face of Christ in this holy shelter. Live Jesus in your hearts."

"Forever," the students responded as one.

"Dorothy Day," Annie stated.

"Pray for us."

We loaded up the van and dropped the students off at their homes. Annie and I took a minute to talk about how blessed we were to get paid to teach about Jesus and to act out the Gospels. A grace-filled job. We were tempted to go out and chat over a beer, but realized the evening should end with the high of six wonderful students, Margaret, Felix, Tyrone, and the grateful guests.

After our goodbyes, I thought about Annie. She was the whole package, bright, dedicated, on fire about social justice, and a Jesus freak. If I survive the morrow, I'd ask Daniel if angels can date the earthbound.

I came home to a message from Paddy on my answering machine. "Two thugs killed in your neighborhood last night. Careful, huh, bro? Call when you can."

If he only knew, I thought. I could give him an earful about thugs, and dogs, too, for that matter.

Twenty-Five

*This is God's world and we have no right to consign
it to the Devil. We should be fighting like mad against
the perverse will of men and this fight is for the love of
God and the love of men, the very least of them.*
Dorothy Day

Friday

"Pray for us sinners now and at the hour of our death" echoed in my brain. My free period found me on my knees in the chapel. Earlier, my first three classes were similar to out of focus photographs, with blurry images of students and lessons. My mind drifted constantly to tonight's confrontation with the Locos and my lack of a concrete plan of action. Yeah, a plan – that would be helpful, to say the least. Last night, I thought let's be real. One of me, many of them; one sword versus an unknown lethal arsenal of weapons. Meanwhile, I kept coming back to my faith and trust in God.

My faith has been strong for as long as I can remember. It was always just there. You were born with it, my mother has always told me. She described my first attempts to make the sign of the cross at the age of three. I always knelt next to my bed to say my simple prayers to God and my guardian angel, she explained. I clearly remember the powerful feeling of my first Holy Communion and the thrill of serving as an altar boy for the first time in fourth grade; I continued serving through high school.

Gazing at the wooden cross above the altar, I closed my eyes and prayed the Our Father. "Deliver us from evil" stood out and I embraced the words. Trust in God and increase the power of God's spirit in me, I reminded myself. Let go of all that held me captive from confidence in the Lord.

I controlled the tempo of my breathing, inhaling fully, exhaling completely. Increase. Decrease. Increase. Decrease.

The insistent ringing of the school bell slipped into my consciousness, signaling the need to go to class. I genuflected, pointed to the Tabernacle and said aloud, "Jesus, you and I can take anything on... Together we can do this." I felt more confident in my role as an instrument of deliverance for Manuel and Maria, two innocent high school sweethearts. I caught the scent of roses as I headed out the door.

*   *   *

Walking past the chapel, I spotted Mac on his knees. No surprise there as he usually stops in three or four times a day, even if just for a couple of minutes. He's the face of our Catholic school, the most Christ-like amongst us. He calls everyone brother and sister or I should say in the Mac way, brotha and sista. Whenever I ask the kids to name a person who truly exhibits and lives his faith, Mac's name always comes up. His former students often tell me he brought them closer to God and made them more spiritual. The words of St. Teresa of Avila are apropos when it comes to Mac. "The hands, the eyes, and the heart of Christ."

The angel wires hummed with the expectation of Mac making a move soon to confront the evil faced by Manuel and Maria. Daniel was unsure of the day – maybe, today or tomorrow – but nothing definite as he was unable to pick up any firm vibes about Mac's intentions. We were all on alert, ready to assist if possible. Hear his prayer, Lord, I whispered. Put all your trust in God, Mac. You are in His hands.

*   *   *

Automatic pilot carried me through the rest of the school day and on my walk home. In my apartment, I wolfed down two slices of cold pizza. My last supper flitted through my head but I quickly banished the thought. I reminded myself that my weapons were as powerful as any I could imagine.

"Stand therefore... having put on the breastplate of righteousness... taking the shield of faith... and the sword of the Spirit" (Ephesians 6:14, 16-17).

So armed, I headed out the door to my destination a couple of miles away.

I stood across the street from the Locos headquarters, a marble mansion on the Grand Concourse. It looked like a mini-version of the main building of the New York Public Library with arches and columns leading to the entranceway, and two stone lions on either side of the marble steps.

Mayor Fiorello La Guardia named the lions at the New York Public Library, Patience and Fortitude; he felt these two characteristics were necessary for New Yorkers to cope with the Great Depression. The lions are a New York landmark, part of the fabric of the Big Apple. Festive holiday wreaths are placed around the lions' necks during the Christmas season, and I always make a point of walking by them after stopping to see the gigantic tree decorated with Christmas lights at Rockefeller Center.

Gazing now at the two lions across the street, the names Malice and Greed came to mind for these guardians of the gate. The numerous windows of the mansion, some eight feet in height, were covered with curtains. Architecture aside, I was impressed by the lack of graffiti on any of the walls. The Locos must be bad boys indeed if they're able to scare off the locals from leaving their tags.

I put on my rugby game face – determined and steely-eyed. Time to ruck and maul, I calmly told myself. Before crossing the street, I said a final prayer, not asking for anything specific, just turning everything over to God. I decreased and felt Him increase. The words of Jesus to mystic St. Faustina came to mind, *"My mercy does not want this but justice demands it."*

I crossed the street and walked up the smooth marble steps to the wooden front door. Before my raised fist made contact with the mahogany, it abruptly flew open and framed a well-dressed hombre in a midnight blue suit, with a silver earring dangling from his left ear, and a heavy gold chain encircling his neck.

"Dorothy Day has finally made an appearance," he stated.

"Yeah, it sure has," I responded firmly.

"We were expecting someone sooner or later."

"Well, sooner has arrived."

"You're alone." He laughed.

"Yep, me, myself, and I stand before you... but I never walk alone."

"Really? Looks that way to me." He glanced up and down the street and then looked back at me. My eyes were lifted upwards, looking to the heavens.

"Fat chance. Don't count on it. You're on your own. But what do I know; I'm only Raul, a high school dropout, while you're a teacher."

"Got that right. Religion at that. I'm Mr. McCarthy. I'm here to talk with your boss about Manuel and Maria."

Raul moved aside from the doorway and gestured me into a large foyer. A split second later, I heard the door lock behind me. My glance took in a huge chandelier suspended from the center of the ceiling, two standing lamps about six feet high on either side of the door, and a checkerboard floor of black and white marble. Across the room stood a wide marble staircase flanked by two goons, standing as ramrod straight as the lamps by the front door. Raul signaled to one of them. He came over and stood in front of me.

"Put your arms straight out from your sides," ordered Raul. Following his directions, I held out my long arms and the punk rapidly but thoroughly patted me down. He then moved inches from my right side, folded his arms, planted his feet, and stared straight ahead.

"I'll see if the boss has time for you." Raul turned and left me standing there.

I looked around and noted the numerous paintings on the red walls. No cheap poster art here. My college art history classes came back to me. Somebody knows what they're doing when it comes to art, I thought. The ceiling mural depicted a Bacchanalian feast, a drunken revel celebrating the god of wine. Not an angel, in sight, but plenty of satyrs with lecherous grins. Gazing over my shoulder, I saw a stuffed head of a wolf, his mouth in a grimace, baring sharp-pointed teeth, hanging above the front door.

Raul soon returned, and signaled from the staircase to follow him. On the second floor landing, I was frisked by two henchmen and again on the third by a mean-looking dude with a scar on the left side of his face that curved from his ear to the corner of his mouth. He nodded to Raul, who then tapped on the door, stood aside, and allowed me to enter the sanctum of the boss, followed by two thugs. They positioned themselves besides me at the entrance to the room. The door closed behind us.

The suite was impressive. Two massive stone fireplaces anchored the ends of the room. Crackling fires blazed in both. Three chandeliers with hundreds of bulbs hung from the ceiling, and provided most of the light as three walls had no windows. The only natural light came from sliding glass doors leading to a balcony off the fourth side of the room. A balcony without a view as it overlooked a windowless brick wall about ten feet away.

I studied the man who had risen and now stood behind his wooden desk on an elevated platform in the middle of the room. He was a man of average height with a long black ponytail and black beetle eyes. His charcoal gray-striped suit was well-tailored, and he wore a purple silk handkerchief in his jacket pocket. The thought "built like a brickhouse" came to mind as I observed his well-developed muscular body. He had the perfect Hollywood look of a forty-eight hour beard. A dark aura, steady and pronounced, surrounded him.

"Mr. McCarthy, what can I do for you?" he asked in a raspy voice.

"I don't have a lot to say. We can make this fast. This is not a social outing."

"I know why you are here and it will be brief but indulge me for a few minutes. Ponce, step in."

Ponce, the former Dorothy Day student, stepped in from the balcony. Now sporting a mustache, he no longer looked like a school kid.

"Ponce, you've gotten older since I saw you last. Have you gotten smarter? You left without your high school diploma." Sarcasm dripped from my voice.

"McCarthy, excuse me if I drop the title mister since neither of us are in school now. As for school, I make a lot more money than the chump change you make with your diplomas."

"Touché, Ponce."

"Enough," said the boss. Ponce responded like a soldier,

standing erect with legs apart and arms held straight against his sides. This boss commanded discipline.

"Your name?" I asked.

"I go by many names."

"I bet you do." One name surely had to be devil. His aura was much darker than Ponce's. It was black, making him a demon, according to angelic Agnes.

"Today, call me Mr. Bautista. Now for the record, state your business."

"Simply, leave Maria, Manuel, and the Dorothy Day community alone."

"Why do you care? Your concern?"

"It's a teacher thing. It's what we do."

"That's not all you do. I sent two good men to visit you on Wednesday. I haven't seen them since. Do you know what happened to them?"

I remained silent.

"Ponce said you were trouble. Brother a hotshot cop. You a Jesus freak. Maybe with some muscle." He looked me over. "You're sticking your nose where it doesn't belong. Ponce scouted Dorothy Day. Soon it and the rest of the Bronx will be ours."

"Big words."

"Who's gonna stop us?"

"I'm not scaring the hell out of you? I'm surprised. Shocked really." I had said the word hell with heavy exaggeration. I ended with a hearty laugh.

He did a double take and responded, "Sorry to disappoint you but you don't scare the hell out of me. In fact, I find you rather pathetic."

Anger contorted his face into a grimace. He walked up to me

and spit in my face. His hoodlums each grabbed an arm and pinned them behind me. Bautista went on, with a tone, an attitude.

"You come here alone with only good intentions. And you think that's enough? Where's your weapon? Your gang? Your brother New York's Finest?"

"Alone. You said alone... I'm not alone!"

"Ponce, get a load of that. The religion teacher came with God."

They laughed. But I wasn't alone; I felt the presence of the heavenly hosts. A tranquility and warmth pervaded my spirit.

"Religion teacher, you are amusing me, but that's only temporary. You blame me for threatening Manuel. It was his own flesh and blood older brother who begged to join us for easy money. He came willingly. He knew the rules. Family follows. No exceptions."

"Abel has often had a Cain."

"Clever, religion teacher. Real clever."

"And Boss, how do you rationalize Maria?"

"As they say collateral damage, the cost of business. So American – yes."

"So wrong. Yes, so very wrong."

"You make me out to be a bad guy. Do we force young people to do drugs? You give your pathetic anti-drug speeches in class and they ignore you."

"Not all."

"Small victories, teacher. The war on drugs has been won. The winner is drugs. The kids' own music glorifies drugs."

"And collateral damage is young lives, families, and neighborhoods destroyed, cops killed, and dealers imprisoned," I said.

"It's the cost of doing business." He paused. "The cop, drug user, and dealer choose freely their path," he continued. "Free will, religion teacher. So how can I be guilty? You defend man and man is weak-willed."

"Not all are weak-willed."

"You, Teacher?"

"I'm a sinner but I'm also made in God's image. I'm trying to strive to be in his image."

"God's image? And what might that be?"

"LOVE. Simply love."

"Remember the story. That image died painfully on the cross. That's love for you."

"Not bad. But out of love, He died for us and He rose. His passion offers all of us the opportunity to join Him in resurrection. Archbishop Romero of El Salvador became a martyr because he stood up to your ilk. He said that if they kill me, I will rise up in the people. Boss, you can't kill us all. The Church in Jesus' name will send others to stand up to you and all evil. The Church will not perish."

"How can I let you go? Today you come for Manuel. Tomorrow for someone else. Today you try to stop drugs. Tomorrow, maybe, prostitution. Well, Mr. McCarthy, you'll go, but not by the front door. You talk of joining Him in resurrection, well, it's your time now."

I straightened up, confident and serene. "I once again demand in God's justice that you leave Manuel, Maria, and the Dorothy Day community alone."

"Are you threatening me, Teacher? You, a religion teacher. I'm shocked... totally shocked."

"You've been warned. Leave Fordham, the Bronx, alone."

"Where's your army?" The boss looked around and laughed.

"It's here in the room – the Father, Son, Holy Spirit, Mother Mary, the angels, saints, and prophets. The opposite of you. '*You are of your father the devil, and your will is to do your father's desires... He was a murderer from the beginning...he is a liar and the father of lies'''* (John 8:44).

"Your gibberish bores me. You came alone but I will send you to them. Take him out," he said to Ponce, "and kill him." Bautista turned and went back to his desk.

"I'm baptized. I'm God's and you will not win," I responded.

Increase. Decrease. Increase. Decrease. My powers swelled. I easily shrugged off the two goons holding my arms. Shamrock appeared an instant later. With a swift backhand move, it slashed across the belly of one of the thugs, ripping it open and spilling out his guts. I continued the arc of Shamrock and stabbed the other guy in his chest. He went down in an ever-increasing pool of blood at his feet. A pop-eyed Ponce backed away, stumbled, and fell heavily.

Bautista turned at the noise. I sprang towards him and swung, but he moved rapidly. My sword missed his chest but dug into his shoulder. He pulled away and a machete with a broad blade appeared in his hand. We both hesitated and then with a roar we engaged. Our weapons carved the air and rang out in repeated contact. We jabbed and stabbed, scoring cuts and nicks to arms, chests and abdomens. My gift of heightened senses foretold his main moves, and allowed me to avoid major damage from his flashing blade.

Shamrock blazed.

"You have been weighed in the balance and found wanting" (Daniel 5:27), I bellowed.

With a powerful arm movement, I whacked aside his blade, feigned an attack on his strong side and then went for his weakened shoulder. Another hit, this time deeper than the first. As Bautista backed away, I bull-rushed him, smashing my elbow into his nose and then a shoulder into his body. We both went down but we managed to hold onto our weapons. Scrambling to our feet, he swatted at me; I ducked, came up swinging and backhanded a swift two-handed stroke. Decapitation. His head, with eyes and mouth open in utter surprise, fell off his shoulders, rolled across the floor and landed by Ponce, who was back on his feet. Pointed ears and fangs appeared on the detached head. His headless body transformed into a not-of-this world being. Translucent skin, a four foot tail, three-pronged feet ending in six inch talons, and veins filled with blue and red liquid lay on the floor.

Ponce, retrieving a gun out of his belt, froze at the sight of the changes in Bautista. He stared at the creepy body and head of his boss, the two thugs, and my radiant sword. Spearing Bautista's head with my weapon, I charged him, the bloody head dangling on the end of my blade. Panic set in; he fired his gun wildly as he ran to the balcony. Then Ponce let out a blood curdling scream and jumped. That's the last movement and sound from him. Looking over the balcony, I saw his body impaled on a wrought iron fence below. His death – instant and gruesome.

Ponce's shots and scream led to movement and sounds outside the door. I positioned myself behind the door, Shamrock firmly in hand. My senses were charged and alerted to the max.

My ears picked up on the voices of four people. They were debating whether to enter or not. The sounds followed by silence in the room confused them. Out of the norm, I was sure. I had one chance of surprise before they realized I was alive and not their companions.

Throwing open the door, I caught them flat-footed. They surely expected to see Bautista standing there. Rushing out in full fury, I twisted and turned Shamrock. I slashed left and right. Then I feinted left but went right. A flash of movement and action by my glittering sword. In no time at all, a heap of four bodies lay around me.

Jumping over the human pile, I ran down the stairs and speared Shamrock through a man advancing from the second floor.

My momentum carried me into his partner and we tumbled down onto the second floor landing. In hustling to get back on our feet, I moved faster and split him in half before he could fire his gun. Cautiously peering over the second floor railing, I quickly took stock of the number and location of the people on the main floor. Their guns erupted, bullets whizzed by, as I ducked behind a stone pillar. The element of surprise would again act as my weapon.

Instead of plunging down the stairs, I vaulted the railing and landed on the main floor. My action momentarily threw them off, giving me enough time to get steady on my feet. My hearing and sight picked up every movement and sound in front of me, behind me, and off to the sides, enabling me to anticipate their moves. Shamrock hummed with a life of its own and its sharp blade cut them down. A thrust at one, a swipe at another, a jab to my left, a stab in front, always moving and causing damage. Faith was my shield, righteousness my breastplate as their bullets grazed me but left no serious damage.

Victory was almost complete when I slid on the bloody floor and was thrown off-balance. Before I could recover stability, the last thug put a bullet into my shoulder. I staggered but managed to get back my equilibrium. I lunged forward and with one final swipe finished him off.

Bad boys, in a skating rink of blood, lay sprawled in various positions on the floor. The place was silent – dead silent. The faces of the dead showed no gangster smugness or arrogance. Their death masks had no attitude. They were just dead. Cut up by Shamrock.

My shoulder wound, dripping blood, widened the red puddle already on the floor. Feeling weak, I knelt and then slid down on the floor. I mumbled, *"Yea, thou art my rock, and my fortress"* (Psalm 31:3). Darkness quickly followed.

From a distance, I heard someone calling my name and I

caught the faint scent of roses. But both remained far away in a fog of confusion. Slowly, the sound and the scent became stronger and within my grasp. I opened my eyes to find Annie Ferber, kneeling next to my sprawled body. A brightness outlined her body. I managed to laugh softly. My angel was an angel!

"I came thinking you might need help," said Annie. "I'm not a warrior angel so I'm unable to help with the likes of them." She looked around at the bloody death scene. "I chose to be a healer," she continued.

Annie examined my injuries. "The bullet went straight through below your clavicle. No damage to major organs," she said. She placed her hands over my shoulder and the bleeding stopped. She then ran her hands over the multiple wounds on my body. They healed immediately.

Excusing herself, she left to make sure no one else needed healing. Returning in a few minutes, she confirmed the Locos were wiped out. We looked at each other. Silence

"Rookie angel, you beat them all," said Annie, breaking the hush.

"Annie, according to G.K. Chesterton, 'the most incredible thing about miracles is that they happen.'"

"That they do," she responded with a smile on her face.

She helped me up and we proceeded to survey the rooms on the first floor. Plastic bags of coke, pot, heroin, and pills were stocked on shelves in four of the rooms. The basement warehoused their weapons: handguns, machetes, shotguns, and assault rifles. The second floor had rooms of money. Piles of it. Surveillance video and computers filled the third floor. I thought of destroying today's film with a crushing blow from Shamrock but Annie assured me it was unnecessary; film cannot capture an angel form.

I surmised the place must be sound proof because no sirens

were heard after the gunfire. I dialed 911.

"A drug battle at the Locos mansion by Fordham Road on the Grand Concourse. Please send multiple units."

I wanted a multitude of cops because the money and drugs could be tempting to a cop making a working man's salary. Time to cut down on temptation. One rotten apple brings bad press to all the honest cops.

Before leaving, we knelt and prayed for the dead. We unlocked the front door for the police and we headed out the back. Ponce hung grotesquely, speared by the top spikes of an iron fence. He had lived ugly and died ugly. We hit the street, and every so often looked over our shoulders but we saw no one. We walked slowly as the rush was over and I felt exhausted. Needing support, I leaned on Annie's arm. We took in the usual Bronx street symphony of cars, buses, trains, and voices on a Friday night. In the distance, police sirens wailed.

On the way home, Annie shared some of her story. After a swimming accident at her beloved Jones Beach on Long Island, she was invited to be an angel. Like me, she said yes; unlike me, she chose to be a healer.

Annie decided to live in a poor neighborhood, making their world her world. She showed the face of Christ by being a loving neighbor: running errands for the elderly, buying groceries for a destitute family, comforting an upset parent, counseling the young, and performing any task necessary for those in need. She became the light in their darkness of despair. Her healing touch lessened the scar tissue of their hearts and souls, and drew out the Christ in them.

She gripped my elbow firmly, and assisted me into my apartment. I invited her to stay for a cup of tea.

"Another day. Much has happened tonight. Pray well and rest. You earned it. You are forever changed and there's no going back. You know this already but it bears repeating. You are not alone. The local angels were told to keep an eye out for the new kid on the block until you got your angel legs. I think you got them."

She stopped talking, raised up on her tiptoes, and kissed me on my forehead. Smiling, she turned around and walked out the door. The smell of roses remained in the air.

Twenty-Six

Your sins are forgiven
Luke 5:20

Saturday

"I was expecting you." Father Bonaventure stood framed in the doorway of the Sacred Heart rectory. A golden hue outlined his slender body. A young priest in his 30's, he sported wire-rimmed glasses and a bushy brown beard, in stark contrast to his traditional white Dominican habit.

"My missionary look," he told me as he gave his facial hairs a gentle tug.

The Bronx could surely use missionaries, I thought. He beckoned me into the rectory like a monk following the rule of St. Benedict: *All guests to the monastery should be welcomed as Christ.*

The rectory was located in the Highbridge section of the Bronx, north of Yankee Stadium. The neighborhood is named after the original bridge built to link the Bronx and the isle of Manhattan. It's New York City's oldest standing span.

When I was a kid, a young Puerto Rican fell to his death trying to hang the single star flag of Puerto Rico from the bridge in a spirit of nationalism. His death led me to the realization that the world was more than play, that there were things worth fighting for, maybe, even dying for.

The rectory was empty except for the two of us. The other priest was visiting nursing homes and not due back until early afternoon. Father Bonaventure led me into the living room furnished with two worn armchairs and a small sofa. The mantle over the fireplace held two brass candlesticks, and a painting of Jesus, heart ablaze with sacredness, hung above it.

"You've been quite busy from what I hear. The angel wire service has buzzed since late last night."

I nodded.

"Not just the angel wires but TV and radio as well."

"No word about me in the newspaper articles that I read," I said. "For that I'm grateful."

"'A Death Blow to the Locos' read one headline," he responded. "A rival Central American gang using their trademark machetes was blamed for the killings. Another article even mentioned the slaughter of the dogs of the Locos. I see you put on God's armor."

"The breastplate of righteousness, the shield of faith. The teaching of Agnes guided me on my angel path."

"And the violence?" he inquired.

"I'm still grappling with violence in the name of Christ... Father, was the warrior angel option tempting to you?"

"I'm a Dominican. Our founder, St. Dominic said *'arm yourself with prayer rather than a sword.'* You chose the warrior path. Your sword enables you *'...to stand up against the Devil's evil tricks. For we are not fighting against human beings but against the wicked spiritual forces in the heavenly world...'* (Ephesians 6:11-12).

"Shamrock has a life of its own," I said. "I just hold on tightly."

"Shamrock? Your sword?"

I nodded.

"You defended Maria and Manual, Dorothy Day, and the Bronx. You lived the radical Gospel message of love. One needs to stand up for it, to live it. As St. Teresa of Avila stated *'What He needs is the resoluteness of our will.'*"

"The will to trust in God."

"And yourself," the priest gently responded.

"I came for confession," I stated.

"I know." He smiled.

Confession, also known as the Sacrament of Reconciliation, is the means to the forgiveness of our sins. *"A tribunal of mercy,"* according to Pope John Paul II. It allows us to cleanse our souls and start anew.

Jesus knew that humans in their fallibility would sin and need healing. In Confession, sins are forgiven, and the penitent reunites his soul to God. Grace increases in the soul, and draws one closer to Him. Dorothy Day, as well as many saints, went to weekly confession in their pursuit of holiness.

On Easter Sunday, Jesus told his Apostles: *"Receive the Holy Spirit. If you forgive the sins of any, they are forgiven; if you retain the sins of any, they are retained"* (John 20:23).

The power to forgive sins in Confession rests with priests. They would tell us that Jesus commands all of us to forgive.

I had a beautiful confession. Father Bonaventure was tender, kind, and understanding as he walked with me in this new stage of my earthly journey. Angels with free will are not perfect, he assured me. We stumble, fail, and need healing. Confession takes our sin from darkness to the light of His love where sin and demons cannot abide.

"I absolve thee from thy sins in the name of the Father, and of the Son, and of the Holy Spirit. Amen," concluded Father Bonaventure as he made the sign of the cross.

Father Bonaventure walked me to the door. He wrote down the name and number of an angel doctor in case I needed medical assistance in the future. He wished me well, reminded me to stay on guard, and promised prayers of support. He left the door metaphorically open. It's the Bronx after all!

*   *   *

"He's okay, both physically and spiritually," said Annie. She looked around at her fellow angels, gathered for their Saturday morning breakfast at Gracie's.

"He had a good teacher," said Mrs. Epstein, looking over at Agnes.

"Good material to work with," she responded. Humble Agnes continued, "'*The Lord loves those who hate evil*' (Psalm 97:10). Let's give thanks to His holy name."

Over steaming cups of coffee, plates of eggs and toast, heads bowed in silent prayers of thanks. Daniel broke the silence.

"Mac's gotten a bit of his angel legs. He's an angel-in-training but he's getting there. We still need to keep an eye out for him, however, to be ready to assist. We need him in our ranks."

"The more the merrier," said Herb, "to fight for the City of God and the Kingdom of virtue versus the City of Man and the Kingdom of vice."

"Amen," all responded in unison.

*   *   *

I realized I needed Father Bonaventure's reminder to stay alert. After yesterday's events, I had slipped into a false sense of complacency, thinking the next battle was not yet on the horizon, that I had time to recover and regroup. Maybe not, I told myself. As I walked home, I looked around and searched the street; I neither saw nor felt anything of a menacing nature. I contemplated the words *Be not afraid*," spoken to Mother Mary by the angel Gabriel. Father Bonaventure mentioned that those words make up the most common phrase in Scripture. Used over 1000 times!

The deep blue skies, the laughter of people walking by, the

locked arms of two lovers, a baby crying in his mother's loving arms. The beauty of my surroundings reminded me of words from a song by Louis Armstrong: "the bright blessed day, the dark sacred night..." Indeed, Louie, indeed. What a Wonderful World!

The blinking light of my answering machine greeted me as I walked into my apartment. Two messages. The first from a concerned and worried Mickey, inquiring if I arrived before, during, or after the bloodbath. "Please call." His message took me aback as Mickey had not reached out for ages. I returned the call, leaving a message that "all was well."

Paddy had also called. "Brother, your part of the Bronx is hopping. I know you heard of it. Your prayers have been answered. Bet you're not surprised, old altar boy. You believe so much in the power of prayer. The Locos are no more. Taken out at the top. We retrieved their film and computer records. Your Manuel will be okay. Threat gone. I'll catch up with you on St. Pat's for a celebratory beer. This case has a lot of cops doing overtime. Talk to you soon."

Restless, I made my way to the Bronx Botanical Gardens, a bit of heaven in the Bronx, with 30,000 trees, 1 million plants, 250 acres, and the most beautiful rose garden in the United States. Being in nature always helps me to reflect, gain a perspective, and put myself back together. I prayed as I walked amongst the trees and bushes. Inside the building, the sweet smell of flowers lightened my thoughts and led me to a sense of peaceful contentment. I was clear on who I needed to turn to for protection and to keep on the right path. Thanks be to the grace of God.

A day with no responsibilities. No rugby. No coaching. Taking advantage of the down time, I had a cup of tea with Louisa, my landlady. A perfect day to visit as I was content to be still. We sat on her porch and watched the Bronx walk by. We both were satisfied.

Take-out Chinese for dinner. Beef and broccoli, a couple of egg rolls, and won-ton soup. I sipped green tea and relaxed in my armchair. Closing my eyes, I meditated. A gentle movement of air and a strong pine scent announced his arrival.

"Hello, Daniel. I was expecting you."

He stood in front of me, a foot away. Up on my feet, I hugged and got hugged. I held on tightly, comforted by Daniel's touch. His high-top black Converse sneakers and his pink and green striped socks poked out from the bottom of his baggy black sweatpants. I smiled at the sight.

"You fought well. I'm not totally surprised you won but I never know. I take nothing for granted in these battles. Anything can happen."

"The thanks are appreciated," I said. "I'm still trying to get my thoughts together but they're scattered to the wind."

"Understandable."

"Do veteran angels ever get used to...?"

"Never," Daniel responded. "If you do, you've crossed over to the other side. Violence can be seductive, just like any sin. We must be centered in Him through the guiding principles of prayer and love. Our strength flows from there."

"Daniel, the battles ahead... worse than yesterday?"

"Your biggest battle will not be with drug dealers, pimps or brigands. It'll be for the souls of your students."

"Say what? That demon was no walk in the park. Granted, teenagers give me a run for my money at times but none have come at me with a machete or any weapon for that matter."

"They are the future – the kingdom builders. Their generation needs to be ready to serve. Your job is to get them to embrace God, to realize they are special because they are children of God. You're up against some pretty powerful forces in society."

"Technology plays a big part. The kids interact with machines more than people," I said. "They always need to be in touch with the latest news, sport scores, friends... the list goes on and on. The distractions of the modern world – phones, iPads, texting, computers, gaming – keep them away from God and shut out His voice."

"No time for developing a relationship with God. It takes prayer and the desire to want to know the Lord."

"They often come without a relationship with God, not even a wee one, and no desire to have one. Their parents or whoever they live with 'don't do God' so it's very difficult for kids to develop a connection. Parents are usually the ones to pass on the traditions, the faith, the desire."

"Add to that a Western culture that has become more secular. It leads..."

"To the slippery slope of relativism," I chimed in.

"No absolute truth. No moral values that are absolute."

"Students often tell me that they can guide themselves to live a moral life and that spiritual help is unnecessary. Not embracing the God story leaves them more vulnerable to amorality, shallowness and evil."

"It's all about me, myself and I, huh?"

"They're feet people, Daniel. They look down at their own feet and not out at the suffering world. Not just the young, but pretty much all ages."

"Walking in Jesus' footsteps takes real effort. It's easier to fall into materialism or a self-centered attitude, caught up in one's own problems, own life. I don't envy your task."

"When I see the spiritual light bulb go on in some of the students, it carries me on a wave of love. They engage on their own spiritual ladder, trying to move closer to God. The day I stop shouting from the mountaintop about our loving and merciful Lord is the day I need to retire from teaching."

"I repeat, your future battles with the devil will be easier." Daniel laughed.

"Will I always recognize him?"

"Right now, some of the time. You'll get stronger and better as you..."

"Increase and decrease," I responded.

"The creature you destroyed yesterday was not at the top of the demonic scale. There will be tougher foes for you to face. Our ancient enemy takes fallen men and fallen angels and distorts and twists them into powerful forces. You won't see horns, a pitchfork, and a tail as he cloaks his identity. Yet, you'll know him for what he is. His minions will be around suffering, violence, killing, rape, genocide... He does not know joy but thrives on chaos. His purpose is to disrupt God's plan."

"To quote the book of Genesis, '*And God saw everything that he had made, and behold, it was very good*'" (Genesis 1:31), I said.

"Your battle will be to create a world of good. One student and one person at a time. Make your classroom, and your relationships sacred ground. One soul at a time, build God's earthly domain. The innocent children are our hope. No child, no human being is expendable. For them we must always fight. The price of failure is too costly."

"Amen," I responded.

Prayer time. My living room floor became our pew as we both knelt down.

Minutes later, Daniel said, "Off to a neighborhood gym. You're not the only angel who needs to stay in shape."

"So that accounts for the sneakers and the sweats."

"Like a couple of old friends. They've been with me for a long time. Comfort shoe instead of comfort food."

"A fun question for you."

"Shoot."

"I just found out Annie Ferber is an angel. She's the whole package. Are there any angel rules about dating?"

"Second time today, I've been asked that question."

I threw him a quizzical look.

"No rules with our good God except love," said Daniel. "Love Him and love thy neighbor. Lead with love."

"Take care of yourself. Be safe."

"Always. And you, too. Your world has become a lot more dangerous. Now allow me to end on a fun note. Annie is definitely the whole package. Good luck."

He winked at me and laughed hard from his belly. He was still laughing as he disappeared.

His merriment triggered my own. I lay down on the floor and the joyous sound filled my apartment for a solid ten minutes. The weight on my shoulders released, and I fell into a deep sleep.

Twenty-Seven

I will not have you hold conversations
with men, but with angels.
Locution to St. Teresa of Avila

Sunday

The Sabbath – a day of rest. I keep it that way. No chores, no shopping. Not even for groceries. I refuse to get caught up in the attitude that it's just another day of the week. My Sundays always center around mass.

I looked forward to getting my Brigid fix, her outpouring of pure love, at morning mass. I always know when and where to find her and Mom on Sundays. They attend 10:30 mass at St. Barnabas Church and sit up front in the second pew on the right side, close to the priestly action on the altar.

Big wet snowflakes accompanied me as I walked to church. The snow was laying down a pure white blanket over bushes, trees, and grass. I enjoyed the moment, knowing the pristine condition of my surroundings was only temporary. I felt giddy with the joy, the gift, and the beauty of life. I playfully tried to catch snowflakes on my tongue but they mostly landed on my face and mustache, melted quickly, and left behind a soft film of moisture.

I paused in the vestibule of St. Barnabas, taking satisfaction in the familiar. Like the feeling one gets when slipping on a well-loved worn jean jacket. I walked up the center aisle of the church, flanked by twenty five rows of wooden pews. If I was unsure where to look for Brigid, I would have found her anyway. A brightness shone all around her, and an aureole surrounded her head. She fingered her rosary beads, deep in her prayers with her eyes closed. Praying with flowers – the word rosary comes from the Latin word "rosarius," which means garland of flowers. I marveled at her witness to faith and to God. I slid into the pew and knelt next to her. She looked over, smiled, patted me on my back, and returned to her prayers.

The words of Mahatma Gandhi, the Indian nationalist and spiritualist, best explain her prayer life: "Prayer is not asking. It is a longing of the soul... It is better in prayer to have a heart without words than words without a heart."

I always find solace in the routine of mass, especially in hearing the Word and in receiving Eucharist. During the collection, Brigid proved the exception to the mass routine. Unlike the other ushers, who remained silent while gathering the money offerings from the parishioners, she thanked everyone, whether they contributed to the basket or not.

After mass, the snow shower had stopped and the sun had made an appearance. Mom planned to join Mrs. Kramer, Mrs. Duignan, and Mrs. Fleming, her three best friends from the neighborhood, for a drink. The four always meet at church and afterwards, go out to their favorite bar, The Hideout, for one drink apiece before heading home to cook Sunday dinner. They talk about their husbands, children, the neighborhood, and bingo, their favorite past-time.

It was a running joke in our family about Mom and drinking. Dad drank hard and regularly and we said nothing; mom occasionally had a drink and we teased her endlessly over it.

"In the spirit of Dad, of course," I said with a wink.

"Hush you," she said "and your siblings." She hurried off to catch up with her friends.

Brigid and I walked slowly home, content in each other's company and the white blanketed surroundings. A block from home, she tensed up and slipped her arm through mine.

"I feel something and it's not good," she told me. "Scary."

I felt it, too. The vibrating air snapped and popped. The weather now loomed ominous, as the sun had slipped behind the clouds and the wind blustered. Snow threatened again and the sky appeared to tremble with a pent up energy ready to unleash a veil of white. I started to hurry Brigid along when I heard the squeal of car brakes behind us. I thrust myself in front of Brigid as I turned towards the sound. A horn blared and the car pulled up beside us.

"Mac, how are you?" asked Abdul from the open window.

"Much better seeing that it's you," I said. My adrenaline rush began to subside.

"He has color," said Brigid. She let go of her grip on my jacket and planted herself firmly beside me.

Intent on protecting Brigid, I had not paid much attention to Abdul. I looked closely at him now and my jaw dropped.

Abdul broke the silence. "We're a festival of colors, religions, sizes, and shapes. No two alike but all of us children of God."

"Well, I'll be," was all my dumbfounded self could manage to say.

Brigid had no problem speaking up, and introduced herself. She walked over to the car and shook Abdul's outstretched hand.

"I'm not afraid, anymore," she said. "Do you know your color?" she inquired of Abdul.

"Indeed, I do. And it happens to be my favorite shade of..." Before he could finish, his radio squawked and he heard the call for a pick-up.

"Gotta go. Nice to meet you, Brigid. And you, Mac, stay wary," he said hurriedly.

Abdul drove down to the end of the street and turned left. Off to ply the city streets and cope with city traffic.

The rest of our trip home was uneventful. We canceled our planned baseball catch due to the inclement weather. We settled into Parcheesi, a board game, instead. When I first taught Brigid the game, I often let her win. The tables have now turned and I sometimes wish she would return the favor. Quite adept at tactical movement of her pieces, she usually wins. During games, she chats incessantly, and I often tease her about her weapon of distraction. I listened as she told me about her school aide job, especially the service day project in the second grade class. They had made greeting cards for the residents of St. Joseph shelter.

I reflected on Brigid's big heart. "The greatest challenge is how to bring about a revolution of the heart," Dorothy Day once said. Brigid never needed a revolution as her heart has never lost its connection with God. Born one with God, her connection has remained unbroken.

Mom walked in just as Brigid declared victory. I smiled, a gracious loser, once again. I turned down Mom's invitation to stay for dinner. If there was evil following me, I wanted to lead it away from here.

As I turned the corner of my block, I saw fireman Herb leaning on a car parked near my home. My nose tingled from a burning smell and I promptly determined the cause of the stench. The remnants of a fire sat at my door.

"What happened?" I asked as I turned my gaze toward him. It was the second time in a short span that my jaw slackened. I noticed the soft rosy color outlining his body.

"You're an angel?" I finally sputtered out.

He nodded.

"Have you been protecting me?" I inquired.

He nodded again. "Abdul let me know trouble was brewing as you walked from church. I figured it might be at your place." He pointed to the fire rubbish. "It might have gotten bigger but we got to it in time."

"We?"

"Abdul joined me after he left you and Brigid."

"A thanks is in order, to the both of you."

I leaned next to him against the car. We both became lost in the solitude of our thoughts. Minutes passed.

"Were you born an angel or given a choice like I was?" I finally asked.

"Some people are born angels but not me. I was saving the rabbit of a kid named Jonathan in an intense fire when my time ran out. Time stood still and I was given the choice. Continue to serve or go and meet my maker."

"Tempting, right?"

"Sure. But He created me and I'm a worker bee for the Big Guy. So here I am."

"Protecting the new guy."

"We all need protection, especially in the beginning. We're most vulnerable then. You'll grow strong quickly though, kid. You already have."

"It's only two days since my battle on Friday... no respite in the war, huh?"

"Nope. No days off from our enemies. We need to be ready 24/7."

He moved away from the car and urged me to follow.

"Let's clean this up. We both have work tomorrow. Some rabbit might need saving," he said with a laugh.

Then Herb turned and looked at me, his face more serious. "You need to save kids."

Twenty-Eight

...until we meet again
may God hold you in
the palm of His hand
Irish Blessing

Monday

The wearin' of the green. Scarves. Hats. Sweaters. Even faces painted with solid green shamrocks or the tricolors of the Irish flag in green, orange, and white. All were in evidence on the subway as it rattled its way downtown. The mood was light and celebratory with young people laughing, singing Irish songs, and a few even managing to dance Irish jigs in the narrow center aisle of the swaying train. Show-time on a New York subway. I settled back in my seat to enjoy the gaiety.

The majority of us exited at Grand Central Station and were swept along by the crowd. At the top of the stairs, I moved to the edge of the stream of people so I could progress at my own pace. A long passageway led to the main concourse of Grand Central.

No matter how many times I walk into the cavernous space, I never cease to be impressed. My attention is always drawn to the expansive ceiling – one hundred and twenty five feet above – with its astronomical figures, including Orion, Gemini, Taurus, and a host of other constellations. I walked past the main information booth topped by a four-faced clock, situated in the center of the concourse. Grand Central has landmark status but the booth alone deserves that designation in my book. It's a popular meeting spot; today was no different, as some stood nearby, searching the crowd for the awaited familiar face.

I worked my way to a Gaelic Mass at St. Agnes, a block away from Grand Central. A bagpiper, dressed in a tartan kilt of green, purple, and black, stood at the foot of the church steps. A lilting Irish tune emanated forth from the pipes and accompanied me into the church. A color guard, carrying the Irish and U.S. flags, marched up the center aisle and planted the flags, one on each end of the altar. The mass was in Gaelic, the Irish language, and it stirred my Irish soul. The British were fairly successful in wiping out the language when they occupied Ireland. Today, Gaelic is spoken and understood by only a small number of Irish. Hence, the homily was in English. At the end of mass, I left the church humming "Danny Boy," a popular Irish song, played by the piper at the back of the church.

The mass and the piper added to my joyous mood. I love celebrating my Irish roots on St. Patrick's Day. The New York City parade is the oldest and biggest in the world. It dates back to colonial America. Today, 150,000 marchers would wind their way north up Fifth Avenue.

I worked my way to the Dorothy Day HS meeting spot at 41st, two blocks off 5th Avenue. A usual five minute walk took triple the time. The crowded streets were filled with parade goers, assisted by police, who directed foot traffic at intersections. Overflows of people spilled from packed bars onto the sidewalks.

I met up with the Dorothy Day band and chatted with the students and the band director, Ms. Bari Maris Hammann. Soon after, the parade marshal urged our group to move forward towards the parade route. Turning the corner, we began our proud march up Fifth Avenue and passed St. Patrick's Cathedral. The sound of pipers and bands filled the air with Irish tunes, and the thick crowd along the parade route was a sea of green. I marched, waved, and felt a love that was tangible, that could be held in your hand. In tricolors, of course. A wet snow marched with us but it bothered no one and made the day more magical.

Late afternoon found me at Mom's, a beehive of activity. I stepped into a welcoming home of food, drink, family, neighbors, and music. I made the rounds. Hugs and kisses abounded. Post Locos, it felt great.

The party settled into its normal St. Pat's rhythm. Mom pushed plates of corn beef and cabbage with Irish soda bread at each and every one of us. As she often said, "I can't stop the drink but I can slow it down." That she did. A couple of my brothers sang Irish ditties and most of the gathering joined in with gusto. My sister Mary Claire, the only one in the clan who took Irish dance lessons, entertained us with Irish step dancing a couple of times this special night. Brigid had her own variation and danced most of the evening. Her energy increased as the night wore on.

Nursing a cold Guinness, I stood in a corner of the living room and soaked up the clan. Captain Paddy came over.

"I'm really happy for you and Dorothy Day. The Locos were real bad hombres."

"Who's responsible? Any ideas?" I asked.

"The surveillance cameras captured everything except those who stopped them. All we see is a blurry silhouette. The experts are perplexed. No way one guy did it! Only a single figure until near the end of the tape, when a second fuzzy silhouette shows up. No one is working real hard to figure out the mystery. Our Bronx is better off without them. Much better. Let's toast to that." He tapped my Guinness with his bottle of Harp, patted me on the shoulder, and moved on to mingle with family.

I went back to viewing the crowd, and enjoyed being around my siblings and their dear families. I watched a contented Brigid dancing alone. Well, not exactly alone, as her aura danced along with her. I lifted my beer and silently toasted her. Oblivious to the festivities around her, she was caught up in a God moment of pure joy. Unlike me with a degree in theology, Brigid never needed to study the Beatitudes. She was living them in the flesh, especially the pure of heart.

All too soon, goodbyes were made. Tomorrow was a work day. Mom hugged us tightly. We all knew she was hurting; Mickey was a no show again. We couldn't help her.

"I called a cab, Mac. I'm not up for the subway or the bus. We'll drop you off; it's on the way," said Seamus, one of my brothers.

"An offer I can't refuse. That includes you paying, right?" I smiled.

"It's here. Let's go."

"Hi, Mac. We meet again," said Abdul.

"Abdul, what the..."

"Not planned. It just happened. I was the next one to head out when the call came in."

"You two know each other?" asked Seamus.

"Abdul and his cab, yeah, we've met a few times," I replied. "He's got my back."

"Huh? A cabbie's got your back? ... What's that about?" inquired my brother.

I shrugged it off and settled into the ride.

"Abdul and Seamus, good night and may St. Patrick bless you both." I alighted quickly, crossed the yard, and opened the door. The blinking answering machine light alerted me to a message.

"Please call," said Mickey. "Sorry about tonight. My demons got me again."

I returned his call, surprised that he was home on this party night. I cut to the chase as I was upset about Mom's pain. No polite chit-chat.

"How come you were a no-show again? Mom's hurt. Are you trying to do that?"

"Bro, I'm truly sorry. I mean it. I fully intended to come. I had a bellyful of beer but not enough to embarrass Mom. I stopped home for a brief rest but the thought of showing up paralyzed me. Earlier in the day, I lit a candle in Good Shepherd's Church for Mom's party. I prayed that everyone in the family had love tonight. I just felt I could not be part of it. My demons are hard to beat and I'm unable to shake 'em... Don't give up on me and tell mom not to give up. I saw some light even though darkness has been the norm."

"We want to love you. To provide the light of love. You don't let us. Try baby steps. Start by seeing Mom and Brigid alone. No party. Break the ice. Would that work?"

"I'll think about it. Really, I will. But tonight I was crippled. I thought of going to the Bronx and the old Ogden Nash poem kept coming back to me, 'The Bronx? No thonx.'"

"Mick we loved that line when we were kids but we aged and so did Ogden Nash. He later amended the poem: 'I wrote those lines, The Bronx? No thonx; I shudder to confess them. Now I'm an older, wiser man I cry, The Bronx? God bless them!'"

"And you, bro. Remember, plenty of people call the Bronx home. Come home, Mick. Come home."

Twenty-Nine

I beg you. I beg you. I beg you.
Every day of your life get down on your knees
and pray to God to teach you how to love.
Monsignor Thomas Wells

Tuesday

Five classes in chapel today. No better way to spend the first day back to school after my encounter with the Locos. I gave my veteran teacher self a pat on the back. Last week, while planning for the week ahead, I knew if I made it through Friday night, the best lesson would be our monthly chapel visit.

In general, religion teachers bring their students once a month to chapel. We need to nourish their souls, their spiritual beings, to get them closer to God, to give thanks for what they have, to lead with love, and to teach them how to pray.

Prayer, like most things, needs to be taught and developed. A religion teacher directs students in how to pray. I never assume they know or had it explained to them. Two things are necessary for the person praying to enter more deeply into God's presence: first, trust in God, next in His mercy.

Do we mess up, make mistakes as humans? Of course. Don't wallow in your errors. Turn to God, who loves you passionately. Let God into your life. Your spiritual survival depends on it; you can't do it alone. So how? How to love and believe in mercy and trust? Pray. Again, how?

In the first month of school, I teach my students to pray the Examen, a prayer routine developed by St. Ignatius Loyola. He believed that God was present in all things. Take time to reflect on God's presence in your daily life. The Examen focuses on gratitude, not sin and guilt.

I walk the students through the five steps of the Examen. Start by praying to God to help you look at your day through your eyes and God's. To see where God was present. Still your heart. Listen. Let the Holy Spirit guide you to understanding.

Gratitude is the key to the second step. Be grateful for the gifts of the day. What are the gifts? People you interact with, the beauty of a flower, the food you ate, your clothes, your families... Look on the positive, the treasures of the day, I urge my students.

The next step: pay attention to your feelings. Focus on the emotions you felt during the day. Anger? Joy? Empathy? Impatience? Review and reflect on the day. Where could you have done better? Where did you not lead with love? Where did you fall short? What is God saying through your feelings?

Fourth. Forgiveness. Ask for it. When? For the times you missed recognizing God's presence in your day. For not acting more Christ-like. Recognize the problem and move closer to God. Sinners – we all are. But we are loved by a merciful God. Ignatius wrote "*God loves me more than I love myself.*" Own up to sin. Let go. Let love. Let God.

Finally. Look ahead to tomorrow. What's coming up? How does it appear? Good? Stressful? Have a game plan. Where will you need God's help? Ask for guidance.

"In as far as you advance in love you will grow surer of the reality of God and the immortality of your soul," wrote Dostoevsky, a Russian author.

"Dorothy Day embraced and lived this thought. You do the same," I often tell my classes.

When we go to chapel, I encourage the students to follow the

Examen. A positive approach to God not a negative one. God is loving, kind, and merciful. Nothing negative about Him.

I usually meet my students in the school lobby, outside of the chapel. Today was different. I met them in the classroom, as I wanted to emphasize the evil of the Locos and the power of love. Love beat out evil in my battle with the Locos.

I had turned to Mother Teresa for my daily feast day quote. Her sentiments reflected my own:

We have been created for greater things. Not just to be a number in the world. Not just for diplomas and degrees. We have been created in order to love and to be loved.

Students looked at my board when they entered the room. Their reaction was immediate.

"Love, Mr. Mac. Not the Locos. They wouldn't know love if it hit them in the face," said Thomas.

"No worries about them," responded Ty. "Kiss them good-bye."

Manuel burst into the room. Happy. No, too mild a word. Ecstatic. That's more like it. He whispered that his brother was not in the headquarters on Friday night and was vowing to clean up his act, no more 'thuggin.' We'll see, I thought.

My class headed to the chapel. Outside of it, I double-checked clothing to see if they were looking good for Jesus. I reminded them to genuflect – acknowledge God's presence – before the altar and encouraged them to be like Jesus in the garden of Gethsemane and get on their knees before their loving God. Most did.

Gregorian chant music provided a rhythm for their prayer. I set out copies of the *Catholic Worker* newspaper and the *Maryknoll* missionary magazine at the back of the chapel for those not ready to pray a full class period. The majority are usually not. The publications emphasize the church's preferential option for the poor. Hopefully, students see the face of Christ in the stories. The power of love.

I stood at the back of the chapel. Pleased with what I saw – students praying and trying to find God – and then pleased with what I smelled. Roses.

I turned and saw Annie at the door of the chapel. We locked eyes and we both smiled. She gave a thumbs up before heading on her way.

I turned to gaze at the cross behind the altar. Increase. Decrease. I reminded myself. I realized the road ahead was clearer, and I had a partial idea of where I was heading. I was definitely uncertain, however, where it would end.

With trust in God, I will not fear for He is ever with me and I will never be alone.

Epilogue

There is no saint without a past;
no sinner without a future.
St. Augustine

Wednesday

Spring Break. Sweet sweet music to my ears. No school on Holy Thursday, Good Friday, and all of glorious Easter week. Alleluia. I'm content in my teaching job and unable to imagine any other vocation that would give me such pleasure. But I love my free-time and can fill every minute of it. Retirement looks quite appealing to me. I have an older friend, a teacher for 34 years. When I asked him about retirement, he gave me an incredulous look and asked "What would I do?" I bit my tongue. If I had been honest with him, I would have said what wouldn't you do.

In the front office, I chatted with the secretaries, killing time until Sister Sam's meeting with Aaron and his mom, Ms. Brown, finished.

They came out a few minutes later. Smiles abounded. Aaron and his mom were perfectly dressed; he in a shirt and tie with pressed pants, and her in a flowery dress. She thanked me profusely for her son's opportunity. The Wall Street ruggers were generous, I told her, but the key was Aaron. She nodded in full agreement.

"The prodigal son was touched by God and now he gets to witness," I said.

"It's miraculous and the answer to my prayers," responded Ms. Brown. No one disagreed with her.

Johnny Bernard, a student on the varsity hoop team, walked into the office. He and Aaron recognized each other.

"Aaron, what are you doing here?"

"I'm enrolling in September."

"Dang. I didn't know you could handle Catholic schools, rules, discipline, God..."

"Sometimes, things change."

"So, no more running the streets. You gonna run for Dorothy Day instead?"

"Bet."

"Hoops?"

"And football."

The two young men chest bumped and engaged in one of those teenage handshakes, which I always fail to follow as they are too rapid and change frequently. Hip doesn't stand still for long.

"Mr. Mac, Aaron can flat out play. I gotta tell coach and the boys that we got some big time help for next year. Have a good day, Sister Sam and Mr. Mac."

"Sister Sam, school and sports for Aaron?"

"Young Mr. Brown was wonderful in the interview, thoughtful in his responses, and earnest about doing well. And he has a very supportive parent, who I gather never gave up on him. He'll be with us in September."

"Excuse me, Sister Sam, I hafta ask." said Aaron. "Aren't nuns named after saints? I think that's what my mom told me. Is there a Saint Sam?"

"The prophet Samuel but my real name is Sister Anne Mary. S for Sister. A for Anne and M for Mary. Thus Sam."

"Cool. Some student give you that?"

"No, a fellow nun. Nuns can be cool, too." We all laughed.

"Kevin, your spring break the usual?" asked Sister Sam.

"Pretty much. School baseball as the season kicks in. My treat